WILDFLOWERS

WILDFLOWERS

Terri Morrison Kaiser

Hardcover ISBN: 979-8-9936004-2-0
Paperback ISBN: 979-8-9936004-0-6
eBook ISBN: 979-8-9936004-1-3

This book is about sisters and mothers, and is, therefore, dedicated to my sisters, Jacqueline, Betti, Sandra, and Kathleen. And to our own little Mamka, our mother, Arlene Loula Morrison.

Sometimes clouds get in the way, cover up a sunny day;
Clouds can take a cityscape and turn it mighty cold.
But I know a place where I can sing no matter what the weather brings,
'Cause there the sun is shinin' in my soul.

From the song *Emery*, written by Ron Simurdiak

ONE

1993

Willa Grace

I am seated front and center of Mrs. Heier's third-grade class to speak on my *Wildflower Girls* series of children's books, about growing up on a northern Wisconsin farm in the 1920s. My stories, loosely based on my family, revolve around five sisters and their misadventures on the farm. They are funny, heartwarming, and unpredictable. I had brothers, too, but they can write their own stories.

On my lap is the latest addition, book number six, *Poppy Rides a Cow*. I never said they were works of the highest intelligence, still, I am proud of them. Children these days need to be aware of the simple pleasures in life.

I wait for the twenty or so wriggling, giggling bodies to settle into their neat rows of desks before I begin. A spitball sails through the air, and a boy in the back makes fart noises with his hand in his armpit. Mrs. Heier hurries into the room with a box of tissues, an apologetic glance my way, and rushes to the side of a snotty-nosed girl.

At the room's entrance stands my daughter Janie, leaning against the door jamb, her slim body clad in an ankle-length green dress over brown leather boots and a salt and pepper braid draped over one shoulder. She is my ride today. She hauls the books for me, makes sure my clothes match, that I've combed my hair, and reminds me not to swear. She grins and gives me a nod of confidence, not that I need it.

I shift my weight back and forth, having no idea how long my butt will stand the unforgiving chair I've been given with no thought to my advanced age. Damn it, I should have brought a pillow.

The scent of chalkboard dust hangs in the air and brings me back to a time long gone. These little poops have no idea how lucky they are. In my day, lunch was a butter-and-jam sandwich, a drink of water from the pump, and a big rock to play on, and on the coldest of winter days, our coats stayed on.

To my left, a boy with sandy hair is picking his nose. Good grief, there's at least one in every class. To the right, a girl with blond, fuzzy hair has a pencil stuck in her ear. That's new. And in the middle, about three rows back, sits a skinny boy in a button-down shirt leaning forward, elbows on his desk, a notepad and pen before him, with beady little eyes focused on me, waiting for my every word. That child is my audience.

I spend a good deal of my time running around to schools, county fairs, and libraries, talking about my books and those five adventurous girls. You'd think an old grouch like me would shy away from all the attention, but it's not half bad. When most people my age are slowing down, I'm busier than ever.

From her desk in the corner, Mrs. Heier puts her fingers to her lips and lets loose with an ear-splitting whistle. Holy hell, I'm not sure that was necessary, but then it's quiet. Mrs. Heier gives me a brief introduction, and I begin my now-familiar spiel, looking forward to the questions I'll get at the end.

When my talk is finished, Janie drives me toward my farm in Emery Township. The county road dips and climbs through the northern Wisconsin countryside, the last of autumn's colors holding on. Everywhere I look, I see memories ingrained in my soul so deeply that they are in every breath I take. It is always this way for me on these roads.

Soon, we crest the hill where the remains of Viola Villa Hall lie. I pass this way hundreds of times a year, but today, there is an unexplainable pull. Then I remember. It's Daisy's birthday.

"Stop the car," I say.

"Is something wrong?" Janie swerves to the shoulder.

After a tussle with the seatbelt, I exit and nearly tip into the ditch.

"Mom, what are you doing?" Janie bolts to my side of the car, takes my arm, and helps me through the weeds to the sad and lonesome remains.

"Viola Villa Hall." My withered, age-spotted hands are at my heart, my tired eyes look upon the jagged mess of what once was the gathering place for our little farming community.

The hall, so vital in years past, collapsed long ago. White-flecked siding juts at different angles into the earthy, woody autumn air. Glassless window frames lay about, and the once-proud cupola, still intact, crowns the long-forgotten heap. Skinny popple trees, weeds, and wildflowers push through it all—the yellow of goldenrod and black-eyed susans, lacey white yarrow, with purple asters and phlox—brilliant life among that which is dying, which is dead.

I close my eyes, gathering memories. Shadowy images of weddings, town meetings, dances, and parties circle me.

And funerals. Too many funerals.

I see my sister Daisy and me as we pull up to peek in the long windows. Our Mamka and reluctant Tata hop-twirl on the dance floor, Mamka singing along to Škoda lásky, the *Beer Barrel Polka,* while our younger siblings scatter about. Faces from the past swirl and dissipate.

And then there is my Henry, tall and handsome as ever, his eyes scanning the crowd for a wayward girl with a big imagination and a thirst for adventure so strong he could barely hold on.

The caw of a blackbird brings me back.

I give a quick shake of my head to stop sentimental tears from dripping down my face.

A cardinal gracefully alights on a buckthorn. It's Daisy—no doubt. This is her way of watching over me all these years.

I quietly gasp and hold my breath. A now-frequent stab to my chest radiates to my jaw and left arm. I don't want Janie to see. Just as quickly, the pain is gone. I take a gulp of delicious country air and turn to face my daughter, a smile pushed into the wrinkles of my face.

Looking to the sky, I say, "Get ready, Daisy. I'll pester the hell out of you before too long."

"Mother!" Janie glares. "Don't talk like that."

"Don't argue with an old woman." I roughly link my arm with hers and grin at my beautiful girl. "Let's go."

I take a quick look back over my shoulder to see a daisy poking through the debris, completely out of season. Its white petals and sunny yellow center look happy, as if it were a glorious June afternoon, rather than this cloudy September day. Was it there when we first arrived?

TWO

1933

Daisy

I stood at the entrance to Viola Villa Hall, searching for my sister, Willa Grace. The bride and groom had left the reception a while ago, yet many remained. Mr. Glissendorf's band swung into *Happy Days Are Here Again* and dancers bobbed and twirled as though they didn't think a thing wrong with the song choice. The Depression had finally reached northern Wisconsin, with falling milk prices that sent our farmers scrambling to make ends meet. My family, the Maruskas, included. Happy days were hanging by a thread.

Under the glow of hazy light, men argued FDR's 'New Deal' as they smoked, while women wiped drippy chins and planned the formation of the Emery Sewing Circle. Children darted in and out of the adults, shrieking with laughter.

"Hey Daisy, wanna dance?" Clarence, a friend of our brother George and a full head shorter than I, slid up in front of me.

I shook my head. "I need to find Willa Grace and get home. Have you seen her?" I raised on tiptoes and scanned the tops of heads. Normally, I would dance with Clarence, but it was late, and the desire to kick up my heels no longer there.

"Last I saw, she was out back." He angled his round face and studied me.

"What, Clarence?"

"What's with the sour face?"

"Willa Grace and I leave Monday morning for Chicago. It's all I can think about." Besides, Harold Smidl, the one boy I hoped would be there, hadn't shown.

"With milk prices going to shit, I bet your folks are happy you girls are gonna help out. Good luck to you. Now, how's about that dance?"

"Sorry. It's getting late."

"Your loss." He shrugged and moved on to Minnie Dudek.

The goddamn Depression, as the menfolk took to calling it, was upon us. The bank in Phillips, eight miles west of us, threatened foreclosure of our farm, and Tata couldn't keep up. His damaged pride wore on him like a heavy, rain-soaked rug, as fear clouded Mamka's eyes.

With all hands doing their part, it still wasn't enough. Willa Grace came up with the idea that she and I should go to Chicago, as some others in our community had done. The two of us had been working at the creamery down the road, but the pay didn't amount to much.

I didn't want to go, but how could I say no? The family needed us, and besides, Willa Grace would go alone if I didn't. I shudder to think how my impulsive, reckless sister would make her way in the big city without me.

The train ticket on my nightstand back at the farm hung like a shadow over my shoulder. Chicago. A place so huge I worried I'd be swallowed up forever. Worse, I wasn't sure I could forgive Willsy if her wild adventure didn't go as planned.

Oh, of course, I would forgive her. I always did.

Where was that sister of mine?

The song ended, and Mr. Rosicky took center stage with his concertina and launched into *The Laughing Polka.* His was my favorite instrument of all, and this, my favorite song. He held the instrument close to his chest as the boxy instrument breathed in and out, the air flowing like an extra set of lungs, his thick fingers flying over the keys as everyone sang, danced, and clapped.

There wasn't a face I didn't recognize here. What a fine thing to be able to say about one's home. In this, I was blessed. Would have been nice if Harold had shown.

I was grabbed from behind and whirled about with such force that I nearly lost my balance and tumbled down the stairs. Willa Grace.

"Geez, Willsy!" I regained my footing with a hand on the metal railing.

"I was just out back, and you wouldn't believe it." Willa Grace was breathing in great gulps, her face flush, chestnut curls stuck to her forehead, her blue skirt a mess of wrinkles.

Sometimes, it was hard to remember she was seventeen and not seven.

"The Stetina boys brought shine from their still," Willa Grace giggled. "Good stuff." She licked her lips.

"Oh, for heaven's sake, it's late." I took back my arm. "You stink of liquor. If Tata smells that on you, you're in big trouble."

Willa Grace put a hand up to her mouth, blew into it, and sniffed. "I only had a sip. Wanna try? They're just beyond the outhouse."

"No! Táta won't be happy we dawdled so long. The family is probably home by now." We had a two-mile trek ahead of us through woods thick as blackberry jam, and our father would be waiting.

"Why have you been such an old crust?" Willa Grace nudged me with her elbow.

"I am not." She was right.

"Are too." Although we were the same height, Willa Grace was bigger-boned and often mistaken for the older of us.

"Let's go." I went down the few stairs, then glanced over my shoulder to see Willa Grace following unhappily.

"Oh, put away that pout," I told her. Willa Grace was cute as the dickens when she pouted, pulling her brows together like little worms, her mouth forming a knot.

She caught up and tugged on the sleeve of my dress.

"You know, the sooner we get home and hit the sack, the sooner tomorrow will come and then Monday."

I stopped in my tracks and sighed. Monday, our whole world would change. If only I could hold back time.

Willa Grace took off down the path into the woods.

I followed, leaving the light of the hall's long windows behind. The scent of evergreen filled my lungs while the happy sounds of celebration faded into the background.

Silvery moonlight dusted every branch and leaf, making the white bark of the birch glow, and fireflies began their jitter-twitter dance to light our way.

Ahead of me, Willa Grace repeated a flat rendition of *Roll Out The Barrel*, jigging from side to side and swinging her brown, shoulder-length curls. I had to grin. The girl loved to dance, but it was a sorry sight to see. And as that thought crossed my mind, Willa Grace's foot caught the root of a tree, and down she went, sprawled in the middle of the path.

I stood over her and extended a hand. "And to think part of your name is Grace." I pulled her up, then brushed pine needles and dirt from her skirt.

"Look at me. How can I show up in Chicago with knees all scraped to hell?"

"No one will care. Trust me." I pulled a twig from her hair, and then a prickle of intuition caused me to straighten. I looked to the left, then right. The nighttime forest was still, yet something was different. Then…

"Daisy, look." Willa Grace grabbed my elbow and pointed to a clearing beyond a stand of birch. A deer nibbled away in that grassy space among the trees in the moonlight. It was nearly all white.

I pushed aside a branch to get a closer look. While the deer's head and upper back were brown, its legs and most of its body were white.

As if sensing our presence, the animal stopped feeding and looked up, its beautiful eyes searching.

"It's the Reaper," Willa Grace whispered.

"Reaper?"

"You know, the Reaper, herald of death."

"That's a ridiculous name for such a peaceful animal."

Willa Grace rested her chin on my shoulder to watch. "I overheard Mister Pesko telling Tata it's a piebald deer. It's like any other except that half its body is white, making it look like the good Lord wasn't quite finished with it yet."

"I suppose it does."

"Mister Pesko says they gave it that name because it has special powers. He swears it appeared outside the window the night their Matty died of tuberculosis. As soon as the deer disappeared into the woods, Matty breathed his last. Mister Pesko said it's a sign."

"Oh, stop," I said. "Anything that beautiful could never be a sign of something so awful. You should know better than to believe what Mister Pesko says."

"I know. Tata says Mister Pesko doesn't know his arse from a hole in the ground, but I think there's something to what he says."

"I don't believe it."

"How do you explain that deer in the field when Mister Jakobec had his heart attack and died?" Willa Grace flicked my arm.

"I never heard that."

"It's true. The Havelka girls said so, too." Willa Grace's wide brown eyes picked up the moonlight.

"Anyway, poor Matty. Can you imagine not being able to breathe? To me, there is no worse way to die."

"I could think of a few." Willa Grace pushed the branches farther apart to get a better view.

I sighed. "If I could afford new paints, I'd paint her just like this with the silver of the moonlight dusting her and the clearing."

"Come on," Willa Grace tugged on my arm, "just in case old man Pesko's right. One of us might be next."

"Oh, Wills, don't say such a thing."

The deer startled and looked to the forest, first one way, then the other, and bounded off with a flash of its tail like a paintbrush dipped in white.

A cloud suddenly snatched the moon, and the forest darkened like when the wind blew the door of the root cellar shut. We stopped, double-checked the direction of the trail ahead, then continued.

"It's a bad time for us to be gone, what with harvest time coming up. Not to mention the new baby." It was true. Our poor mother had just added to the family one more time. This would make eight children, four girls, and four boys, counting Teddy. Do you count someone who only got four years and has been gone so long? Of course, you do.

Willa Grace once again grabbed my arm. "Mamka told us to go. See what's out there. If you ask her, she'd say she and Tata should have stayed in Cleveland."

"If they had, oh, never mind." I just couldn't help myself sometimes.

"Don't do this, Daisy." Willa Grace covered her ears and squeezed her eyes shut. "I mean it. We had such fun at the hall, and you'll only ruin it."

A partridge protecting its young drummed a warning a few feet away.

"I'm sorry. My emotions are getting the best of me. It's…I don't know." This was not the time or the place to discuss Teddy. I knew that. I linked my elbow with hers again. "I'm glad we're doing this together. You're right. We'll see a city, earn money, and help the family. We'll be back before we know it."

"Speak for yourself. I can't wait to live in the city." Willa Grace stuck her nose in the air. "Might not come back, either."

The moon slipped out of the clouds.

"Oh, you'll be back," I said. "You have to. Henry couldn't take his eyes off you tonight. As if that's anything new."

She frowned, then gave me a shove.

"I peeked into your secret hiding place and saw the paper with Missus Harold Smidl and Daisy Jane Smidl written about a hundred times. Gah!" Willa Grace pretended to wretch, then ran ahead.

"You didn't! Willa Grace, you little..."

The chase was on.

Arriving back at the farm, we tucked away the English, as was the rule, and spoke in Czech. The huge, black shape of the barn stood over us as we rounded the pig pen and crossed the yard toward our mostly white paint-worn house with a kerosene glow from the kitchen. It wasn't until we reached the glassed-in porch out front that we noticed Tata and Mamka sitting there waiting for us, a single candle between them, dusting them in gold. A table in the corner held Mamka's many violets, and Tata's barn jacket hung from a hook by the door.

Rather than the expected scolding from Tata for being late, he gave us a glare over the top of his wire-rimmed glasses, holding his pipe steady in front of him. Mamka held baby Rosalie to her chest and gently rocked from side to side.

Careful to hide her liquor breath, Willa Grace quietly said good night and went into the house. I pulled up a chair next to Mamka.

"The music tonight was so good, wasn't it?" I said, trying to be cheerful. Moments so peaceful were rare in the Maruska household.

"It was." Our mother smiled and began to hum a tune—the *Harvest Polka*, I think. Rosalie buried deeper into Mamka's generous chest.

"Jste připraveni na pondělní ráno?" Tata leaned forward to look me in the eye. You ready for Monday morning?

Mamka stopped humming.

"No. But, yes." My heart rose into my throat. I tried so hard to hold back the tears but lost the battle.

Mamka shifted the baby and put a hand on my face. With her thumb, she brushed away a tear. "Nemusíš odcházet, sladká holka." You don't have to go, sweet girl.

Tata looked over his glasses again. "Josie, you said they needed to see what's out there." His Czech pride would never allow him to admit the family needed the money.

"Isaac, what do I know?" Mamka's eyes watered, too. "Oh, I know what I said."

"They are good girls. They know to keep themselves out of trouble." He cleared his throat.

"Of course, but..." Mamka glanced at him.

Tata waved her off with a grunt.

"Things happen sometimes that are out of one's control." Mamka threw up a hand.

"This is your worry talking." He leaned forward and looked me in the eye. "Your Mamka's being silly."

"You better hope I am being silly." Our mother glared at him, then sighed. "You worry, too old fart! Just too stubborn to admit it."

Tata slapped the arm of his chair. "Let's go to bed." He rose from his chair, snuffed out the candle, and left us in the dark.

"Men!" Mamka patted my hand. "Always has to be such a tough guy all the time."

"He's right. We'll be fine." I didn't want to add to their worries and wished I could be as strong as Willa Grace.

Mamka sighed and lightly patted Rosalie's bottom. "Every night I worry so. As long as we stay healthy, anything else, we can handle. I don't know that I've ever worried so much."

I turned toward her, unsure if I should probe. "Mamka?"

"Never mind me. It's probably my age. I thought I was too old for more babies, but along came our Rosie." She kissed Rosalie's golden head. "I told Tata, 'No more babies.'" She must have seen the shocked look on my face. "Too much? You're a big girl now. I've had babies since I was a year older than you."

"I will be nineteen in just a few months. Babies won't happen for a while, but you never know. Harold Smidl might look my way yet, although with Willa Grace and me leaving…I don't know." Until now, only Willa Grace had known of my crush on Harold.

"The Smidl boy. Humph. He will be a lucky young man when he sets his sights your way." Mamka leaned in and kissed my cheek. "Patience, girl. Don't wish your young years away. Go to the city, see what's to see, and come back if that's your desire. Then you can be satisfied with your lot. I wish I'd had that chance. When the train pulled into Phillips from Cleveland, I saw a tiny town trying to keep its head above the muck and mud. It crossed my mind to stay in my seat and run back to Ohio." She waved her free hand in front of her face. "Ack, I'd have followed your father anywhere in those days. I still would. But no more babies."

"For you, I will see what Chicago has to offer." Then I grinned, "Willa Grace can't wait. She thinks the city is just waiting for her to arrive."

"That girl." Mamka put her forehead to mine, and we held hands for a time as silver spilled across the yard.

"One more day…" I sighed.

Willa Grace

"That's it." I forced my cheap brown suitcase shut. "The clothes I have on and the pajamas I wear tonight will stay behind. I'm out of room." My little heart was beating with the speed of a train flying down the tracks. One more day, and my whole world would break open wide. I couldn't be more excited as I thought of the opportunities ahead. But then, there was my sad-sack sister.

"Hmm." Daisy gazed out our second-story bedroom window, her eyes on the yard below. She fingered a black curl on her shoulder. The pink of her blouse showed off her black hair, her creamy skin, and smaller features. Daisy didn't know how pretty she was.

You'd think I was marching her off to war, off to certain death and destruction, never to be the same. Daisy wasn't usually one for dramatics. That was me.

I looked around this room she and I had shared for so many years. It wasn't that long ago that we helped Mamka put up the blue floral wallpaper. Daisy and I sewed the quilt on our double bed, patched together from old dresses. Daisy's side of the room was always neat as a pin. Mine, not so much. She kept a bouquet of wildflowers in a

Mason jar on the stand beside the bed. In winter, it was balsam boughs and dogwood branches. My side was piled with books and a candle, for me to read at night.

I went over to my stack of books and straightened them. I was sorry to leave them behind. These worn and tattered books were my escape to other worlds, my door to adventures, a way to see other people and places I hoped to meet one day.

Daisy stood at the window, the lace curtain in her fingers. She'd been there too long.

"I sure hope I like my new job. We were lucky to have found work."

We'd both found work in the suburb of Berwyn, only a hop, skip, and a jump from the big city of Chicago, where I hoped to end up eventually. According to Tata, Berwyn or Cicero were our only choices because of the many Czechs there. He said it would be safe.

"Daisy-do, hello?" My sister was ignoring me.

"I suppose." She let out a long, weary sigh. Oh gosh.

"You'll enjoy being a companion to that older lady...what's her name?"

"Lucille Winterthur."

"You've always been a better nurse than me." It was true. I had no patience for sickness, not that the woman was sick, but she was old. "Kitchen work in a big house isn't exactly what I would choose, but it'll do for now. Maybe I could be a secretary someday."

"I can see you as a librarian, Wills, with your love of reading, but for now, you know your way around a kitchen fine enough to be a big help." She could have added, 'As long as they don't let you cook.' I know she was thinking that.

I went to the window and peered over Daisy's shoulder. Mamka was hanging wash on the line. Two-year-old Albert hung on her skirt with his little fists, pulling the fabric taut over her still-swollen belly after having Rosalie.

"Poor Mamka, she can't go anywhere without Albert hanging off of her," I said. "And now, one more. You'll never catch me in that situation. I don't want anything to do with having babies."

"You'll change your mind once you find a fella you want to marry. I wouldn't be surprised if you end up with a whole passel of babies at your feet." Daisy looked back at me and grinned.

"Oh, no. If I allow a man to marry me, he has to know, no babies."

"You say that now." Daisy focused on Mamka once again. "Look at her awful apron. I'm sending her a new apron before we come back."

Daisy *would* say something like that. She was always thinking of others. It made me feel like a louse at times.

"There must be years of cooking, baking, canning, and wiping sticky faces on that one."

Daisy let loose with another sigh, then let go of the curtain and sat on our bed.

Our younger sister, Isabelle 'Issy', entered and spread her arms wide. "This will be mine tomorrow. All mine!" She plopped backward onto the bed next to Daisy. Issy's auburn braids jutted out in opposite directions, her skinny legs and arms at angles, and a slight hint of boobs under her blouse. Issy was fifteen, going on twenty, and obsessed with boys. If you ask me, it wouldn't get her a darned thing in this world.

"Try not to be too sad about our leaving," I said. "Besides, little girl, we will be back to visit. Then where will you be, huh?" I gently tugged one of her braids.

"Maybe I'd miss you if you were nicer to me." Issy swiped at my hand and stuck her pointy little nose in the air.

Daisy leaned over her. "You and Addie are needed all the more now, with the new baby. And don't forget, harvest is right around the corner."

"Cripes, now that I think of it, maybe I should go to Chicago, too." Issy sat up. "I could find me a job."

"Think of all the hearts you'd break if you left," I said as I checked my dresser drawers one last time.

"True, but I know girls my age who live in boarding houses and work in restaurants. I could do that." Issy never suffered from a lack of confidence.

"Next year, or as soon as milk prices rise, I'll be back for good. Maybe you can replace me at my job when the time comes. That would be a perfect solution, wouldn't it?"

I gave Daisy a withered look.

"Who knows when that will be?" Issy slapped the quilt in frustration. "I wish I was grown and could do what I want."

With some luck, and if I could help it, Daisy'd come to love the city and stay. After all, I couldn't imagine my life without her.

"Think of all the boys you're going to meet." Issy grinned and got all dreamy-eyed, which made her look like Baumgartner's old bloodhound. "There will be so many to choose from."

"That's the last thing I need," I said, joining them on the bed. "You need to settle down with this boy-craziness. It's going to get you in trouble one of these days."

"Oh, shut up. Mamka's life would be much easier with *three* of us out of her hair."

"Don't be stupid." I hit her with a pillow, she threw it back, and it landed on the floor.

"Yep, I can't wait for my new bedroom. You two need to skedaddle." Issy pushed off the bed with a weary squeak of the springs, shut the door behind her, and stuck her head back in. "Forgot to tell you, Willa Grace, Henry is here." She stuck out her tongue, shut the door again, and ran down the hall.

"Ugh," My shoulders slumped. Henry was a nice guy, but he wanted more than I had to give him. Besides, I'd known him all my life. What fun was there in that? He should be eyeing Daisy. She'd be the perfect farm wife.

"Oh, go be nice. I'm sure he's come to say goodbye." Daisy rose and smoothed the quilt. "He'd been looking for you last night but got tired of running after you."

I rolled my eyes. "There were too many people to see to spend the night sitting with only him."

"You two will make beautiful children someday," Daisy smirked.

"Go jump in a lake."

In the kitchen, Mamka was washing a large kettle of green beans. "Your Henry is here."

"Yep." I looked beyond her and out the kitchen window. Henry was talking with our brother George out by the barn. "He's not *my* Henry."

"Oh, sure he is," Mamka chuckled impishly. "Go. And put on a smile," she called as I went out the door.

"Hello, Willa Grace," Henry said, holding a brown fedora. He was dressed in brown trousers and a white shirt. I, in contrast, wore overalls, a blouse, and shoes that had seen better days.

"See ya later, Henry," George winked at me and left for the barn.

"See ya then," Henry said, bobbing his head before turning his attention to me. "I wasn't sure you'd be at the ball game this afternoon, but Georgie says you're going. I could pick you up, although I have to be there early for warm-ups." He pursed his lips together, brows raised with a hopeful look in his pretty brown eyes and features more handsome than most boys around here. I always thought he looked more like a school teacher, but he loved his farm. And there, dear Henry, lay his downfall when it came to me.

I looked toward the house. Mamka, Daisy, and Issy watched us out the kitchen window. When they saw me, they quickly disappeared, but not before Issy waved—little stinker.

"Um, I.....we'll walk there with our brothers."

"Oh." He opened his mouth to say more, but stopped. I toed the dirt at my feet. An awkward silence followed.

"Okay. I'll see you at the game, Willa Grace. I didn't want to miss a chance to say goodbye and wish you well." He started toward his old truck, then turned. "What time does your train leave tomorrow?"

"Nine-fifteen." I nervously picked at a fingernail. *Please don't offer to drive us.*

"I could drive you and Daisy to the train if you'd like." He turned his hat over, fingering the brim.

"Tata's driving us in." Then I remembered Daisy's advice to be nice. "Kind of you to offer, though." I put my hands behind my back to stop picking.

Seven-year-old Joey ran through the yard chasing Ranger, our dog. Most of the animals ran when they saw Joey heading their way. He was a little shit if there ever was one. He put his dirty hands on either side of his freckled face and made kissing noises at us. I glared. Henry chuckled. Then Joey ran off.

"Say, do you mind if I write to you?" he asked.

"I'm not much of a letter writer. Maybe you could write Daisy instead. She's always writing someone or another. You should see the list of addresses she's got."

"I want to write to you. You don't have to write back to me if you don't want to."

"I guess that would be okay."

"Might I have the address?" He had a bead of sweat on his forehead.

"Oh, sure. I'll be right back." I went to the house. The three spies were in the window again and ducked when they saw me coming.

I wrote down the address of Thorpe's, my new employer, while Issy teased. Mamka and Daisy sat at the table with silly grins and snapped beans.

"Enjoying the show?" I rolled my eyes at them and went back out.

I handed the piece of paper to Henry, who folded the note in quarters and put it in his shirt pocket.

"By the way, did you hear about Willy Blaha?" He put on his hat.

"No. What about him?"

"He died last night at Viola Villa. Didn't you hear? I assumed you were there. They figured it was a heart attack. It happened just as the band was finishing their last song. The poor guy collapsed in the middle of the dance floor. Right in front of his wife."

"Oh, no. We left just after dark," I said. I remembered seeing Willy and his young wife twirling amongst the dancers. They grinned at each other so that I almost felt I was intruding by watching.

Then I remembered the deer.

"Oh my gosh! The Reaper." I put a hand on Henry's forearm, then quickly removed it.

"What was that?" Henry's brows came together.

"The piebald deer that people are saying shows up when someone dies. Daisy and I saw it outside the hall on our way home." Goosebumps rose on my arms.

"Just a silly rumor. Don't pay any attention." Henry grinned.

"This isn't just a rumor. I can't believe it. Poor Willy." This was too much to absorb. Willy was a jokester, the life of the party, but he was also devoted to his sweet wife and three children. It was unbelievable that such a bright light was now snuffed out forever. And the deer Daisy and I saw in the woods had signaled his death. Henry and Daisy could think what they wanted, but I knew people were right about that damned deer.

"Well…" Henry looked as though there was something more he wanted to say. I prayed there wasn't. "I will see you later then." He put his hat on.

"Yep. Bye." I turned toward the house, giving the three at the window a dirty look.

"Wait a moment."

I stifled a groan and turned.

"You know I've taken a fancy to you, Willa Grace. I can't hide it anymore."

I bit my upper lip and focused on a squirrel at the base of a mossy stump, probably the same critter that chewed the pumpkins I planted. I'd have to get out the BB gun.

"I want you to know I'll still be here when you return," Henry said quietly.

"I don't know, Henry. I may not…."

"I'm not a dummy, Willa Grace. I know you don't feel the same as me." He removed his hat again and nervously ran the brim through his hands.

"I don't know what you see in me, Henry. I'm not pretty, I never seem to say the right thing, and I can't dance worth a lick."

At that, he chuckled. "You're a breath of fresh air. Not like the other girls, and I mean that in a good way. And I think you're very pretty."

I knew my face was as red as one of Mamka's zinnias. We stood there silently for a moment. Thank goodness he didn't say I'd make a good farmer's wife. I might have clobbered him. Of course, I could. I didn't want to.

He broke the silence. "What do you say we write just as friends and leave it at that for now."

"I think that would be fine." I smiled, grateful and relieved. "Thank you for understanding."

He angled his head and studied me. "Safe travels, Willa Grace."

"You, too. I mean…um…all the best to you, Henry."

Daisy was in her glory that Henry came to say goodbye since she'd had him pegged as the perfect fella for me. She teased me steadily after he left that day.

A bit later, I got a chance to pay her back. She and I sat on a log at the edge of the pasture to put together a bouquet of wildflowers we'd picked for Mamka.

"Aw, geez." I closed my eyes and shook my head. Harold Smidl was coming across the field.

"What?" Upon seeing Harold, Daisy practically threw her flowers at me, straightened her shoulders, and smoothed her white blouse. "Oh my, I didn't expect this." She brushed a burr from her brown pants and crossed her legs all ladylike.

"Gosh, I can hardly wait," I said as I watched him approach.

Dressed in black slacks and a blue shirt, Harold had his black hair combed severely over to one side. To me, he always looked like he had a stick up his backside. A fierce blush crept up Daisy's neck. How cute, but nauseating.

"Hiya, Daisy. And you, too, Willa Grace." Harold's voice was deep and so very manly. He kept his eyes on Daisy even as he said hello to me. I don't think Harold thought too much of me after I clocked him once with a baseball at the Villa's annual ice cream social. It wasn't my fault. He should have paid attention to where he was walking.

"Hiya, Harold," I said, nudging Daisy and trying not to laugh at his effect on my sister.

Harold's eyes were glued to Daisy as she scooted over, and he took a seat on the log.

"Heard you're headed to the big city tomorrow. That's quite brave of you."

"Thank you. I will surely miss the farm and…everyone here. You can be sure I will count the days until I can return. Our little piece of Wisconsin is all I need."

Could my sister have been more obvious?

"Well, Daisy, the city could be quite exciting," Harold said. "I'm thinking of going there myself. Just for a visit, mind you. It won't be the same here once you're gone."

"It would be lovely if you could visit while we're there."

"Uhh, I think I'm going to throw up." I rolled my eyes.

"Willsy!" Daisy gave me a shove with her shoulder, and off the log, I slid. "Don't mind her. She's just jealous." It seemed like a good time to leave. So, I did.

That night, Daisy was sound asleep, and I was counting cows. Sleep never came easy for me, and this night, I knew that the fight was not worth spit. Thoughts of the city and all that lay ahead had me so excited I couldn't stand it.

I eased out of bed, slipped on loafers, and, with a spare blanket over my nightgown, stole down the stairs and out the back door.

A full moon and stars made for a beautiful night. I followed the well-worn path to the creek, careful to stay away from the northern swing of it. A cooling breeze moved the hair on my shoulders, and the clean country air filled my lungs.

I sat on the hillside overlooking the creek, tightened the blanket around my shoulders, and pulled up my knees. The creek was a ribbon of sparkle. The willow tree across the way swished in the soft breeze, mixing with the scent of grasses and wildflowers. Far off, an owl hooted a few times, then silence. Dawn was still hours away. My heart never took for granted the beauty of our piece of Emery Township.

Yet, I was so willing to leave it behind. Why was that?

I was a complete mystery to myself at times. I suppose that would never change.

Farther down the creek, the dreaded northern curve of it, a movement in the shadows of a cottonwood caught my eye. Like a puff of fog, it formed, frittered away, and formed again. I narrowed my eyes.

It was a silhouette I recognized.

"Teddy?" I whispered. A prickle crawled up my spine, but I wasn't afraid. "Teddy?" My heart thumped in my chest as I blinked and held my breath.

I'd spent many a night sitting by this creek. This had never happened before. Why now? Was he telling me goodbye? Was this a warning of some kind? Or has he been with us all along, and I never paid attention?

"I'm sorry," I said quietly into the night, and with the hush of a breeze, he was gone.

THREE

Daisy

To my shock, Harold had come to see me off to the city. He and I sat on the log along the field for quite a while, talking about general things: the fine weather we'd had, milk prices, and whatever news we could think of in Emery Township and beyond. We were both nervous, but in the end, we exchanged addresses. He didn't kiss me goodbye, but I could tell he wanted to. I would have let him.

If I thought leaving was hard while I simply hoped Harold had noticed me, it was nearly painful now that he had. If ony I had said no to Willa Grace's wild adventure from the start. It was too late to back out now. As flattered as I was that he'd come to bid me goodbye, I almost wish he hadn't. Well, not really.

Saying goodbye to the family was beyond difficult, but knowing it was temporary helped. Yet, I had an upset stomach for nearly the entire trip on the train, and I wasn't sure if it was nerves or the rocking of the passenger car that was giving me motion sickness. Since morning, I've also had a stiff neck from trying to sleep sitting up. As the train rolled to a stop in Chicago, I made up my mind to do as Mamka said—see what there is to see, make some memories, and know that Emery Township was waiting for me when our time was done.

As I stepped off the train behind Willa Grace, I held my purse and suitcase close for protection and took it all in. After the long trip on the train, it felt good to have my feet on solid, steady ground, but I was ill-prepared for this new place.

Chicago Union Station was like nothing I'd ever seen. The grandeur of the soaring arched ceilings, fancy pillars, scrollwork, and all that marble was nothing like I expected. There were elegant staircases and balconies. Sunlight streamed in through tall, curved windows. The artistry of the design was unexpectedly breathtaking and intimidating. What wonders man creates!

I looked over to Willa Grace, who stood with her mouth gaping and eyes wide. I couldn't help but grin at her. Looking around, it was as if we'd been dropped on another planet. I nudged her with my elbow, and we giggled. I wasn't sure if we were laughing because of nerves or the ridiculousness of the drastic change in our location.

"Do you believe this?" Willa Grace grabbed the fabric of my light coat, trying to contain her excitement.

"We've arrived." This was something. I wasn't sure what.

Bustling crowds pushed in around us, and I suddenly felt closed in, which was silly in such a massive space. I held my suitcase close and realized I was holding my breath. So many people, so many different faces, all hurrying to heaven knows where and why. The air was heavy with all the aromas, pleasant and otherwise. I tried not to breathe too deeply, already missing the scents of evergreen and newly cut hay.

I swear, I think the station held more people than lived in all of Emery. Men rushed by in tailored suits and fedoras tipped over their foreheads, and women in fashionable dresses and slacks, their heels clicking on the marble floors.

I was suddenly aware of how 'country' my sister and I must appear. The women wore their hair short and bobbed. Tata wouldn't allow us to cut our hair in a bob. He didn't want his daughters to look like boys, or worse, flappers. Our dresses looked like potato sacks compared to theirs.

"We look like we're fresh off the farm," I said to Willa Grace.

"Who cares? We'll fit right in before you know it."

A man in a navy blue uniform with gold trim and a matching captain's hat approached. "Do you ladies need help?" He looked down on us over wire-rimmed glasses.

"Sure." Willa Grace stepped forward, set her suitcase down, and dug in her purse for our addresses.

"Willa Grace," I whispered, leaning into her, "we don't know him."

"We don't know anyone." She took a piece of paper from her purse and held it out to him. "We need to get to these places. Those are our new jobs. We've never been in the city before."

I pinched the underside of her arm and gave her a look.

"Ouch." Willa Grace rubbed her arm and glared at me.

This stranger didn't need to know how out of place we were. For all we knew, he could be a criminal in a nice suit.

Mr. Uniform Man pushed his gray brows together, frowned at us, and then turned his attention to the addresses again. He handed the paper back to Willa Grace. "You ladies need a taxi. Follow me."

Willa Grace took off behind him, with me following, my eyes sweeping here and there for any trace of danger. A young boy crossed in front of me, and I nearly tripped over him. An elderly man hobbling over a cane slowed me down just as a young woman dragging a child by the hand cut me off. When I looked up, Willa Grace and our guide were out of sight.

"Willa Grace!" I called out, and people turned in my direction.

"Hurry up," Willa Grace appeared through the crowd, only feet away.

Once outside, the true size of Union Station could be seen. I was in awe and felt mighty small.

Our leader hailed a taxicab from a line of them waiting along the busy street, then bid us farewell and disappeared into the crowd. A tall, skinny man with black curly hair and skin nearly as dark jumped out of a yellow car and came around to stand before us.

I embarrassed myself by gasping. I'd never engaged with a black man before, and neither had my sister, although a couple bought a farm on the northeast side of Emery. I'd never seen them, but I'd heard they were very pleasant people who mainly kept to themselves.

"Cedric, at your service. Where to, ladies?" He had a wide, toothy smile and a slight accent I couldn't place. We hadn't actually been exposed to very many.

Willa Grace gave him the addresses.

"Well, these aren't too far away. Hop in." Cedric opened the trunk, put our suitcases inside, and then slammed it shut. He opened the back passenger side door and waited while we slid inside. "What brings you to our fine city?" he asked as he got in on the driver's side and returned the paper with the addresses.

Willa Grace had her face up against the window, so I answered. "We have jobs here."

"You're lucky to have found them. Jobs not easy to find. No matter what, I hang onto this job for dear life." He adjusted his mirror and smiled at us.

Willa Grace scooted forward, leaning her elbows on the back of the front seat, and asked, "Where are you from, Cedric?"

"I am from England, most recently. Jamaica before that. Been here a while now, so I know the city 'bout as well as my big toe." He laughed at his joke.

I settled back in the seat, my shoulders pulled in, trying not to breathe too deeply and looking for anything worrisome. There was none, and the interior of the taxi was clean with a slight cinnamon scent. The cab scooted forward into traffic. From behind, a horn tooted.

"Will we get to see the city on our way?" Willa Grace's face was at the window again. "We've never seen a skyscraper. I can't imagine how tall they must be. I would just love to see one. Could you show us?"

"Willa Grace, I'm sure he has better things to do," I said, my hand on her sleeve.

"It would be an honor to show you ladies our beautiful city. That will be no problem at all. I will make a loop through the heart of it on our way."

Willa Grace clapped, looking ready to burst. "Yippee!"

Oh, dear heavens, that sister of mine.

Cedric chatted happily, patiently answering Willa Grace's rapid-fire questions. Then, we were in the thick of it. Chicago, Illinois, in all its glory. Buildings were so tall they seemed to push against the sky, people everywhere, cars and trucks zoomed around the trolleys. I craned my head upward, feeling very tiny in this concrete forest.

Looking closer, Chicago was not as grand as Willa Grace promised. So many buildings stood vacant due to the Depression, I could only imagine, yet people were everywhere. With so many on the streets, crime had to be around every corner.

It was a warm day, and Willa Grace rolled her window down. I did the same. The city's noise was astounding—motors and horns, people yelling and cursing. And the smells—exhaust from the vehicles and smoke from chimneys, cars, trucks, taxis, and buses all trying for their place on the street, and people of so many shades of color and styles of dress.

The buildings hung over us like giants, casting shadows on everyone below. I had to crane my neck to see the tops of them. Then, I remembered hearing ghastly stories of the crash in '29. Desperate bankers and investors jumped to their deaths from these tall structures. Bodies raining down on the sidewalks, all because of money. The gruesome pictures in my head made me shiver.

I knew right away that this wasn't the place for me. I would do my duty to help my family, but I was heading north as soon as possible.

As we rounded one corner, Cedric indicated one of the bread lines we'd heard about on the radio. Long rows of people looking desperate, exhausted, and humiliated.

One young man stood out to me, reminding me of our brother George in a way. It was the tall, proud cut of him. His dirty, brown shirt hung like a sack on his bony frame, and the sweat-stained Fedora covered the tops of his ears. He and I made eye contact as we passed. His eyes haunted me, so full of hatred for whatever placed him in that line. He spat on the ground and defiantly pumped his chin, never shifting his gaze. I quickly downcast my eyes, feeling guilty for our good fortune. We weren't hungry and had a home with family who loved us.

Willa Grace stuck her head out the window like a dog needing fresh air, taking it all in. She was in her glory, gawking at everything. She paid no attention to the bread line, the closed banks, department stores, and hotels.

Suddenly, Willa Grace yelped. I jerked my head around as she pulled her head inside, bumping it hard on the door frame. "Ow!"

"What happened?" I asked, reaching for her arm as she rubbed the top of her head.

"I swallowed a bug. Yuck!"

Cedric and I laughed as Willa Grace spit a few more times and wiped her mouth on her sleeve.

"Thanks, Wills. I needed a laugh." That sister of mine could always lighten the mood. "Are you sure you're all right? You hit your noggin pretty hard."

"Good as new. Look at the size of that building ahead!" The bug incident was forgotten.

"That," Cedric explained, "is the Chicago Board of Trade Building. Forty-four stories high."

"Holy moly, can you imagine the view from up there?" Willa Grace's head was out the window again. "Someday, I'll find a way to see it myself."

At that, I had to stick my head out as well. I had to admit, I found what people could create to be impressive.

Suddenly, Cedric jammed on the brakes, and we slammed against the door and back of the front seat so hard I was sure I'd have a crick in my neck.

"Sorry, ladies." Cedric jumped out of the cab and ran around the front. Willa Grace baled out as well. I couldn't see anything, so I followed her, horrified at what I found.

A young boy had run across the street and collided with the front of our cab as we pulled to a stop at the intersection. The scraggly child wore pants two sizes too small that were ripped at both knees. His shirt was dirty, and his shoes had holes in the soles. He held a loaf of bread to his little chest as if it were a treasure, no doubt the only food he had to feed his family. I wanted to scoop him right up. Thankfully, he only suffered a cut on his head. I rushed forward with the handkerchief from my coat pocket and offered it to him. The whiteness of my handkerchief was striking against the filth of his hand as he grabbed it and held it to his cut. I started to reach for his head to push his hair away from the cut and reassure him he would be all right, but Cedric blocked my hand and shook his head.

A large man with a messy white apron tied around his girth came into the street, cursing the boy and taking back the loaf of bread. The poor child had tears running down his cheeks.

"Sir," I said, and Willa Grace's eyes flew open wide in shock, "can't you let him have it? It's just a small loaf. He looks hungry."

"No!" The man shouted, turned, and pushed back through the crowd.

"Let me help," I said. "I have a few coins I can give you."

The boy's tears stopped, and he nodded, not saying a word.

"There are ways to get food without being a thief," Cedric said.

"He's a child." I gave him a quarter from the purse hanging on my arm.

The boy took the coin and ran off. The crowd moved on.

"That was a kind thing you did there, Miss. He'll be able to buy more than bread with what you gave him. I didn't want you to touch him for fear of lice. Can't have my cab infested."

"Nice going, Daisy." Willa Grace said. "That could have been so much worse."

Cedric checked his cab for damage and, finding none, we were on our way, but it would be a long time before I could forget the terrified look in the boy's dark eyes. I hoped my measly quarter would do him some good.

I breathed a hefty sigh of relief when we left the city behind for the suburb of Berwyn. I'd seen enough. As we approached, streets narrowed, and neat homes came into view with pretty yards and big trees. Children chased balls and rode bicycles. Mothers pushed babies, and old men visited on corners. Berwyn's quaint shops lined the streets, selling everything a person would need to get along. It looked like a fine community for our temporary situation.

Still, I'd already seen things that made me long for home.

Willa Grace

Chicago was a revelation. I'd seen it described that way in one of my books, and it wasn't a lie. When we stepped off the train, I didn't want to blink for all there was to see. Sky-high ceilings and marble everywhere. I'd never been anywhere with so much activity in one building. People rushing here and there, surely with important places to be. And the sounds. Train whistles, the hiss of the engines, people calling to one another, babies crying, boys calling out the latest headlines trying to sell newspapers, and men in fancy uniforms hollering out train schedules.

I nearly tripped over a suitcase next to an elderly gentleman as I swung my head from side to side to take it all in. If Daisy hadn't been there for me to grab the sleeve of her coat, I'd have been a splotch on their marble floor.

There were people of every nationality. I stood still for a second and could make out at least three different languages. German, Spanish, and, music to my ears, Czech. It was a sign. We were going to be just fine here. I could have stayed there all day to take it in.

"Look at that guy over there." I pumped my chin toward a stocky man in a finely tailored suit, hat dipped nearly over one eye, and a mighty stern look on his pockmarked face while he puffed a thick cigar. He tipped back and forth on his heels while studying the crowd of travelers. I wondered if he carried a piece hidden under his coat. "He's got that Chicago look about him."

"We're in Chicago."

I rolled my eyes to the ceiling and drooped my shoulders. "You know what I mean. He looks like a gangster, doesn't he? Maybe he's eyeing up the place, looking for his next hit."

"For goodness' sake, Willsy. Do you want me to stay or not, because I could get right back onto the train."

"No, you couldn't. You can't afford the ticket back."

A woman dragging a child behind her bumped into me and nearly knocked me over. "Geez, Louise!" I righted myself.

Daisy was starting to look about as petrified as a tombstone.

"Where do we go next?" she asked. If she hugged her purse any tighter, she'd be wearing it.

"No idea."

As if on cue, a lovely man offered to help us get where we were going. I gave him the addresses, and we followed him to an entrance. He then got us a taxi, just like that. Our driver, Cedric, was the first black man I'd ever been close to. I walked up to him, held out my hand, and introduced myself.

Daisy's eyebrows nearly disappeared into her hairline.

Cedric kindly shook my hand, nodded to Daisy, placed our bags in the trunk, and we were off. He was so interesting as he shared his journey from Jamaica to England to Chicago with his young wife and children. I now knew someone from Jamaica and England, and I hadn't been in Chicago for more than an hour.

Daisy was peeved that I asked Cedric to drive us through downtown Chicago, but why not take advantage of the ride? Besides, Cedric generously obliged. Oh, the sights we saw. He pointed out his favorite eating places and grocery stores while navigating the busy neighborhoods and city streets. Here and there, he threw in a historical tidbit.

Me, Willa Grace Maruska, was really, truly here.

I rolled down my window, gawking at everyone and everything. I hated to blink for fear I'd miss something. The noise, the people, the architecture, the shops, one after another, offering anything a gal could want.

There were a few vacant buildings due to the goddamned Depression, but things would rebound, they had to, and these places would thrive again like they always had. Henry said old FDR would bring the country back stronger than ever. Daisy and I were there at the perfect time to see the transformation that was sure to happen. How thrilling.

To those on the street, I suppose I looked like an absolute country bumpkin leaning out to see all I could. Who cared? I was in the city.

On State Street, I saw a young woman bustling down the sidewalk in confident strides, dressed in a white form-fitting short-sleeved jacket belted at the waist, a mid-calf black skirt flaring at her knees, silk stockings, and shiny black shoes with pointy toes and high heels. Her blond hair was short and crimped, covered partially by a black hat tilted stylishly to the right. Under her arm, she held a black clutch. Where was she going? Surely, an office high in the sky where she took notes, attended meetings, and knew very important things.

As we passed, she looked in my direction, and I waved. Her expression was one of confusion. Was I someone she knew? It made me laugh.

Someday, that would be me. Yes, it would.

I felt like I had waited all my life to be part of this energy, to walk these sidewalks, dart in and out of the stores and cafes as though I'd been here my whole life, to wake up each day and wonder what new experience lay ahead.

It was going to be torturous to spend my time in Berwyn, just a hop, skip, and a jump from Chicago, but that was where we found jobs with Tata's approval.

That was fine for now, but I had a plan. After the family no longer needed our help, I would save enough to afford an apartment in Chicago and find work there. I looked over at my sister. My first task would be to make sure Daisy liked this place and wouldn't leave me.

Daisy craned her neck, looking for the tops of the buildings. I tried to sense her reaction, but Daisy was reserved as always. I reached over and grabbed the sleeve of her coat.

"Do you believe all this, Daisy-do? What an adventure we're going to have."

She pulled her head back and grinned half-heartedly.

"Oh, come on. Can't you see the opportunities here?"

Finally, I got a genuine smile from her. "You're right. This is quite amazing."

"Told you! Wait and see. We're going to have such fun on our days off together."

All of a sudden, Cedric bellowed, "NO!" and slammed on the brakes. Daisy and I careened against the back of his seat, both of us screeching in shock.

"What happened?" I asked as Cedric bolted from the taxi.

I flew out of the back seat with Daisy right behind me. There, in front of the taxi, lay a young boy at odd angles with blood spurting from a cut above his eye.

People gathered around as Cedric bent over the scruffy-looking boy holding a loaf of bread. A hefty man, balding and in a white apron, ran forward, shouting, "Thief!" The man stood over the boy, raising his fist high. Cedric bent over the boy and held up an arm to shield him.

The boy started to cry. It was a pitiful sight as tears ran down his dirty cheeks. His pursuer, the man who looked like a shopkeeper, took back the loaf of bread and stormed off. What a jerk.

Before I could think what to do, Daisy came around me and did what Daisy does best. She handed the boy her handkerchief, the one Mamka had embroidered for each of us as a going-away gift. I cringed. That handkerchief was never going to come clean after this.

"You're going to be okay, little guy," I said, but nobody noticed. Then Daisy dug a quarter from her purse and gave it to him. Again, I cringed. We didn't know this kid. He could be a professional thief for all we knew. And besides, neither of us had money to spare.

I quickly got out a quarter as well, but the boy took off before I could give it to him.

Daisy never got her handkerchief back. I was secretly glad I didn't offer mine.

"Damn, shame, that is," Cedric said when we were back in the taxi. "Glad he wasn't hurt more and no damage to my taxi."

I hated to see the city fade behind us as we entered Berwyn, but I soon realized Berwyn had nice things to offer as well.

"Daisy, there's a movie theater! Do you think we could go? Gosh, I'd love to see a movie."

"That'll be fun." She could have said that with a tad more enthusiasm. My sister was nervous that we were close to our new jobs and would be separated. I felt that, too. I reached over, patted her knee. She squeezed my hand in response.

Cedric stopped at an intersection, and I pointed. "There's Sokol Tabor." We'd learned of the Sokol from neighbors who moved to Emery from this area.

"The Zellinger girls said they have dances and plays, classes for all kinds of things, and parties on the holidays. I sure hope we can take part with our work schedules." Somehow, I'd make sure we'd attend.

"Almost to your destinations, ladies." Cedric glanced back at us. "Miss Daisy, your stop will be first."

That's when it hit me. For the first time in our lives, we would live apart. How would it be to have my own bed? Daisy and I had always shared a bed. I loved those nights we snuggled together, whispering secrets or telling stories. Daisy was my best friend. She knew me better than anyone.

I looked at Daisy, and she looked at me. I raised my brows and nodded. She smiled in that reassuring way she had, even though this was the last place she wanted to be.

Soon, we would be separated and on our own. If only we'd known what lay ahead.

FOUR

Daisy

Cedric pulled up along the curb on Longcommon Road in front of the home of my new employer, Mrs. Lucille Winterthur. Her sizeable Victorian house was painted yellow with white gingerbread trim and sage green in the peak and around the windows. Pink clematis wound its way up a trellis on one side of the wide porch that held white wicker furniture with floral cushions. From baskets on the porch rails, petunias in pink, purple, and magenta spilled over. Paned windows showed delicate lacy curtains on the inside. A wide chimney rose in the middle of the roof, suggesting cozy fireplaces. A massive maple tree graced the yard with sturdy branches stretching over the grass and shading the walk. Hydrangeas in hues of pink and white caressed the front of the porch, their blooms large and puffy as snowballs. Hollyhocks and zinnias of every color danced along the white picket fence, which finished the scene, making it picture-perfect. One day, I promised myself I would paint this beautiful place for my memories of the time we sisters went away to help our family.

As if Willa Grace, scrunched alongside me to see out the window, had read my mind, and said, "It's like one of your paintings, Daisy." If only my paintings were this good.

"Come with me," I turned to Willa Grace. As welcoming as this place appeared, what if it hid terrible secrets? What if, upon entering,

I felt the need to run? Cedric wouldn't leave without Willa Grace or without being paid. I wanted to be sure, and I wanted my sister's opinion to back my own. First glances are telling, and I didn't want to miss a warning of any kind.

Our driver quickly removed my suitcase from the trunk and handed it to me with a big smile. "I hope you'll be happy here, Miss Daisy."

I smiled back, wanting to remember his face for some reason, maybe because he'd been so kind in indulging Willa Grace's desire to see the city, and a bit of guilt at my wariness of him.

"Thank you, Cedric. All the best to you."

"You as well, Miss." He returned to the taxi to wait for Willa Grace.

I walked up the front steps, me carrying my suitcase, grateful that Willa Grace was with me for support. It was too bad I wouldn't be there for her when she met her employer for the first time.

Before knocking, I filled my lungs with sweet, floral-scented air, then looked to Willa Grace, who gave me a wink of encouragement. Through the oval leaded window, I could see movement. Willa Grace reached over and squeezed my hand.

A plump lady in a gray dress, starched white collar, and a white apron opened the door. Gray curls wreathed her round, fleshy face. She was a dull contrast to the colorful exterior of the home.

"Yes?" She didn't smile and didn't look like someone who smiled often.

"Daisy Maruska. I'm the companion for Missus Winterthur," I said and smiled. "This is my sister, Willa Grace. She's seeing me settled before she goes off."

The woman looked me up and down, then Willa Grace, with an expression that showed no interest in us whatsoever.

"I'm Gerda, head of the house."

"It's nice to meet you, Gertie," I said, unsure whether to offer a handshake.

"It's Gerda. Come in," she said without turning around. I realized I may have to tread lightly with her. I'd already made a mistake with her name, and I hadn't yet entered.

Willa Grace made a face at Gerda's back, which would normally make me grin, but I was too nervous. I gave her a nudge with my elbow.

The front hall was something I'd never seen before. The walls were papered with a botanical pattern of leaves, ferns, and berries in various shades of green on a blue background. A table stood against the wall in a rich wood tone with an ornate lamp in gold. The parquet floor gleamed under a Persian rug in blues, reds, and greens. A grand staircase eased down from upstairs with a graceful banister and a runner to match the rug. To the left, a living room with a stately fireplace and cozy, overstuffed furniture in floral patterns. To the right, the dining room with furniture as fancy as that I'd only seen in books and magazines.

A lovely woman floated down the staircase. Her silver hair swept up at the back of her head. She had perfect posture in a stylish blue dress that fell mid-shin, a simple belt to match, and a bodice in white lace. Gerda introduced her as Mrs. Winterthur. Her shiny black shoes lightly touched the rug as she came toward us.

I set my suitcase down as Gerda introduced both of us.

Mrs. Winterthur stopped just short of us. Her complexion was soft with a warmth that shone through as she smiled, her cheeks a peachy blush with few wrinkles, and the kindest blue eyes I'd ever seen.

"Welcome, girls." Mrs. Winterthur's voice was soothing, and I immediately felt welcome. She took my hand and enclosed it in both of hers. These were hands that had never milked a cow or picked rocks in a field, or so I assumed. But I admired her sense of beauty and her grace.

"Pleased to meet you, ma'am," I said and curtsied. I didn't know why I did this, but I immediately wanted to kick myself in the rear. Willa Grace pulled in her chin to stifle a grin.

"Oh, my goodness, dear, I'm not royalty, for heaven's sake." Mrs. Winterthur patted my hand. "We're going to be wonderful friends,

Daisy. Nice to meet you as well, Willa Grace. Both of you have such beautiful names." She then shook Willa Grace's hand.

"Thank you, ma'am." Willa Grace nodded.

We made small talk about the weather and the beauty of her gardens for a few moments before we heard the toot of Cedric's horn. We'd completely forgotten about him waiting.

"I'm off to the Thorpes. I'm going to work in the kitchen," Willa Grace said.

"I'm sure you will enjoy working there, as I've known Missus Thorpe for a while now. Willa Grace, you're welcome here anytime. Gerda and I will make sure Daisy settles in just fine here. I promise you that."

This was it. The time we both dreaded.

"Well…" I shrugged and opened my arms. I don't know how I held back the tears.

Willa Grace stepped into my arms, and I held her close. My heart screamed, 'No, I'm not ready to say goodbye.'

And so, our separation began. I let go, then once more hugged Willa Grace tight as though I were breathing her into my body before stepping back to allow her to leave. I had the clarity of knowing that our youth had slipped away. We had to be adults now. Those carefree days of life on the farm were gone. Even when I returned, I knew it would be different.

My sister's eyes were watery as well, but in true form, she squared her shoulders and gave a clipped bump of her chin to let me know she was ready for the challenge before her.

"Oh, girls," Mrs. Winterthur said, looking as though she knew what we felt, "you'll be able to see each other on your days off."

"We will," I said through my teary gaze. "Good luck, Willsy.

"See ya, Daisy-do." Willa Grace turned and marched out the door.

With my heart in my throat, I watched her leave. I put my hands over my heart. This really was it. The adventure Willa Grace and I had talked about for weeks was about to begin.

I turned to face my new future. 'Chin up,' as Mamka would say.

Mrs. Winterthur put an arm around my shoulder, and her rosewater scent wafted about us.

"You'll be happy here, Daisy. I promise."

I took a deep breath and relaxed. "Thank you." I gazed around the warm and cozy home. How could my stay here be anything but happy?

An oil painting of a garden over the mantel in the living room caught my eye.

Mrs. Winterthur followed my gaze and asked, "Do you like that one?"

"Oh, yes," I answered. "The colors are so bright and alive. Is this your garden?" I was drawn in, interested in the play of light and shadows.

"I painted this last year." Mrs. Winterthur coughed, cleared her throat, and continued, "Excuse me. I enjoy putting brush to canvas. It's my hobby. Busy hands are happy hands."

"The Missus here," Gerda interjected from behind us, "is quite modest. She's known city-wide for her fine work."

"How exciting!" I'd found a kindred spirit. How unexpected.

"Now, Gerda, you're giving me a big head. Please show Daisy to her room, won't you?" Then, she said to me, "After you settle in, come find me in the garden."

A tiny, white terrier pranced in and ran to Mrs. Winterthur's side, putting tiny paws on her leg. "Oh, this is Poppy, my little buddy." Mrs. Winterthur reached down and scratched Poppy's ears.

"She's adorable!" I knelt beside the dog and let her lick my cheek as I petted her silky fur—all of this and a pet.

"Come, Poppy. I'll take her on a little stroll around the yard before dinner." Mrs. Winterthur left us, the little puffball on her heels. "See you in the garden, Daisy." She pointed to a set of French doors off the living room as she left us.

Gerda looked me up and down again and sighed. "Come on." I followed her up the staircase. "The Missus has a room on the left here. You and I are at the other end of the hall."

Gerda opened a door and indicated the bathroom she and I would share. Indoor plumbing! The pink tiled room had a white sink, clawfoot tub, and toilet. I was certain I'd get a bit spoiled here. Even I had to admit it might be hard to go back to waiting for my turn to use the tub behind the curtain in the corner of our kitchen and squatting in the outhouse in winter.

"You and I will work out a bath schedule and such. Towels are in the armoire. My room is across the hall." Gerda swept her hand toward a door opposite. "I like to go to bed early, so I would appreciate your being quiet."

"Of course."

I then followed Gerda through the next door. "This is your room. All we ask is that you keep it clean. Breakfast is at eight, and lunch is served at twelve-thirty. Dinner for you and the Missus will be in the dining room at seven. She also likes a cup of tea at four in the afternoon."

"Where will you eat?"

"In the kitchen. I eat before serving the two of you." Her tone was a bit harsh.

"Oh." I felt I'd said something I shouldn't have as Gerda's mouth drew into a tight bow, and her eyes flashed green.

"That's how it's done." She pulled down the shades on the two windows. "Let me know if you need anything. There's an extra blanket in the closet if you're chilled at night."

I nodded. "This is all very comfortable. Thank you."

"The Missus is a very kind and generous woman. Don't abuse that. She is a woman still mourning, and you are to respect that."

"She's a widow?"

"Mister Winterthur passed away a few years ago. Heart failure. Earlier this year, she lost her only child, a son, David, to cancer. It's hard for her to speak of, so don't bring it up."

"Poor Missus Winterthur. How awful."

"You are here to help her move on. She realized hiring someone to keep her company was in her best interest. She and David were close."

"Did he live here?

"St. Louis. When he became ill, she moved him here. We both nursed him at the end." Gerda maintained her stern expression.

"I'm sorry, Gerda. That must have been hard."

"How old are you?"

"Eighteen." I straightened my shoulders and pushed my chin a tad higher. "Nineteen in a few weeks."

"That's plenty old enough to know how to behave. Make sure you do."

"I will do my best," I answered with all seriousness. How much trouble could I get into with Willa Grace gone? I grinned at that thought, and Gerda pursed her lips. I think she thought I was making fun of her.

With a clipped nod, Gerda left me to my new room.

The walls were covered in pink wallpaper with white stripes. The comfy bed had a brass headboard and pink chenille cover. Against the opposite wall stood a chest of drawers with a mirror. I didn't own enough clothes to fill every drawer.

I had never had a room of my own before and found I was quite pleased. To think I came here, dreading every mile on the train, only to find I might be happy. Temporarily, of course.

Setting my suitcase down, I plopped back onto the bed, arms spread wide, just as Issy had done in our room at home in her glee to have our room.

Why had I been so sure this move would be the death of me? So silly.

Willa Grace

Leaving Daisy left a hole in my heart. If I hadn't felt confident she would love it there, I'm not sure I could have left. The only worry I had was the sour-faced Gerda, but I was sure Daisy would win the old bag over. There wasn't a person alive who didn't love Daisy.

It was only minutes before Cedric announced our arrival at Thorpes. He pulled the taxi up to a fancy-pants iron gate where a stern-looking fella let us through. The paved drive curved through woods thick and green.

We went around a bend, and there it was. My new home for now. A massive stone house with turrets on both ends.

"Holy Christ!" I blurted and leaned over the front seat to get a better view.

Cedric's head swung sharply in my direction, and he burst into laughter.

"Sorry. I didn't expect this. Wait until Daisy hears." The house was enormous.

Cedric grinned. "Welcome to the Thorpe estate."

"I'm speechless, and that rarely happens. Why the heck does someone need a house this big?"

"Beats me," Cedric said, "but I'd like to try it out sometime." He drove past the gardens surrounding a fountain out front. These gardens weren't as colorful as Mrs. Winterthur's, but still impressive.

Cedric pulled to the side of the house by a stone carriage house, which is what he called it, with large wooden doors that opened to show a few autos inside and a grand old-fashioned carriage in the back. A man all in black was polishing a large automobile while another swept the floor.

Behind this was a large barn painted white with maroon trim. I have to admit, seeing the barn gave me a twinge inside for home. A young fella came around the barn leading a golden brown horse with white over the hooves. I knew it was a Belgian from the horses used on the logging jobs up north. This horse was not a logging animal by a long shot. They disappeared inside as Cedric parked alongside the house.

"Good luck!" He said as he hopped out and retrieved my suitcase.

"Thanks," I slid out, and took stock of these new surroundings. "This really is it." I shook hands with Cedric and turned toward the doorway to this adventure I'd dreamt of for so long.

"Hey!"

I turned to see Cedric staring at me, brows raised.

"I don't work for free."

"Oh, sorry. What do I owe you?" Daisy and I had pooled our money for a taxi ride, with me holding on to it as we knew I'd be let off last.

Cedric held out his hand, palm up. "That'll be two dollars and fifty cents."

"What! Two dollars and fifty cents? You've got to be kidding."

"The way things are these days, I'm lucky to keep gas in my tank. Besides, I hauled you all over creation today. I ain't getting rich here." Cedric's face lost all previous friendliness.

"Fine." I dug the money out of my purse and reluctantly pressed the fare into his hand. "You could have warned me."

Cedric shrugged, shoved the money in his pocket, and took off.

I looked around at the workers in the yard. No one paid me any attention. Before the heavy wooden door where I'd been told to report for duty, I checked my blouse and skirt for wrinkles and stains. There were wrinkles galore, but not a stain in sight. I knocked. Waited, then knocked again.

The door swung open, and a short, round woman in a blue dress just above her ankles and a hairnet over her reddish curls shot with gray looked back at me. She wiped her hands on a soiled apron.

"I'm Willa Grace Maruska." I held my breath.

"Right on time, ya are. I'm Blanche McGill." Her round face broke into a welcoming smile, and her blue eyes sparkled. "Bonnie was supposed to watch for ya, but that girl's run off. God knows where." Her voice, a pleasing Irish sing-song.

"Nice to meet you, Missus McGill." I extended a hand.

"Ack, it's just Blanche to you. I'd be the head cook." Her hand was still a bit moist from whatever she'd been working on before answering the door. I didn't mind. "Come on in. I'm happy for another pair of hands around here."

I followed Blanche as she waddled down a long, paneled hall, then down a narrow staircase.

"Well, girlie, I'm to take ya to Miss Mulchaey before giving ya a tour. She's the head of the whole shebang here."

Blanche led me past a room where two gals in similar uniforms with shorter hems than Blanche worked over ironing boards, and another worked over a large tub. They smiled as we passed.

"Everyone is working extra hard today," Blanche explained, "as the Thorpe's have important company coming tomorrow morning."

"Anyone I know?"

Blanche stopped, turned, and looked me over.

"Sorry. Just being a goof. I run at the mouth when I'm nervous."

To my relief, Blanche chuckled like the tinkling of a bell, one hand on her tummy, the other on my shoulder. "I like you already," she said.

Blanche explained that the mayor of Chicago, Edward Kelly, his wife Margaret, and three children were coming to spend a few days at the estate.

"We've got plenty to do, and Bonnie will get a talking-to when she shows up. Ack, that girl. The Thorpe's normally give us more notice for their hoity-toity visitors, but I don't mind. Gives us a chance to show what we can do, and I feel honored to cook for the mayor."

Blanche's sense of humor and easy way made me feel I'd found a kindred spirit. Then Blanche stopped outside a paneled door, and the smile slid from her face.

"As I said, before I take ya off to the kitchen, you must meet Miss Mulchaey. She oversees the household and wants to meet all the help." She leaned into me with a hand shielding her mouth and whispered, "Just a warnin', she's a hard one. Don't let 'er scare ya none."

I took a deep breath and, with a quick bob of my head, said, "Let's get on with it."

Blanche winked and knocked. "Enter," came from the other side.

I followed Blanche into the dark paneled office, which was neat and tidy. I held my suitcase tight before me, as much for support as for a shield. My purse dangled from my elbow.

A thin, older woman with white hair pulled into a severe bun at the back of her head sat at the desk with a ledger of some kind before her. She wore a black dress and a white collar.

Miss Mulchaey looked up, and the air in the room felt heavy. The woman had sharp grey eyes behind thick, black-rimmed glasses. She was skin and bones. Everything about this woman was severe.

"This is Willa Grace Maruska, the new kitchen help, Miss Mulchaey," Blanche said as she backed toward the door. She winked at me again, then said, "I'll wait outside."

"Hello, Miss Mulchaey," I said, deciding to meet her head-on, and held out a hand. Tata always said to offer a firm handshake. It sets a good example.

Miss Mulchaey pushed up from her chair, kind of like a spider stretching out its long legs. She kept her hands on the desk and ignored the hand I offered, then looked me up and down like a side of beef. "You're a farm girl?"

"Yes, ma'am." I took my hand back and stood tall and straight, head high.

"Good. In my experience, a farm builds a good work ethic, if not an academic one. You'll do. Do what you're told, and you'll be fine. Mind you, I don't put up with foolishness." She glared at me for dramatic effect. The way she worked her mouth when she talked reminded me of an old horse, as if her teeth were too big for her mouth. I widened my eyes to keep from grinning.

"The Thorpe estate is a fine home and runs with the precision of a clock. No fraternizing with the boys." She leaned forward, eyes narrowed. "I mean none. No, staying up past bedtime, nine o'clock on the dot, and up every morning at five-thirty. You'll get Sundays off and half a day every other Saturday. There may be times we need you to work those days as well for a special event. Refusing is not an option. You'll mind your manners and not make eye contact with the Thorpes should you meet them in the hall or anywhere on the grounds. You are never to be seen in the main living quarters. They prefer the help to remain invisible."

"Yes, ma'am. I'm happy to have a job. It means a...."

"We are not here to visit, Miss Maruska."

"I'm just being polite, ma'am." I kept my eyes glued to the older woman's face. "We're like that on the farm." I smiled sweetly, amused that the farm that I couldn't get away from fast enough was coming in quite helpful. Daisy'd enjoy that. But honestly, how dare this woman dress me down when I was trying to be friendly. I couldn't give two spits for her.

Miss Mulchaey's gaze narrowed, and I feared I'd made a fatal mistake.

"I didn't mean to be impertinent, ma'am," I said with all the seriousness I could muster. Miss Hegstrom, my grade-school teacher, used the word impertinent on me more times than I could shake a stick at, so the word and I had a relationship of sorts.

"Well, you are impertinent, and I don't like it. Mind your manners," the old horse lady spat.

"Sorry," I pulled in my chin.

Miss Mulchaey cleared her throat and continued. "You'll sleep on the third floor with the other female staff. Take your turn in the bathroom. You get five minutes, not a minute more." Miss Mulchaey went to the door, opened it, and said to Blanche, who was still waiting in the hall, "We're done."

"Thank you, ma'am." I slipped past her. "I will do my best."

"Keep an eye on this one, Blanche." The sneer on old Miss Mulchaey's puss made her look like a dried apple until she showed those horsey teeth of hers.

The kitchen was bustling, all in uniform, with two girls cutting vegetables on one end of a work-worn wooden table and a girl kneading bread at the other. At the stove, another person was stirring a steaming pot that filled the room with a delicious beefy aroma. Like Blanche, they wore blue dresses, white aprons, and hairnets. I wasn't too excited about the hairnets.

They all looked my way with hellos, reassuring smiles, and nods of welcome.

Suddenly, a shriek gave us all a fright, and I jumped along with the other girls. The sound came from the girl at the stove.

She dropped her wooden spoon into the kettle and huddled in the corner. A dead mouse lay under the stove.

"Oh, Jesus, Joseph, and Mary. It's just a damned mouse, Bonnie." Blanche tsk-tsked and shook her head. "By God, girlie, buck up. By the way, nice of ya to show up for work." Then to me, "You afraid a mice?"

"Nope." I marched over and took the skinny tail between a finger and thumb. "Where do you want it?" I held the dead rodent in front of Bonnie's face. Bonnie pulled in her chin, and it looked like she wanted to throttle me. What a ninny! The other girls chuckled until Blanche gave them a look.

"It's a good thing old Horseface didn't see that," the bread kneader said. "She'd have our heads."

"Ya got that right. Toss it in the fire." Blanche indicated the stove. "Mice ain't something we often see in my kitchen, just so ya know."

I opened the fire door and tossed the little bugger in.

"Horseface?" I asked as I turned around. It didn't take much to know who they referred to.

Bread kneader pushed her chin down, lips pulled back to show her teeth. All the girls giggled.

"Now, girlies, be nice." Blanche's eyes glinted with mischief.

"Aw, come on, Blanche. You know it's true," pot stirrer said.

"This here's Colleen," Blanche indicated the tall, green-eyed, red-haired girl kneading bread, who nodded, "and these two are Bertie and Tilly. They also help the cleaning staff part of the day." Short and with blond curls, Bertie gave a little wave with a knife in her hand, and Tilly, an exotic dark-skinned beauty with black hair, stirred. "This one is Bonnie, course you just had a dose a her." I turned to the fraidy cat in the corner. Bonnie stood, arms crossed before her. She was slender and shorter than I, with storm clouds in her blue eyes. I gave her a fake smile to let her know I wasn't impressed.

Blanche showed me around. The kitchen was three times the size of Mamka's, with long tables against the walls and between them, the most oversized sink I'd ever seen, and an ice box bigger than our outhouse. And the stove, which I'd barely noticed as I disposed of the mouse, was something I'd never seen before, with knobs everywhere and burners to cook so many dishes at once. Gleaming copper pots and pans hung from the ceiling over the center table. There were some things I had no idea how to use. Then Blanche took me into an adjoining room, which was very plain but had a huge table and at least fifteen chairs around it—the staff dining room.

Blanche explained that one of my jobs was to keep the staff dining room clean after meals, take care of leftover food, and wash the dishes. The staff had breakfast at seven o'clock, lunch at one, and dinner early at five thirty before the family ate at seven.

I had no doubt I would do an excellent job. "Will I get to help with the cooking?"

"In time."

"Good, because I'm an excellent cook." Daisy would have choked to hear me say that.

"Confident one, aren't ya?" Blanche grinned. "Let's get ya settled upstairs."

I retrieved my suitcase and followed Blanche down the paneled hall and up two winding, narrow staircases to the attic bedroom, a long room with yellow walls, gleaming hardwood floors, and ten single beds, five on each side covered in plain green bedspreads and white pillows. A small window was at the far end of the room, with two gable windows on each side and green gingham curtains. My bed was the last one on the right. I had a small two-drawer dresser, and the rest of my things were to stay in my suitcase tucked underneath the bed. I also had a small lamp so I could read at night. During my time here, this would be agreeable.

I put on the uniform Blanche gave me, pulled my hair into a ponytail that I then tucked into the net, and checked myself in the mirror on the back of the door. I'd do for now.

Downstairs, Blanche set me to washing the pots and pans used to prepare lunch for the Thorpes. The others bantered about as they worked and often included me. Despite Miss Mulchaey, or Old Horseface as they called her, and this Bonnie person, I thought this would be a happy place to make a dollar.

That night, in the attic bedroom, I got to know the other girls who worked as housekeepers or laundresses. Everyone was pleasant. Well, except Bonnie, who gave me the cold shoulder and, unfortunately, had the bed next to mine.

I settled into my comfy bed, listening to a few whispers of the others and someone snoring softly. Through the small window across from my bed, I watched the moon pass and thought of Daisy in her pretty house on Longcommon. I hoped she was happy with her arrangement.

As always, sleep was hard to find. There was too much to think about.

Blanche woke us before the sun was up. My arse was dragging, but I was anxious to start this new adventure.

Everyone dressed quickly and ran downstairs to the kitchen. Blanche already had the fires stoked. She sent Bonnie and me, of all people, out with baskets to gather eggs. Bonnie didn't say a word, just stuck her little nose in the air as I followed her on the path to the fanciest hen house I had ever seen. Our chickens would think they'd died and gone to heaven here.

As we arrived, a young man ran around the corner and nearly bowled us over. I'd noticed him from a distance when I'd arrived.

"Watch where you're going, fella." Then I saw how pretty he was.

He stopped, pulled in his chin, and gave me a 'well, excuse me' look. I guessed him to be a bit older than I. His tanned skin highlighted honey-blond hair that crossed his forehead over soft brown eyes. Then he grinned, showing his cheekbones.

"Sorry. I'm late for milking." And he took off again, lickety-split.

"That's Jode. All the girls here have goo-eyes for him. Not me."

"Does he have a girl? Not that I'm interested. A fella is the last thing I need." Although I watched him leave as we continued to the henhouse.

"I don't want nothing to do with boys. Had enough of my brothers back home."

"Wicked, were they? I've got a few of my own, but they're good eggs." Then I realized what I'd said, and laughed. Grim-faced, Bonnie started filling her basket with eggs. I did too, but then Bonnie stopped.

"I'm the only girl in six. Life was good until our mother died a few years ago." Her gaze lowered, and she bit her lower lip.

"I'm sorry to hear that. I suppose you were spoiled with all those boys looking out for you."

Bonnie's face was as close to horror-stricken as I could describe.

"What's that look for?"

She took a step back from me, shaking her head. "Nothing."

"What?" I asked again. Then, I saw a glimpse in her eyes of some terrible thing in her past that shaped her in ways I couldn't imagine. Her hands shook, and her face was pale.

It seemed like a good time to change the subject. "Tell me about the Thorpes."

Bonnie started gathering again. "Missus Thorpe, she comes down to the kitchen sometimes—a nice lady. If you meet her in the hall, she always says hello. Mister Thorpe won't. He likes to entertain a lot. Missus doesn't so much, but she's a good sport."

"Good to know."

"Mister Thorpe only comes down to the kitchen if something is wrong. That's only if he can't bitch to Horseface, so if you see him, look sharp. Blanche handles him well enough. Actually, I'd rather get a chewing out from him than Horseface."

"I can't stand that woman, and I've only been here a day."

"Me too. Mister Thorpe is a fine-looking man, and he knows it. Pretty uppity, he is."

"Hope I don't run into him. Is this a forever job for you?"

"I plan to be here until they make me leave. This is better than anything I could have thought up. Nice house like this, decent pay, and Blanche is like family to me, even though I piss her off at times. I don't mean to, just, I don't know."

"I want to work in the big city someday. There are opportunities around every corner. It's amazing. This job is nothing more than a stepping stone for me." I realized I'd given her some ammunition against me. "Way in the future that is."

"You forget about the way things are these days? You'd better hang on to this job as long as you can, girl." She nodded and pulled her lips into a straight line, showing off her dimples.

"I'm grateful to be here. I am."

"As much as I like it here, my job here is hanging by a thread. I can't seem to do anything right." Bonnie rolled her eyes and smacked her forehead. "Wicked old Horseface doesn't like me for a few reasons. Last Monday, I broke an expensive gravy boat right in front of her."

"Who needs a gravy boat anyway?" I gave her a nudge and a grin. "How'd you get the job?" I brushed chicken shit off my skirt.

"The gardener caught me sneaking through a hole in the fence to steal from Thorpe's garden. It just happened that Missus Thorpe was helping to prune her rose bushes and took pity on me. I said I had no home, which I didn't anymore, and she took me in. Horseface had a fit. She gets pissy when she isn't in control. Of course, she'd never let on to Thorpe's. She takes it out on us."

"Why didn't you have a home?"

She stopped, hugged the basket of eggs to her chest, and said, "We better get these eggs into Blanche."

I followed her up the cobblestone walk from the henhouse toward the kitchen. We were just about there when Bonnie tripped on a loosened shoelace and fell forward with the eggs. At least half the eggs were shattered and cracked, leaving a gooey mess on the walk.

"Oh no!" Tears sprang from her eyes as she scurried to gather what eggs she could.

I set my basket down to help.

"Oh my gosh, I'm going to be in so much trouble."

"Don't worry," a male voice came from behind. It was Jode, the boy from earlier. "I'll run to the well, fill a bucket, and rinse this away before anyone knows."

"Thought you had milking to do," I said.

"Naw. Otto filled in for me. I overslept." He ran off, then came back quickly with the water, which he sloshed over the mess.

"Thank you, Jode." Bonnie and I quickly gathered what eggs hadn't broken. "I guess it could have been worse." She looked into her basket, which now held only a quarter of what it once had. "And there's company coming. Blanche is going to be so mad."

"Ah, she ain't gonna fire you. Not for something like this. Just tell her the hens are takin' time off." Jode winked at her.

"Don't worry about a thing." I took her basket and gave her mine. "I can take the blame. I'm new. Blanche won't think twice about it."

"That's nice of you, but Blanche'd never believe it. She knows how clumsy I am."

"You haven't seen me in action. I can drop eggs as well as anybody." I led the way, and once in the kitchen, Blanche took one look and said, "What in the dickens happened?"

"It's my fault. I tripped and broke some. Sorry." I held my breath. I didn't like lying to someone I liked and respected.

Blanche blew out a sigh and stared at me for a long moment. "This is a fine mess." For a split second, I feared she knew I was lying. "We'll have to make do." Blanche took the baskets from us and went to the worktable.

Bonnie smiled at me and gave me a light nudge with her shoulder. This Bonnie girl needed a friend, and so did I.

FIVE

Daisy

It was a snowy December afternoon with big, fluffy flakes floating outside the paned-glass windows. Mrs. Winterthur and I expected Gerda to call us to lunch at any time now. A fire crackled and spat in the fireplace. Mrs. Winterthur eased back and forth in her rocking chair, reading *To a God Unknown* by John Steinbeck, occasionally stopping to sip a cup of tea. I sat on the sofa, knitting a long green scarf to send to Tata as a Christmas gift. Little Poppy lay beside me, her furry body rising and falling in slumber.

I was the luckiest girl in the world, being paid to sit snug and warm in this beautiful, peaceful home with a woman I adored. I never expected such good fortune as the result of a journey I dreaded. Of course, I missed my family, but that was temporary. I also missed seeing Willa Grace every day. However, during my time in Berwyn, I had been happy.

Gerda bustled in with the day's mail. She handed Mrs. Winterthur a few envelopes and tossed one toward me. I caught it and rolled my eyes. There was always Gerda to bring me a dose of reality. Little did she know, I found her amusing.

The letter was from Harold. I quickly tore into it.

Dear Daisy,

I have some exciting news to share. You know I've been saving every penny working at the feed mill in town. Being an employee has never been my calling. Well, I can finally say that I've saved enough to buy my own business with a bit of help. My Uncle Fred, who owns a creamery down in Wood County, has agreed to front me what I lack as long as I pay it back in two years.

Last week, I purchased Mr. Allendorf's Cheese Factory. Yes, finally, I will be my own boss. Mr. Allendorf is retiring, and no one from his family is interested. All his employees agreed to stay on. What I need now is repairs on one of the milk trucks and signed contracts with the farmers. I have my own home because the house is attached to the factory. It's small and needs a woman's touch, but I hope to add on a few rooms after I have a solid handle on running the business.

I must say, Daisy, I am thrilled to start this new venture. Everything is falling into place. I have such plans for the expansion of the creamery. I can't wait to show you around when you come home next.

Take care,
Harold

Anticipation zipped through me so strongly, I could have leaped from the sofa. Harold was thinking of the future. Our future. I kissed the letter and held it to my chest, feeling the rapid beat of my heart. I closed my eyes and felt tears pricking the corners of my eyes. Could my lot in life be any better? No amount of restraint could wipe the smile from my face.

Mrs. Winterthur angled her head and raised her brows. "I assume that's a letter from your young man?" She set her book on her lap.

"It is. Harold bought a cheese factory. He now has a house and a business with employees. He says everything he's wanted is falling into place." I knew my cheeks were blushing with anticipation for the life ahead for Harold and me. It was hard to believe that Willa Grace and I had been in Berwyn for over four months, and the time had flown so quickly. It wouldn't be long, and we'd be back home in Emery Township, and I'd have a wedding to plan.

Mamka had written that milk prices had not recovered, but surely they would soon enough, and then, we'd be home. Willa Grace could bluster all she wanted about city life, but she'd come back with me. And Harold would be waiting.

I had written Harold twice as much as he wrote me, but now I knew why. He'd been busy securing our future. Going forward, I reasoned that I might hear from him even less, as he would likely be extra busy with organizing a business and furnishing a house.

Mrs. Winterthur chuckled. "Daisy, you're wearing the deepest blush I've ever seen."

I put a hand on my cheek, feeling the warmth of my excitement. I still could not stop grinning like a fool. "Harold gave a tiny hint at a proposal, saying the house needed a woman's touch. I'm sure it's coming. Even so, we would take time to make plans for our future once I get back. For now, my family still needs my help, and Harold needs time to build the business."

"I'm happy for you, dear. I remember those young years when life seemed so full of possibility." The soft lines of her face clouded for a moment. I wanted to ask after it, but she brightened and continued. "You and your Harold will make a wonderful life. I'm certain of it."

She brought a hanky to her mouth and started to cough. It was a deep, guttural sound that caused me to set aside my knitting and move to the edge of my seat, until Mrs. Winterthur waved me back and the coughing ceased. Her cough was more frequent.

"I'm fine." She sat back in her chair and, with the back of her hand, motioned toward my knitting project. "Keep on," she said. So I did.

Mrs. Winterthur and I had spent many happy hours together in her gardens as fall wore on, and now, with winter at the doorstep, in her art studio, a glassed-in solarium off the south side of the house. She was a wonderful teacher, explaining different techniques with paint and brush, her favorite medium being oil, and my work wasn't half bad if I may say so myself.

The two of us took long car rides in the 1930 Packard Club Sedan Mr. Winterthur bought shortly before he passed away. She loved to drive and took me all through the Chicago suburbs, carefully avoiding the downtown as she wasn't as confident in her driving skills anymore. I had no wish to visit the downtown area again, but I was able to see that the Chicago area was not the big, bad monster I'd imagined.

The Missus, as Gerda referred to her, and I worked puzzles, shared books, and played Kings Corners, a card game she taught me. Sometimes, I felt guilty about taking a paycheck, but that pay was so desperately needed, and I'd begun setting aside a tiny amount for a trousseau.

Gerda was still her crabby old self, but her jealousy of my being Mrs. Winterthur's 'playmate' softened a tad.

Sundays, our joint day off, Willa Grace came to visit. It turns out that being apart all week gave us plenty to talk about. Willa Grace was full of rumors circling through the Thorpe estate and funny stories of the goings-on there. Some Sundays we'd ride bikes into Berwyn and see a movie, other times we'd go to ball games in the park, or take a long walk and get lunch. Rainy days and winter had us staying in my room as Willa Grace wasn't allowed visitors. One particular rainy day had us cutting each other's hair into a bob, which was all the rage here and up north as well. Tats was going to spin himself into the ground when he saw us next, but we decided we'd deal with that when the time came. That was my first and only act of rebellion.

"I'm so happy for you, Daisy. Your Harold is sure to come through with a proposal. You've made him sound like a worthy young man." Mrs. Winterthur coughed again. Then, I noticed the deepening gray pallor on her skin.

"You need to see a doctor."

"No doctors. You know my stance on that. That will not change." Mrs. Winterthur leveled a glare at me, the first time I'd seen any sign of temper. "I don't trust them, and if I had bad news coming, I wouldn't want to hear it. Just let me live my life my own way." She dabbed the hanky at the beads of sweat on her forehead.

"Your cough is getting worse."

"It's nothing."

"Please? Maybe call your sister? Sisters are always good for honest advice." I set my knitting aside, went to her side, and squatted down to where we were eye to eye. "Your cough is starting to frighten me. I wish you'd get a quick check on it."

Mrs. Winterthur breathed in slowly, her voice raspy. "I appreciate your concern, but no." She pulled a second hanky from her sleeve and brought it to her lips.

"I hate to see you suffer, is all."

Mrs. Winterthur raised a finger. "Enough. I know you mean well, Daisy. Don't you be worrying about me. Now, go finish your knitting."

I did as I was told but kept a careful eye on her. Fifteen minutes later, the coughing returned. Out came the hanky again. Mrs. Winterthur gave me a warning glare, but then a coughing spasm took over so ruthlessly that she doubled over with its force, hands over her mouth.

"Gerda, come quick!" I yelled toward the kitchen, then knelt beside her chair, one hand on Mrs. Winterthur's knee, the other on her back.

Gerda ran into the room, wiping her hands on a dish towel. "Oh dear, I'll get the cough medicine." She disappeared into the hall.

Mrs. Winterthur gasped for air for another minute, then lowered her hands to her lap.

"Missus Winterthur!" I looked down to see the hanky and her hands splattered with red.

"Oh, goodness." Mrs. Winterthur whispered and held her hands to me, her eyes pleading for help.

I grabbed a linen napkin from under her teacup and used it to wipe her hands. "Let me get this wet." I ran to the kitchen for water, passing Gerda and the cough medicine.

I was only gone for a split second, but when I returned, Mrs. Winterthur tilted her chin and opened her mouth like a tiny bird waiting for dinner as Gerda gave her two teaspoons of the dark liquid, which seemed to do the trick.

She took a few deep breaths and settled back into the chair.

I finished cleaning Mrs. Winterthur's hands as best I could. She was embarrassed and, in a voice just above a whisper, said, "I am so sorry."

"I am here for you, whatever you need." I put an arm around her shoulders and gave her a squeeze. Gerda returned to the kitchen without a word.

"Don't call a doctor or Sylvia. Please. Promise me." Mrs. Winterthur took my hand in hers. "Doctors killed our only son, David. I don't trust them. Never will."

"I don't understand." I used the wet napkin to clean my hands as well.

"My boy had cancer that was misdiagnosed for nearly two years. I knew something worse was wrong, but he downplayed the pain in his back. The doctor said it was nothing serious. Well, it was. We followed the doctor's instructions to the letter, but nothing seemed to work. Finally, we consulted another doctor, but it was too late. David didn't have to die."

"I'm so sorry."

Mrs. Winterthur pushed back a shock of white hair. "He was only thirty-one."

"That's way too young." Tears pricked my eyes.

"This is nothing more than a case of bronchitis, and the force of the cough has ruptured a blood vessel. My father suffered from bronchitis on and off for years and had the same symptoms. I suppose I am prone as well." She patted my hand and then hung on. "And promise me, no doctors and no Sylvia. My sister is a nervous wreck as it is. She'd only make it worse."

I agreed and returned to the sofa, but out of the corner of my eye, I continued to watch this lady who had come to be so dear to me. Maybe it was simply bronchitis, and I was overreacting. My lovely little lady took a deep breath to regain her composure, and I reassured myself she was fine. Her cough was nothing serious.

I looked down at my now clean hands. But what if it wasn't?

Willa Grace

I called Daisy on a Sunday afternoon for a chat when I got my turn at the telephone in the upstairs hall by the staff quarters. Because of the blizzard raging outside, we couldn't meet up for our usual Sunday afternoon visit. I'd pilfered a chocolate chip cookie from the kitchen when no one was looking and nibbled as I dialed.

"I had a dream last night," Daisy said after our hellos.

"Oh, geez. You and your dreams. What this time?" I brushed crumbs from the front of my sweater. Daisy loved to analyze her dreams. They were always so vivid, and sometimes a bit spooky. The night before our grandpa died, she dreamt he had a stroke. He did.

"Now, don't get mad. I need you to listen to me."

Yikes. Something told me to take a seat and hold on. Since there was no chair, Horseface's plan for keeping our calls short, I sank to the floor and sat there cross-legged, stretching the phone cord as far as I was able.

"You're making me nervous." I took a bite.

"It was about Teddy."

"Dammit it, Daisy," my voice was muffled by cookie.

"Shush. You're the only one I can tell."

Daisy was right. I was the only one. Lucky me. Mamka and Tata surely couldn't talk about Teddy, and the others were either too little or not born yet. This unspoken, awful thing bound Daisy and me as tightly as our love for each other as sisters.

I wiped my mouth with my sleeve. "It's too hard, and I don't understand why you're bringing it up after so long and after I've told you I can't. I can't talk about it."

"Him. You can't talk about *him*. He was a person. Our brother. Besides, this was a dream."

"Why bring…why?" I checked the hall to make sure no one was listening.

"He deserves to be remembered."

"I know that. You don't think I do? I can't, that's all." I brought a knee up, resting an elbow, and cradled my forehead in the palm of my hand. I felt a headache coming on.

The cookie rolled around in my stomach.

"I dreamt he came to me." Daisy paused, trying to stay calm as her voice hitched. "He wore the same clothes as that day. This bright light surrounded him, so white I had to squint to see him, but there he was, plain as day." Was she crying?

"Oh, for pity's sake." I felt like ants were crawling up my limbs. I brought my shoulders up and squeezed to stop the sensation. But no such luck.

"He smiled so beautifully, and when I reached for him, he turned away and disappeared into the light. What do you suppose that means?"

I didn't respond but focused on the pattern of roses on the runner in the hall.

"I could smell him, Willa Grace. He smelled like chicken soup. Remember? That's what Mamka was simmering on the stove when we left the house that day."

"Don't do this to yourself, Daisy-do." Now I had a leaky eye.

"I feel like it's a sign of some kind."

"Like what?" I pushed up from the rug. "You bring this up when you know I don't want to hear it. So you saw him standing in a bright light. What are you supposed to make of that? I don't know what you want me to say. God, Daisy, I'm trying to be sympathetic, but I don't think your dream means anything. You just miss him, is all."

"Well now, you're just being mean."

She was right.

I never told her about seeing Teddy's ghost, if that's what it was, by the creek the night before we left. I knew if I did, she'd make something of it, although it was strange. Why would we both see him now after all these years? I was more curious than I wanted to admit. And a little scared.

I apologized and we talked about other things.

After, I remained sitting on the hall floor. Our little brother's death was like a black monster that followed me everywhere. I wasn't so out of touch that I knew it was partly why I needed to get away from the farm. I pretended I wasn't running away from that terrible day, but I was.

Daisy once told me that she was terrified she'd forget what he looked like, the sound of his laughter, the feel of his hand in hers. Of course, I had those same fears.

I pulled myself up, replaced the receiver, and then went to curl up on the bed.

It was a miserable, wet, and cold March when it happened. I was five, Daisy seven, and Teddy four.

Teddy was a happy boy, always laughing, with brown hair like mine and a splash of freckles across his nose. I don't remember the color of his eyes, but I think they were blue. I recall him on Tata's lap in the evenings, in the corner of the parlor, a kerosene lamp making them glow. The smoke from Tata's pipe made a wreath over their heads, and the rocking chair creaked on the hardwood floor. Teddy was his little man.

Tata was in the barn that morning, and Mamka was in the bedroom feeding the newest baby, George, while two-year-old Isabel napped alongside. George was a fussy little thing, and Mamka asked Daisy and me to take Teddy out to play.

We bundled up in coats, boots, hats, and mittens and went out into the snowy, slushy yard. As I closed the door, Mamka called, "Stay away from the creek. It's not safe this time of year."

The three of us built a sad-looking snowman with heavy snow that packed well. Teddy was having such fun. At one point, I saw Mamka watching us out the kitchen window as she bounced George against her shoulder. The window was frosty, and she looked like an angel, her face surrounded by crystals. I waved and gave Teddy my green knitted hat for the snowman's head. After all, the weather was warming, and I didn't need a hat so much.

I lifted Teddy's scrawny body while Daisy helped him center the hat on the snowy mound. We stood back and admired our work. Teddy named him Peter after *Peter, Peter, Pumpkin Eater*. Mamka had read that story to us a hundred times.

"Can we go sledding?" Teddy asked.

"There's not enough snow," Daisy said.

"There is too," I said.

"Please," Teddy pleaded, his little face scrunched tight.

"I suppose." Daisy relented. "I'll let Mamka know."

"Teddy and I'll get the sled." I took Teddy by the hand, and we ran to the shed by the barn.

We returned, with me pulling the wooden sled with red runners and Teddy riding atop. Daisy came from the house.

"Mamka's napping with Georgie and Issy. Let's go."

The three of us went through the apple orchard and into the scrubby forest beyond. We continued through the snow, between stumps and brush, until we reached the hill that we only ever used for sledding when he was along.

Below, the creek curved like a ribbon cutting through the underbrush, the center of it free of ice, although the edges were still covered in a thin layer.

"We'll have to be careful not to go out too far," Daisy warned.

"We won't slide that far," I said, always the tester of limits.

"We might."

Teddy stared up at us, eating a handful of snow.

"Okay, let's go down the other side." I pointed off to the east.

"Go, go," Teddy rocked back and forth, wanting to get moving. His little nose and cheeks were cherry-red.

Daisy nodded, and off we went. She and I took turns pulling the sled with Teddy. He giggled, so excited, and made us laugh. We sang *Jingle Bells* as we went.

I went to the bottom of the hill as Daisy and Teddy flew down. Then, it was my turn with our little brother. After many trips up and down, I said, "Daisy, let's you and me take a turn together. Teddy, you wait here."

My ears were getting cold, and I regretted letting Peter the Snowman have my hat. Daisy and I ran up the hill. She pulled the sled. I covered my ears with my snowy green mittens.

At the top of the hill, Daisy sat on the front, and I snuggled in behind her, knees up on either side, and wrapped my arms around her middle. Together, we scooted until the sled began to inch down. Then, with one last shove, it took off.

I tried to see over Daisy's shoulder, but a pine branch hit me in the eye, and I veered to the other side of her. The shift in weight swung us to the right as we whooped and hollered, careening down the hill. Suddenly, we struck a large, exposed rock with a crash. Daisy flew forward, and I rolled to the side, tumbling down the rest of the hill. The wet snow clung to my coat, hair, and mittens. I was sure I resembled a snowman by the time I stopped. I lay there on my back, breathing heavily, with snowflakes catching my eyelashes and making me blink. I turned my head to look for Daisy. She was lying on her back, not moving.

Quickly, I picked myself up and raced toward her, kneeling at her side.

"Are you okay?"

She nodded. "Can't breathe," she mouthed.

I pulled her into a sitting position. "You just got the wind knocked out of you, is all." I patted her back until she took a big gulp of air.

"Do you know how scary it is not to be able to breathe?" Her eyes were huge. "I thought I was a goner."

I sat back on the snow and laughed. "Wasn't that fun?"

"No!"

"Aw, come on. You know it was." I lobbed a handful of snow at her. She swiped at my hand and shook the snow from her black curls.

"Where's Teddy?" she asked.

We looked around but didn't see him.

"Teddy!" I called.

The forest was deathly silent.

"Teddy!" We both yelled.

I stood, and my eyes went to the creek. "No!" I took off running with Daisy right behind me. Further down, Teddy stood precariously on the ice at the creek's edge.

"Back up, Teddy," I called as I ran toward him. "Back up. Don't go…" and that's when the ice gave way, and our darling little brother slipped under the ice and vanished. We were only seconds from him.

Daisy got on her belly, pulled herself to the edge of the ice, and put her arms in the frigid water, feeling for him. I jumped over her and into the water. The cold stabbed my lungs, forcing the air from them. Pinching my nose, I went under, my hands flailing this way and that, trying to grasp his hand, coat, foot, anything. The current was too swift.

I came up for air, and as I crawled out, Daisy ran farther down and banged on the ice, screaming his name. I opened my mouth, but nothing would come. I could barely breathe. I'd never been so cold.

A section of ice broke free, moved out into the open center, and nearly took Daisy. She pushed her body back onto the edge, screaming with everything in her.

I jumped up, ran down the shore, and searched. We both screamed his name.

Then I saw his tiny, blue hand come up above the water, and once again, I was waist-high in the razor-cold creek. I wrapped my arms around him and pulled with all my might. The weight of his wool coat and boots held him. Sheer terror gave me the strength to haul him out. He was a sopping ragdoll in my arms.

Just then, Tata, who'd heard our screams, came over the hill. He flew to us, and I will never forget his scream as he gathered Teddy's lifeless body in his arms. In seconds, he was running toward the farm, Teddy's arms and legs flopping with each step, Daisy pulling me as I shook so badly I could only stumble along.

Back at the house, Tata laid Teddy on the floor by the stove and stripped off his wet clothes while Mamka covered him with blankets and held him to her, kissing his face, cradling his head, and rubbing his tummy. Daisy, at Tata's order, helped me out of my clothes and into the warmest clothes she could find and poured me a cup of coffee from the pot on the stove, then one for herself. We hid in the bedroom, cowered in the corner, crying into our coffee, while Issy and George wailed in fright from the bed.

Tata desperately flew from the house and rode the old mare to Doc Kerwitzer's house, who lived not far. Doc came, but nothing could be done. Teddy was gone.

Tata sat at Teddy's feet all night, rubbing his legs. Still holding him, Mamka swayed from side to side, singing softly into his ear.

When George and Issy needed attention, we took care of them. It was all we could do.

Strangely, I don't remember his funeral. The township neighbors came and went, but I don't remember a funeral. Today, a tiny stone marks his grave in Emery Cemetery.

That's all that's left of him.

For so long after, Daisy and I would lie in our bed at night, holding onto each other, weeping silently. Tata hid in the barn for hours, often returning to the house with brandy on his breath. Mamka sat at the window, tears rolling down her face, as though she were looking for Teddy to return. He never did.

Tata was a hardened man after that. For Mamka, it took a long time and more babies before we heard her sing again. Still, there were times when she stared out the window, and I knew her eyes watched for Teddy playing in the yard, her ears searching for his laughter.

Eventually, Daisy and I returned to the creek, but away from the hill where Teddy died. There were other places to sled. For farmers, every bit of land was usable, but that area was left untouched. There were times Daisy and I would sit on that hill amid the wildflowers and watch the creek go by, trying to forgive it for what it had taken from us and, without success, forgive ourselves.

SIX

Daisy

"You've been quiet today, Daisy." Mrs. Winterthur looked up from her newspaper.

"I didn't sleep well. I've got a headache." I leaned my head back against the sofa.

"A cold compress on your neck might help that. Maybe you should try a nap. I may try that myself. I thought we'd shore up the peonies today, but the weather isn't cooperating. Maybe tomorrow." An early spring rain sputtered against the windows.

I took her advice and napped soundly for an hour, but I didn't feel any better. After lunch, the rain had moved off, so Mrs. Winterthur and I went to the garden to sit in the sunshine and play with Poppy. She decided the peonies could wait.

Mrs. Winterthur's cough had come and gone a few times over the winter months; yet, each time it returned, it was stronger than before. Her explanation of bronchitis seemed reasonable, although her refusal to see a doctor was not. All my pleading went in one ear and out the other.

Hummingbirds were out in full force, and we watched them flit from flower to flower. Poppy briefly tried chasing after one, only to end up tumbling like a snowball against a lilac bush.

We laughed as she righted herself and took off after a butterfly.

Suddenly, a forceful, phlegmy cough caused Mrs. Winterthur to double over. I jumped to her side as she sat up and wiped her mouth with a hanky.

"I'm fine," she assured me, waving off my concern.

"Are you sure?"

Mrs. Winterthur bent from her chair and picked up Poppy. "Tell you what, let's go for a drive. I want to see the lake and the gardens in bloom. My husband and I spent many a Sunday afternoon at the lake, and I'm feeling pulled to go back there today."

"Are you sure you're up to it?"

"Maybe the fresh air will take away that headache of yours and do me some good as well."

The drive did, indeed, put us both in better spirits. The Missus loved to drive. Back at the house, Gerda, who'd voiced her displeasure at the Missus going out for a drive in the face of feeling unwell that morning, shooed Mrs. Winterthur off to bed right after supper.

The following day, my headache returned. I was tired, suspected a fever, and had a persistent cough. I went down for breakfast but knew the rest of my day would most likely be spent in bed.

"I suppose we should have stayed home resting yesterday rather than driving all over creation," Mrs. Winterthur said at breakfast, "but I hate giving in to illness." She put a hand on mine. "I coughed a good deal last night. I apologize if I kept you from sleeping."

"If I may, Missus," Gerda said as she spooned scrambled eggs onto my plate, "you might consider who you're spreading the illness to. Daisy here isn't the sturdy one I am, and she's not feeling the best. I suppose I'm next."

I held my breath as I'd never heard her talk back to the Missus, who gazed over the tops of her glasses and said, "I'll stay in my room. You can bring my meals to me from now on." To me, she said, "Daisy, you're on your own."

After breakfast, I went to the kitchen. Gerda was scraping leftovers into the garbage.

"Gerda, I'm worried about her."

"What am I to do?" She glared at me. "The woman has a mind of her own."

I coughed lightly, then cleared my throat. "She does."

"Get yourself to bed. I don't need to be running my arse off after both of you."

"Fine." I went up the stairs with Poppy on my heels. I spent the rest of the day in bed, sneaking down the hall a few times to check on Mrs. Winterthur. The next morning, I still felt sickly, but forced myself to dress and go for breakfast.

As I reached the top of the stairs, I could hear Mrs. Winterthur's constant cough. Gingerly, I turned the knob of her bedroom door and slipped inside. She was lying flat on her back, staring at the ceiling, gasping for breath between racking coughs.

"Missus Winterthur!" I rushed to her side.

She looked gray in the light of the bedside lamp. I put my hand on her forehead. Her skin burned with fever. On the floor lay a handkerchief spattered with blood. This time, I couldn't ignore how sick she was.

"You poor thing."

Her voice was raspy and weak. "Get me a cup of tea and some aspirin, please."

"I'll be right back." I ran down the stairs and into the kitchen. Gerda looked up from whatever she was mixing in a huge bowl. "Missus has a terrible fever and is coughing up blood. We need a doctor."

"She won't like it." Gerda wiped her forehead with the back of her hand, then wiped her hands on a towel.

"We have no choice. She can be angry with me all she likes. I want to make sure this isn't something serious."

Gerda simply stared at me.

"You must know of a doctor to call."

"I do. You're sick as well. I'll make the call and then fix you both some tea. Go back up to her." Gerda put a hand on my forehead. I felt the coolness of her touch and leaned into it. "I can't tell if you're feverish." Then she did something so uncharacteristic. She patted my shoulder and gave it a squeeze. "We must take care of her. She's all I've got."

Dr. Bennet Ferguson, a long-time friend of Mrs. Winterthur's through the Art Council, knocked on the door just before noon that day. He was a tall, kindly gentleman with graying brown hair, bushy brows, a tweed jacket, and a black case. We followed him up the stairs and waited in the hall.

"You didn't mean that, did you?" I asked Gerda, who stood across the hall from me. The tension was heavy between us. "That she's all you have?"

I could see the walls rise up around her.

"Don't be silly. I have plenty of folks of my own." She stuck her pug nose in the air and refused to look at me.

Dr. Ferguson quietly entered the hall, gently shutting the bedroom door behind him. I held my breath, silently praying I'd overreacted in having Gerda call him, and that my dear employer could forgive me.

He sighed, took off his glasses, and rubbed his forehead.

"Well," Gerda asked.

The doctor shook his head and put his glasses back on. "Lucille is a very sick woman. I suspect tuberculosis. She's had it for quite some time."

"What!?" We both exclaimed, trying to keep our voices low. Deep down, I knew this was going to be the diagnosis, but hearing it from a doctor was shocking.

"That can't be," Gerda said, shooting the doctor a glare. "It's just bronchitis. You don't know her like I do. Her father suffered from it. She's had this cough for so…" Realization stopped her.

"I know tuberculosis, and this is a classic case." He closed his doctor's bag. "If there's any chance to save her, she needs hospitalization immediately."

I backed against the wall for support, and it took every ounce of strength not to sink to the floor. *If there is any chance to save her?* How can this be? Poor Mrs. Winterthur. My thoughts went to Matty Pesko, who'd passed last year from the dreaded disease. The stories we'd heard of his final months were terrifying. Whole families could be infected. I couldn't bear the thought of Mrs. Winterthur suffering such a fate, gasping for her final breath.

I put both hands on my heart and bent over, fearing I would faint.

Gerda, a horrified look on her round, red face, backed away from the doctor and me.

"What if we have it?" she asked, panicked. "This one," she pointed at me, "has also been sickly."

Dr. Ferguson pulled his brows together and studied me. "Is this true?"

"Well..." Was I really that sick? "I think I'm suffering from a bad cold. Maybe the flu. That's all. I've never had the cough she has."

"You'll both need to be tested and x-rayed as soon as possible. Mantoux tests, the skin tests, won't return results for a few days, but we might see something on X-ray."

"Oh, dear God!" Gerda breathed fast and hard, her eyes watery and bulging. She put a hand over her mouth.

I sank to the floor, squatting. Tuberculosis affected breathing. I could breathe just fine. There was no chance I had this. Could there be?

"Now, ladies, let's not make assumptions. We'll need an ambulance. Please direct me to the telephone. I'll make the call." Dr. Ferguson tried to reassure us. I stood, trying to stay calm. Gerda looked as though she might lose her mind at any moment.

"How bad is she?" I looked at the closed bedroom door.

"We'll know more at the hospital. As soon as the ambulance arrives for Lucille, I will send you both for testing. You both can ride with me."

"We'll do whatever you think, Doctor." My ears were buzzing, and my eyes struggled to focus.

"But I don't have symptoms." Gerda shook her head, eyes wide with fear. "I'm as fit as a fiddle. Look at me." She spread her fleshy arms wide. "I can't have this. I simply cannot be sick."

"Calm down, Gerda," Dr. Ferguson said, "We need to be sure. Tuberculosis is only transmitted by prolonged exposure. I'll give you both masks to wear to the hospital, and you'll need to wash your hands thoroughly and often."

"Will she be all right?" I asked, my voice breaking.

Dr. Ferguson shrugged. "Her age is not helping. She's a very sick lady."

Tears seeped from Gerda's eyes. I put a hand on her shoulder, but she bolted away from me.

"You brought this with you!" She glared at me.

I couldn't believe my ears.

"Gerda, no, I…you said yourself she'd had these symptoms before."

"There's no telling where she came in contact," Dr. Ferguson said. "We know that TB can sit dormant in a body for quite some time."

Sweat beaded on my forehead. I closed my eyes, my arms wrapped around me. Suddenly, I felt like I couldn't breathe. My lungs wouldn't let me. This can't be. Tuberculosis would not be my fate. It couldn't be. I was young and had always been healthy. After all, I'd been raised my whole life on fresh homegrown food, breathing pure country air while working a farm and running after my brothers and sisters. But then I thought again of Matty Pesko back home and others we'd heard had it.

The doctor's advice about making assumptions pulsed through me, and I tried to hold onto that, but it didn't prove easy.

I straightened and nodded determinedly—enough of this. I would be fine. Yes, I would. Right now, Mrs. Winterthur needed us. She needed me.

"I need to go to her. Can I?"

Dr. Ferguson nodded. "Just for a moment. Keep your distance. Don't touch anything."

With my hand on the ornate knob. "Oh, God, please, not tuberculosis," I whispered before entering.

Mrs. Winterthur was lying with the blankets up to her chin, her white head propped on pillows. Dark circles wreathed her eyes, her cheeks a deep pink, highlighting her otherwise pale complexion. She coughed once and said, "Don't come near me, Daisy. I couldn't stand the thought of giving you this damned disease."

I edged nearer to the bed. "Let's not think about that. It would be best if you focused on getting better. This might be pneumonia or bronchitis—something like that. You said so yourself. Just like your father had, you'll be back here lickety-split."

"Always the optimistic one." Mrs. Winterthur gave a weak smile.

"Is there anyone I should call? Your sister?" I asked gently.

"Yes, I suppose we should call Sylvia, but not yet." She held up a thin, gray finger. "My attorney's number is in the drawer under the telephone in the hall downstairs. He handles all my affairs now and has strict instructions if I am ill. I would appreciate it if you could let him know what's happened." She then slipped into a frightening coughing fit.

I reached toward her, but she vigorously shook her head, handkerchief to her face.

All I could do was stand aside and watch, terrified.

Just then, we heard the ambulance siren.

I wanted to call Willa Grace, but there was no need until I knew for sure. After all, this was probably nothing to worry over. Absolutely nothing. But my sister's assurance would be so welcome.

Then I stared down at my hands that had cleaned blood once before from the Missus' coughing, and deep inside, a fear roared to life like nothing I'd ever experienced.

Neither Gerda nor I spoke during the ride to the hospital. As soon as we arrived behind the ambulance, Mrs. Winterthur was whisked off down a long, stark hallway. Gerda and I were taken to separate examining rooms. A kindly nurse whose nametag read Arlene helped me onto a gurney and took my vitals. My temperature was 101. She explained, then performed a Mantoux test, injecting fluid under the skin of my arm, which, if red in a few days, would result in a positive tuberculosis reading. Arlene had me change into a cotton gown, then helped me into a wheelchair and left me alone in the cold, sterile room that smelled of alcohol and pine cleaner.

The minutes ticked by. What had just happened to my ideal life?

I couldn't have tuberculosis, could I? And if so, had I infected anyone else? That frightened me more than anything. What if I'd carried it inside me with no symptoms? I'd heard of that happening. What if I'd given it to Willa Grace? Thank goodness we hadn't been home for a visit since we'd arrived.

I sat there, feeling the air move in and out of my lungs, as it had every moment of my life. Nothing, not an inkling that anything was wrong with my lungs other than a slight cough. No, this couldn't be. My body wouldn't betray me with this disease, would it?

But why, oh why, did I not see the signs in Mrs. Winterthur sooner, recognize the symptoms? Perhaps, had I betrayed her sooner, she might have been certain to recover.

I wished for Mamka and Willa Grace with all my might. Mamka would calm my fears, tell me all would be well, and whisper a song in my ear. Willa Grace would come undone with anxiety for me, but would grip my hand and tell me TB wouldn't stand a chance against the two of us. That made me smile a tad. Then I looked down at my arm. If only I could see into the next few days.

A different nurse and an X-ray technician entered, both in masks and gowns. They took me down a hallway to a room so cold that I couldn't stop shivering. Tears slipped down my cheeks, and I wiped them away with my palms.

The tall, dark-haired technician with sympathetic brown eyes touched my shoulder and said, "Let's not worry until we have something to worry about."

"Will this hurt?" I'd never had an X-ray before.

My question had their eyes crinkling at the corners. "Not a bit."

I stood before a large, noisy machine and did what I was told, wondering how in the world this machine could see inside me. I was told to hold my breath, so I took a big gulp of air and held tight. Could I have done that with infected lungs?

Before long, I was wheeled back to the examination room and helped onto a hard, unforgiving gurney where I lay. Still cold, I shivered as though it were ten below zero.

There was a light knock on the door.

"Come in."

Dr. Ferguson, in a white coat, his face covered with a mask, and holding a clipboard, entered. Nurse Arlene slipped in behind him, her blue eyes downcast.

The doctor looked grave, and I knew.

"I'd like to call my sister, please."

Willa Grace

"Ack, girl." Blanche looked down at my pan of kolache. "What kind of mess is this?"

"Sorry," I shrugged and pursed my lips. "Guess something went wrong in the rising."

With our heads at angles, we studied the sheet pans of overbaked blobs of dough, which looked more like puffy biscuits than the buttery, fruity pastries they were meant to be.

"You guess something went wrong?" Blanche tsk, tsked, and threw a kitchen towel over the pan. She looked at me through furrowed brows. "Thought you said you could bake. I ain't seen nothin' to suggest that."

"Give her a chance, Blanche." Bonnie stuck up for me as she washed the breakfast dishes. "That's a putzy recipe if you ask me. Lots of work with little to show for it."

"Little to show? You try tellin' that to the Mister when he asks for them at breakfast."

I grabbed the pan, forgetting it'd come from the oven. "Dammit!" I dropped it on the floor as I ran to the sink for cold water.

"Jesus, Mary, and Joseph, girlie," Blanche jumped out of the way. "Watch what yer doin' there. Christ a mighty!"

Bonnie giggled until Blanche gave her a look.

"Sorry, again." I didn't know what was wrong with me. Well, that wasn't entirely true. The kitchen window looked out upon the yard between the big house and the barn where the horses were kept. Jode was in the yard working with a gigantic Belgian, preparing it for a horse show in the city.

He brushed and fussed for a good part of the morning under a warm spring sun. His muscles bulging and tight, his blond hair sticking to his neck and forehead, his hips moving back and forth with his weight as he moved around the horse. He needed someone to fetch him a cool glass of water. Someone to gently move the hair out of his eyes. Someone to…yikes. Such a fine spectacle of a man made it hard to focus on the work at hand.

Never before had a boy/man been a distraction for me simply for being pretty to look at.

The kitchen door swung open, and we all turned. Horseface stood there looking like a scarecrow, with her skinny body and arms out, her hands on either side of the doorway, her long face looking mighty pissy.

"Hello, ma'am," Blanche said. "What can I do fer ya?"

"This one," Horseface indicated me with a swipe of a long finger. Immediately, I thought, 'What did I do now?' "She's got a telephone call." She was displeased. What else was new?

"Me?" I put a finger to my chest. Why would I have a telephone call? What would be so important that someone needed to call me during work? Then, the blood rushed from my brain, leaving only the thought that this was not good. Someone was sick or dead. Mamka, Tata, one of our siblings?

"Who is it?" I asked, my voice cracking, panic gripping me from head to toe.

"How should I know?" Horseface screeched like an old crow. She turned from the door and disappeared.

Blanche pulled in her chin and raised her brows as she looked my way.

I wiped my hands on my apron and followed the old piss-pot down the hall, wishing she'd move faster. I'd hate to have to run her over, but my nervousness was sky-high.

"You know this is against the rules. I wouldn't have put it through if the call hadn't come from a hospital. I offered to pass a message on, but..."

At that, I pushed around her and ran for the office as Horseface yelped. I didn't pay any attention to her scolding and screeching. I grabbed the receiver that lay in the middle of her desk.

With my heart pounding and hands shaking, I put the receiver to my ear and heard the words that would change my life forever.

"Willsy?" It was Daisy, and she sounded awful.

"What's happened?" My hand was shaking, so I could hardly hold the receiver.

Horseface stood just outside the doorway, working her big teeth, glaring. I reached over and gave the door a shove. It shut in her face as she protested from the other side, but she didn't come in.

"I'm at the hospital in Oak Park." Daisy was crying now.

"What's wrong?"

"I...I...the doctor thinks I have...," she sobbed.

"What, Daisy! You're scaring the shit out of me."

"Tuberculosis."

"What did you say?" I heard her wrong. I was sure of it.

"TB. Tuberculosis. I have it. Missus Winterthur does too. She's not doing well, and they won't let me see her."

At that, I dropped to my knees, still holding the receiver, with my other hand on the edge of the desk holding me upright. I pressed my forehead to my arm.

"Willsy, are you there?"

I swallowed the hard fist in my throat.

"Yes, I'm here," I whispered, knowing Horseface most likely had her ear pressed to the door. "How do they know? Don't those tests take a few days?"

"He said I have a lesion in my left lung. I had an X-ray."

"Oh no…" I was terrified and immediately thought of the poor souls I knew who had this awful disease. I breathed in and out to steady my nerves.

"I have to go to a sanitarium. The beds are all full at the ones here, so they're sending me to the Wisconsin State Sanitarium in Waukesha County."

"Where is that?" I had no idea where Waukesha County was, but it felt like it must be on the other side of the world.

"By Milwaukee, I guess."

"Oh, Daisy. When?"

"Soon. Tomorrow morning."

"No! For how long?" I tried to keep the panic out of my voice, but knew I was losing the battle. I didn't know how long it took to cure tuberculosis. Then, I thought, *can* tuberculosis be cured? Matty Pesko died an awful death.

"I don't know, but I heard someone mention six months."

"Six months! I won't see you for six months?" I heard Daisy sniffle on the other end. She must have been terrified. I had to be strong for both of us. "You'll do whatever is needed to get better. If that's being gone for six months, then that's that. I can certainly manage if you can."

"I suppose. What about my income? Mamka and Tata are counting on me."

"Stop with that right now. I'm coming to the hospital. You shouldn't be alone." Darkness was just starting to fall. I would walk in the dark if I had to. The distance didn't matter.

"You can't. They aren't allowing any visitors this evening, and I don't want you exposed to this. I knew you'd want to come, but the doctor said you can come tomorrow morning. Please don't come tonight. There's nothing you can do."

"I will be there, Daisy. You're not leaving without my seeing you off."

"You have to work. Your job is more important than ever." Daisy yawned. "I'm so tired."

"You'd better get some sleep if you can. I'll see you in the morning."

"Okay." She sounded like a child, not the big sister I adored.

I replaced the receiver. The door of the office opened, and Horseface stood there.

"Life isn't easy or fair. It's time you learned that." The old poop looked smug. I hated her in that moment. A hatred so strong I had to stop myself from strangling her. "So, what's wrong with her?"

Thank goodness she didn't hear the word 'tuberculosis.'

I gave Horseface a hard stare. I wanted to blame her, no matter how crazy that was. I wanted to blame someone. How dare this damned disease invade my sister?

"Answer me."

"I don't know. I'm going to her tomorrow morning. You are not keeping me here."

"You will not. If you do, take your things with you. You're done."

"You need me. Thorpe's fancy dinner party is tonight, and Blanche needs every hand she can get in the kitchen. As soon as Daisy is shipped…as soon as she's shipped into another room, I will be back."

"That smart mouth of yours is going to be the ruination of you. Get back to work."

After I'd returned to the kitchen, I couldn't tell the truth about what Daisy was facing. I couldn't say the word 'tuberculosis.' It would have triggered a panic that would spread throughout the house. I told them my sister was in the hospital, the diagnosis uncertain, and I would be gone in the morning to see her.

Blanche nodded, then asked, "You okay?

"I'll be fine."

That night, I lay in bed, unable to sleep, with tears staining my pillow and dripping into my hair. I replayed our telephone call over and over, trying to come to grips with the truth of what was happening. Was Daisy sleeping? I was certain she wasn't. Was she crying into her pillow the same as I? Of course she was.

The next morning, just as the pink smudge of dawn pushed into the sky, I arose and quickly dressed just as the others were beginning to stir.

"Bonnie," I touched her shoulder. When she failed to respond, I said her name again and gently nudged her.

"Shoot, am I late?" She sat up, rubbing her eyes. Bonnie was always late.

"Tell Blanche that I'll be back as soon as possible."

"Uh, huh." She yawned and rolled over.

In the early morning dusk, I stood under the backyard light, buttoning my coat and gearing myself up for the long walk. I knew where Oak Park Hospital was located and that it would be a long hike without the bicycle I normally borrowed from Otto, who worked in the carriage house and had been gone the night before.

As I rounded the carriage house, there was Otto's bicycle. He must have left it out when he got back last night. Glory be!

SEVEN

Daisy

I lay on the hospital bed in my yellow dress, awaiting transport, still terrified by the turn of events. Every time I silently repeated the word 'tuberculosis,' I felt as though there wasn't enough oxygen in the room.

Tuberculosis, tuberculosis… I wanted to beat my head against the wall to erase that dreaded word. How could this be true?

I thought of dear, sweet Matty back home and how his sister said he struggled for every breath. Would Mrs. Winterthur die? Would I?

I knew then I had to stop this awful fear. I needed a good dose of Willa Grace. With a fist, I pounded the bed rail. No! I was too young and otherwise too healthy.

Dr. Ferguson said tuberculosis was flooding the sanitariums, and it was hard to find an open bed, but he had managed to find one. Unfortunately, it was a far distance from my home up north, but only a few hours from Berwyn and Willa Grace.

I'd just gotten used to being without Willa Grace, and now this. There would be so many letters to write to explain my situation. The first letter would go to Mamka to inform the family of my new temporary home with assurances that I would be okay, and where to write me. Then Harold. What would this turn of events do to our plans to build a life together? Surely, he'd be patient with my recovery, and then we'd have the rest of our lives together, watching our family grow. After all, he was busy with his new business, which would surely help pass the time until I returned.

I was going to miss my dear Mrs. Winterthur dreadfully. She was in critical condition, and I was in isolation for the time being, and if she stabilized, she would be sent on to another sanitarium.

I had no idea how long it would be before I returned to work. Now, the sole burden of sending money fell on Willa Grace, who was already sending what she could. I was needed more than ever, and here I lay. Anger and fear took their turns with me.

I felt like a caged bird as I lay there waiting. I wanted to fly away from this place, as far from tuberculosis, hospitals, and sanitariums as possible. I wanted to circle above the trees and the rivers and find my way back to Emery Township.

I sat up once, but the fever made me dizzy. Despite the medication I'd been given during the night, my fever persisted.

A thought occurred to me. They couldn't take me away if I didn't want to go, could they? I could grab onto the bed rails and refuse to let go.

Yes, I could do that, but where would I run? Mrs. Winterthur's? No. I was confident her attorney had the place locked up by now. Gerda hadn't shown any signs of disease and was sent home. I didn't know where she lived, but if I showed up at her door, she'd surely slam the door in my face. I could walk to the Thorpe estate and Willa Grace. But then what?

Dr. Ferguson had done his best to reassure me that many people have beaten TB. There was no reason this disease shouldn't delay my life much more than six months. I believe that's what he said. Still, six months, at age nineteen, seemed like forever.

Cruelest of all, Willa Grace and I couldn't even say a proper goodbye. The nurses said my sister could come to see me off, but only from a distance.

Just then, the door to the room burst open with a bang and hit a cart alongside. Willa Grace entered with a wild look in her eye, her hair a mess, and her coat barely hanging on.

A dark-haired nurse ran in behind her. "Stay back, Miss. Visiting hours haven't started yet, and I don't think you're supposed to be in here anyway."

"Daisy!" Willa Grace bent over, hands on knees, trying to catch her breath. "I'm so sorry."

Tears slid down my face and gathered in my ear.

"You're here," I choked out.

Willa Grace straightened and started toward me.

"Don't come near me." I held up a hand as though to push her away. The nurse handed my sister a mask, which she put on haphazardly. "Oh, Wills, I'm so glad you're here." I hadn't realized how much I needed to see a familiar face.

Willa Grace's watery eyes softened. "How are you feeling?" She wrung her hands before her.

I bit my lip to stop trembling. "What am I going to do?"

With a determined bob of her head, Willa Grace said, "You're going to get better. You'll go to the sanitarium, do what you're told, and return before you know it. What choice do you have?" She stood tall and proud as she mothered me.

"Keep your distance. You were supposed to wait in the lobby until we wheeled her out," the nurse said. "I'm going to find out who let you in." Out the door she went.

Willa Grace was now the big sister, and I was grateful.

"The doctor said that it doesn't look like a severe case."

"Are you sure the doctor is right? Doctors can make mistakes just like anyone else."

"He showed me the X-ray. It's clear as day. When Missus Winterthur coughed up blood a few months ago, I wiped it. I guess that wasn't so smart of me, but I didn't know what was wrong with her. I'm so afraid for her. She doesn't deserve what she's going through. She's so sick." I rubbed my forehead with my fingers. "I worry I'll never see her again."

"You will. I know you will."

I wiped my tears and shivered, unsure if it was the room's temperature or sheer fright.

"Are you cold?"

"I am. I've been shivering ever since I saw the X-ray."

Willa Grace went to the door, stuck her head out, pulled her mask down, and hollered, "We need another blanket here."

"Willsy!"

"You're cold." She looked back at me and shrugged, then stepped aside as another masked nurse bustled in and tucked a blue blanket around me. It was Arlene from the day before. To Willa Grace, she said, "How did you get in here?"

"I was given special permission because my sister will be sent away."

Arlene furrowed her brow. Then, the corner of her eyes crinkled in a grin, and she left.

"How *did* you get in here?"

"The receptionist was gone from her desk, so I just walked around until I found you."

"I'll just die if you catch it. Maybe you already have." We stared at each other, wide-eyed.

"Can't they give you medicine to make it better?"

I shook my head. "The doctor says they treat it with lots of fresh air, rest, and good, wholesome food."

"Well, you could do that anywhere." Willa Grace held her arms open wide and took a step forward. "Why, I could take care of you. You can get fresh air at home on the farm, and rest is easy to come by. Let's leave. What are they going to do? Call the cops? Tie us to the bed?"

"No, Wills, listen to me. I can't take a chance on infecting anyone else. Besides, the State is monitoring all cases of TB. I'm already branded. Anyway, I'm out of work. I will go to the sanitarium and get well. Then, I'll be back good as new." One minute, I believed that. The next, not so much.

"Mamka will be beside herself worrying about you."

"She doesn't need one more worry. I hate that I'm adding to her burdens. I suppose there is no way we can shield her from this."

"We could pretend..." Willa Grace looked to the ceiling, her gaze searching for answers.

"No, we have to tell them. They'd see my letters coming from a different address, and I wouldn't get theirs. Then there's the loss of my income." I started to cry again. "They so needed our help, and now..." I waved a helpless hand.

Arlene came in with a syringe and a clipboard, indicating Willa Grace. "We need to do a skin test, Miss Maruska. You've been with Miss Daisy here, so you need a test. Are you having any respiratory symptoms, a fever, coughing?"

Willa Grace's eyes widened like pie plates as she vigorously shook her head. She hated needles as much as I hated liver, and that was a lot.

"Don't worry. You'll survive." I wiped my eyes with my fingers.

Willa Grace looked green but stuck her arm out like a trooper." The nurse performed the test, and Willa Grace filled out the necessary paperwork. Arlene told my sister to call in three days for the results and then left us.

"Time won't go fast enough for me to get these results and to have you back." Willa Grace crossed her arms over her chest. I could see the wheels turning. She was trying to find a way to save the day like she always did, but there was nothing she could do. "Maybe I could go with you." Her eyes widened, and she flung her arms out. "I know. I could work at the sanitarium and watch over you. There's all kinds of jobs I'm sure I could do."

"No, no. I don't want you anywhere near all that sickness. Please, don't even think that. You have a good job here."

Her shoulders slumped. "I suppose you're right. What about all of your things? You don't have anything here with you. How can they send you off without a change of clothes?"

"Mrs. Winterthur's attorney and his wife went to the house to gather some things for her and to clean out my room. My suitcase is in the closet here. They dropped it off last night."

"Is there anything I can get for you?"

I shook my head.

"Will you write Mamka and tell her I'm feeling good and looking just fine? And that I'm all right with going to the sanitarium. I will tell her these things, too, but she needs to hear it from both of us."

"Whatever you need, you say the word. I will visit you as soon as I can."

"You can't afford it, Wills. You need to save your money to send home. I'll be okay. We'll write every few days."

Two masked attendants entered the room, followed by two other nurses. It was time.

An overwhelming sense of panic gripped me. Willa Grace and I locked eyes. She looked as panicked as I felt.

"To hell with what they say. I'm hugging you." Willa Grace leaped forward and gathered me in her arms against the nurses' protestations.

I clung to my sister with all my strength. Both our masks were wet with tears.

"Write to Mamka, Wills. Write to me."

Willa Grace

I stood outside the hospital as Daisy was loaded into the back of the white ambulance. The driver, a man with black hair and tanned skin, slammed the door without a glance at either of us. I wanted to punch him between the shoulders as he went to the driver's seat, hit him so hard he couldn't take her away.

Through the window on the side, Daisy smiled from the gurney, head raised off the pillow, and waved as though she were being hauled off to a great party where she'd have such fun. That was so like her.

Hiding her terror to give me hope. I waved back, willing my face to show I wasn't worried, although I was scared as hell. The ambulance pulled away from the curb and began down the street. I waved until long after I knew Daisy could no longer see me.

I closed my eyes, and in my frazzled brain, the ambulance became a black hearse with Daisy in the back, trying desperately to escape. I nearly screamed in horror at my vision. I clamped my hand over my mouth and turned away, tears flooding my face.

My knees gave out, and I collapsed onto the cold cement steps. I was exhausted. Bringing my knees up and hugging them, I tried to make sense of it all. People passed by me, going in and out of the hospital, carrying on. How dare they not see the world had stopped turning? For a moment, I hated them all.

Daisy had tuberculosis. And it was all my fault. The rest of my life wouldn't be worth spit because I'd done this to her. Daisy hadn't wanted to leave the farm. She was never interested in city life. But no, I pushed for the chance to see a city, live somewhere different, and meet new people, not caring a lick for all her doubts. How could I have been so selfish?

And now, Daisy was paying the price. Why couldn't it be me? I wanted to run screaming down the street after the ambulance.

My breath came in short, shallow bursts. Here I was, barely able to breathe, and Daisy, who was breathing just fine, was on her way to a sanitarium. How goddamned absurd. I looked down at the site of the Mantoux test, where they'd stuck the needle under my skin, and willed it to be positive so they could take me too. Just three days were all I needed for the results to come in, then I could go too.

Just then, a presence, all in white, appeared at my side, and for a hopeful moment, I thought it might be an angel.

It was the nurse who did the Mantoux test. She spread her brown jacket on the step and sat beside me, smoothing her skirt around her white nylon legs, a nurse's cap neatly perched on her black curls.

"Are you going to be all right?" She asked sweetly with the kindest of blue eyes.

I nodded that I was fine. It was a lie.

"I saw you still out here after the ambulance left. Your sister will receive the best care. I promise." She smiled sympathetically. "By the way, my name is Arlene."

Again, I nodded.

"My shift is done. Do you need a ride home?"

I swallowed hard and forced a deep breath. "That's nice of you, but I rode a bike." I didn't tell her it was stolen, and Otto must be wondering what happened to it.

"I have sisters of my own, and I know how I would feel if one of them were ill. I don't know what I'd do without them." Arlene gently touched my arm.

"I guess I'm going to have to figure that out." I sniffed and wiped my face with my palms.

"I'm sorry you're both going through this, but your sister needs you now more than ever."

"What if I never see her again?" Nausea swirled in my gut, and tears spilled afresh.

"Focus on what needs to happen next. Daisy doesn't need you wallowing in pity for her or yourself. She needs your strength and support, and to know you are carrying on despite this awful news. She needs to focus on her care, and you need to take care of yourself. Don't give Daisy anything more to worry over."

Arlene was right.

"Thank you. I…I need to get back to my job. I work at the Thorpe estate." I stood, wiping away tears again.

"Why, that's right on my way. You wait here, and I'll get my car. We'll put your bike in the trunk." Arlene stood, took off her hat, shook her hair free, and retrieved her jacket.

"That's very kind of you." It was a comfort to have someone to rely on, if only for a brief time.

Arlene and I loaded the bike, and she tried her best to reassure me on the drive. I had her drop me at the front gate.

"Now, Willa Grace, you remember what I said." Arlene leaned down to see me out of the open passenger side window as I stood on the curb with the bicycle. "This is not your fault. Not at all. TB is everywhere, and new treatments are being tried every day."

"I know." But I still didn't understand why it was Daisy and not me.

I thanked Arlene and watched her drive away. As I stood there by myself with Otto's rusty bicycle, it seemed the ground beneath my feet was slipping away, as though my world had tilted on an angle, and I was sliding, unable to catch my breath, not wanting to comprehend what had happened on this cool March day. I'd always hated March.

How long would it be before I would see Daisy again? I never wanted to take this journey alone. For all my bravado in wanting an adventure, I wanted Daisy by my side.

I was so alone, but shame on me for this monumental bit of self-pity. What was ahead for Daisy? What if the sanitarium was an awful place? Was she going to be in pain? Would she die?

Putting a hand on the cold stone of the front gate, I steadied myself with a deep breath and a determined shake of my head. I needed to carry on, be strong for Daisy and my family, and get back to work while I still had a job. If I still had a job.

I slipped inside the gate and took the path between the stone wall and the tall shrubbery to the back of the house. I put Otto's bicycle where I'd found it and ran through the gardens to the kitchen door. I hesitated before entering.

How was I going to concentrate on work?

I entered the kitchen to the questioning stares of the others and a welcoming smile from Bonnie. Blanche was a dear, as always. She put up with no guff in her kitchen, but her heart was as huge as Mamka's.

I had a decision to make. Do I tell them that Daisy had TB? If I did, it would cause panic, no two ways about it. I decided not to share the diagnosis with anyone until the results of the skin test were known. I knew this was reckless of me, but I needed this job more than ever, so I told them she had an attack of appendicitis. I thought that sounded good.

In the late afternoon, Blanche gave us a short break. I decided to use the time to take a walk and gather my thoughts before returning to prepare for the party Thorpe's were hosting. Bonnie offered to go with me, but I needed time alone.

I skirted the back of the gardens, slipped under a fence, and into the woods, walking along the horse path. My feet pounded the path as if I could beat away my fear for my sister. With my eyes downcast as I moved amid the roots of the trees, I failed to notice the figure leaning against a tree, puffing on a cigarette.

"You escaping too?" He snuffed out the cigarette under the toe of his boot.

"What!" I nearly had a coronary. "Geez Louise! You could have said something sooner." I put a hand on my chest and gasped for breath, with one on the nearest tree trunk.

It was Jode.

"Sorry." He was grinning like a cat. "But are you? Escaping?"

"No, just walking."

"Thought maybe you was in trouble with Horseface again. I heard her griping at you and Bonnie the other day for taking too much time in the garden."

I shook my head. "I'm just walking." A tear slipped down my cheek.

Jode's expression changed from one of mischief to one of concern. "What's wrong?"

"It's my sister." So much was built up inside that I had to let it out. I told him the whole story.

Jode put a hand on my shoulder. "Life can be the shits sometimes."

I wiped my face with my hands. "Daisy didn't want to come here, but I pushed and pushed until she finally agreed. And then, when she told me she had a bad feeling about the move, I told her it was all in her head. How could I have been so cruel? Why didn't I listen to what she wanted?"

"It's not like you tied her up and shoved her on the train. All you can do now is deal with it." He took a step closer.

"You're right. Still, I'm scared for her."

"Come here." He pulled me into his arms. At first, I stiffened. I hardly knew him. "You look like you need a hug," he said with his breath on my neck. I did need a hug, so I relaxed against him. He smelled of horse, sweat, and cigarettes, but I didn't mind.

My arms hung loosely at my sides, and he tightened his embrace to a quick squeeze, then relaxed and stepped back. "All better?"

I shrugged. "Thanks." I didn't know what else to say. I knew I was blushing. This was so crazy. Daisy is fighting for her life, and because of that, Jode was paying attention to me—Willa Grace.

"I'd better get back."

"Yeah. Me too." He pumped a shoulder and grinned. "Glad I ran into you, um…"

"Willa Grace."

"I knew it was something like that. We better not go back the same way. I don't need more trouble than I already got."

I wasn't sure what he meant by that, but it was true. Horseface'd string me up if she knew I was out here with a boy.

That night, I wrote to our family. It was the hardest letter I ever had to write because I knew how devastated they'd be. Of course, I would assure them that Daisy would be as good as new before long. Mamka would do what she could to bolster spirits. She might decide to spare telling the young ones, but I was sure she would spend her grief alone with little comfort from Tata. He would hide his worry with work as he had with Teddy.

My next letter was to Henry. I don't know why, but my soul felt the need to reach out to him. His letters had come regularly every other week. I wasn't so good at answering each one, but I'd warned him of that. Now, I needed his friendship in a way I had never needed it before. He and I shared a history of community, family, and friends that bound us together.

Yes, Henry would know just what to say.

EIGHT

Daisy

As I jostled along in the ambulance, staring at the white roof over me, trying to make sense of my life, thoughts raced through my brain. One moment I was hopeful, the next, terrified. I had to be okay. I had to, for my parents, my siblings. I also knew that I had to try with everything in me to keep a good attitude. Otherwise, I was sunk from the start.

But also, I worried, would I have enough strength to fight this? I'd never been thought of as strong of body, and now my body was being attacked.

What would Willa Grace do? That would be my guide. Willa Grace had never been afraid of anything I could think of, even when Teddy slipped under that sheet of ice. She jumped in without a thought of freezing to death. My little sister had courage enough for the two of us.

Albert, my driver, and I had made a little small talk during the trip, but I was so preoccupied that I wasn't much for conversation. He seemed to understand.

"This is the road in," Albert said over his shoulder. I rose on one elbow and craned my neck to see out the front. Albert turned off the highway onto a narrow paved road. Wildflowers lined both sides of the road, dancing in the breeze as we passed. Two stone pillars rose in the distance, like soldiers guarding a castle. Except this was no castle.

"You're supposed to lie, Miss," Albert said. "You don't want to get me in trouble now, do you?" I could tell he was grinning.

"I'll have plenty of time for that in the next six months. I want to see where I'm going, Albert. I won't tell if you don't."

Albert drove between stone pillars and a sign announcing The Wisconsin State Sanitarium. My heart did a flutter and my stomach a lurch. Ahead, the drive curved to the right, revealing a huge, well-tended lawn dotted with trees where people strolled about dressed as any I'd seen on the streets of Berwyn, looking happy and healthy enough. Here and there, flowers bloomed with splashes of orange, yellow, and purple.

To the right of the driveway was a large, white two-story home with a cupola on top and a screen porch on the front.

Albert bumped his chin and indicated the house. "That's where the doctor stays and has his office. The superintendent, too."

"Nice."

"That brick building over there," Albert pointed to the right, beyond the offices, "is the powerhouse. It supplies all the heat for the entire place. "Ahead is the hospital. That's where I'll be dropping you."

I bent down as far as I could to see a three-story building, white with windows looking out over the lawn where I'd seen the people strolling. I couldn't see the top floor, but the building looked like any other hospital I'd seen in the city. A place where miracles and heartbreak happened hand in hand.

I took a deep breath to steady my nerves and coughed, recovering quickly.

"Behind the big hospital is the dining hall and auditorium, and beyond that are the cottages where those close to permanent release are housed."

I pushed a knot of fear down my throat and said, "You make a fine tour guide, Albert. All I expected to see was a hospital."

"Well, Miss Daisy, it's too bad, but I come here quite regularly."

Albert parked the ambulance at the side entrance to the hospital. "This is the administration entrance. Wait here. I'll let them know we have arrived."

On the lawn, a few young women sat on the grass, looking like they were having a picnic. Two elderly men played a game of checkers at a table nearer the building. Four young men gently tossed a ball.

The place had an almost resort-like feel to it. This might not be so bad after all. There was no dark sense of death, no evidence of evil. All of a sudden, I just knew. I'm going to be okay here.

Within minutes, I heard voices, and the ambulance's back doors opened. A gray-haired woman with glasses in a nurse's uniform and two male attendants, all masked, waited with a wheelchair. Albert stood off to the side. The nurse smiled with her eyes and said, "Welcome, Miss Maruska. We'll get you inside and to admissions." I wanted to see their whole faces, but as I would learn, it was rare to see them without masks.

The attendants wheeled the gurney out and helped me into the chair, and one took my suitcase. I held my purse tight against me for support or possibly protection, in case my first impressions of the place were wrong.

"I'm Nurse Carter," the nurse said with a pleasing sing-song quality to her voice.

"Pleased to meet you," I said.

"May I call you Daisy?"

I nodded and flashed a smile. A tremor of nerves went through me.

"Nice to meet you, Daisy. My two helpers here are Dan and Steve." One waved, the other gave a quick nod. Nurse Carter continued. "This building is the hospital where our newcomers go first. We'll get you all checked in and then see you settled into your room."

"Good luck to you, Miss Maruska, Daisy." Albert gave me a grin as he went around the front of the ambulance to take his leave.

"Drive safely, Albert, and thank you."

Nurse Carter led the way through the double doors as one of the attendants pushed me along. We went down a sterile, white hallway and passed a few offices before entering a small office with a metal desk. The wheelchair and I were parked alongside. The two attendants left. A middle-aged woman in a brown tweed suit with shoulder-length chestnut hair and a mask came in behind us, rounded the desk, and took a seat.

"This is Miss Gregor. She'll get you all signed in," Nurse Carter said. "Then I'll take you up to your room. You'll be on the third floor. Your suitcase will be there waiting for you."

Miss Gregor's blue eyes crinkled over her mask.

"This is scary, I know, but we'll take good care of you here." She pushed an open ledger aside and pulled out a folder with my name on the tab. "The hospital in Oak Park called with your information. Daisy."

Then, she mentioned the cost of my stay, fifteen dollars per week, and my heart hit the floor.

"I have very little money." I never for one moment thought about having to pay for this. How foolish of me. I had seventeen dollars to my name and couldn't, wouldn't, ask my parents to pay. How could they? I nearly panicked at the thought that they would have the burden to pay on top of my diagnosis. Tears stung my eyes.

"No worries, Daisy. As you are a legal adult and this is a state facility, the state will absorb your cost."

"Thank you." A captive breath whooshed out of me. "Oh, thank you."

"You must pay for personal items on your own, though. If your family wants to help you, they can send you these things or the money to buy them here. We will start you with some toiletries if you don't have them."

Once Miss Gregor was done with me, Nurse Carter took me to the third floor, chatting as we went. Once she rolled me off the elevator, Nurse Nelson stepped forward.

"Well, howdy there, sweetheart. Welcome to the third floor." She chuckled as she stepped behind me. Her voice was high, crisp, and a bit loud.

Nurse Nelson was short and round, with curly auburn hair framing her face, dusted with freckles, her nursing cap at an uneven angle, as she wheeled me down the hall, her shoes squeaking on the polished tile floor. It smelled of antiseptic with a hint of newly cut grass from the open windows I saw in all the patients' rooms as we passed. Coughs ranging from dainty to downright hacking chased us down the hall. I was met with several welcoming smiles as we passed room to room, seeing patients of all ages.

Nurse Nelson asked about my home, the size of my family, and what I did in my spare time. Along the way, she also said hello to many of the others.

She stopped at room 302. "This is your new home for now." And once inside, "Meet your roommate, June."

A girl a bit younger than I with short, curly blond hair, a dimpled smile, and a pert nose that made her look like a pixie lay propped against two pillows in the far bed. She and her pink pajamas were tucked tightly into the blue cover of her bed. She set the book she was reading aside.

"Well, Hallelujah!" June said joyfully as Nurse Nelson pushed me between the two single beds with metal headboards.

My bed was neatly made with a blue quilt and a white pillowcase over one fluffy pillow. The room was a sunny yellow, and despite the cool spring temperature outside, the windows were wide open, giving me an immediate chill. A small dresser sat between the two beds, and another dresser was in front of the windows.

"Meet June Hewett," Nurse Nelson gestured toward the girl, who offered a wide grin.

"Yay!" June struggled to push herself up on the pillows behind her. "Nelsy, why didn't you tell me I was getting a new roomie? Gosh, I've been so lonely."

"June, stay down. You've only been approved for a two-pillow incline." Nurse Nelson shook a finger at the girl. "This is Daisy Maruska."

"Hiya, Daisy!" June leaned toward me with a hand outstretched, and we shook. "Oh, Nelsy. Don't be yelling at me in front of my new roommate."

"Nice to meet you, June." I immediately liked this new friend.

"You want me to yell, Miss June? That was nothing, and you know it." Nurse Nelson turned her attention to me, motioning to a small set of three drawers under the windows. "We'll put your things in the dresser over here."

I rubbed my arms. "It's a bit chilly."

"Get used to it," June said. "They don't care one whit about the temperature outside. The windows are open every day, all day. And I mean every day, no matter the season. Right, Nelsy?"

"Winter, too?" I asked.

"Yep."

"How do you survive that?" This was an alarming development. Winters up north had wind chills below zero. "They can't possibly do that to us, can they?"

"Now, June," Nurse Nelson warned. "Don't you be scaring Daisy."

"Oh, they can do it, and they will," June said. "All you can do is bundle up and stay under the covers. You get used to it."

"That sounds like torture." I scooted onto my new bed, and Nurse Nelson pulled back the wheelchair and parked it by the door.

"You two want to get better or not? Fresh air is the key." Nelsy, as June called her, said, "Let's get you on the way to recovery, Miss Daisy." She took my suitcase from the floor by the bed and placed my neatly folded clothing in the drawers.

"Might as well keep out pajamas and a sweater," Nelsy said. "We need you to change and hop into bed immediately. You're on strict bed rest for the next few months. You cannot get up unless it's for treatment, not even to go to the bathroom. You'll get sponge baths and use a bedpan for now."

"Oh. Bed rest…for months?" A knot formed in my throat. This was not what I'd imagined.

"It's not as bad as it sounds," June replied. "Just don't miss the bedpan. That's a pain." She giggled.

"Thank you, Miss June." Nelsy gave her a look over her mask and shook her head. "Positive thoughts are as important as all the rest."

I went behind the panel in the corner to change as I listened to Nelsy describe my new life. It sounded more like punishment than treatment, but nothing I couldn't handle. *I'll be fine*, I repeated silently to myself. Willsy would take this in stride.

"You only get one pillow for now. Two, once you're responding well. Finish changing and get yourself tucked in. I'll be back to check on you in a bit." Then Nelsy squeaked down the hall.

June peeked around the side of the panel. "Quiet," she whispered with a finger over her lips.

I stood in my underwear, holding white pajamas with yellow roses to my chest.

June looked back at the door to our room, seeing no one, turned back to me, and grinned. "I like Nelsy, but all these dumb rules. It gets old. Nice jammies. Carry on." Then disappeared. I heard the springs of her bed announce her return to her nest. She reminded me of my dear Willa Grace, and I knew June and I would be good pals.

I finished putting on my pajamas, a sweater, and white socks to warm my feet on the cold floor. I set the clothes I had worn in the basket alongside the dresser for laundry. I took my perch on the bed and pulled up the covers.

"What are you reading?" I asked.

"*The Great Gatsby*. Want it when I'm done?" June showed me the cover.

"I've never been much of a reader. Now, my sister, that's another story. She's got stacks of books people have given her."

"If I were you, I'd become a reader. It helps the time go quickly."

"Where do you get them from? Books, I mean."

"They bring them around from time to time. People either leave them here or donate them. I pretty much read non-stop. It helps keep me from going nuts. There are also crossword puzzle books. I'm no good at those, but you might be. Writing letters helps, too. Of course, life will be much easier now that you're here and I have someone to talk to."

I smiled. Considering the starkness of the room, staying busy might be a challenge. "Is there anything else to do?"

"Once you're upgraded, it gets easier. Just get yourself through the next three months. I promise. My brother, Theo. He was here last year. He's fine now and back home finishing high school."

"That's good to hear." I fluffed my one pillow before lying back. The bed was comfortable enough.

"I think you and I will get on well together." June grinned. "Do you snore?"

"Not that anyone has told me, and as long as you don't sound like an old hound dog when you sleep, we'll be just fine," I said with the start of feeling at home. "I like to sing, do you?"

"I do! Maybe we can work on harmonizing. Do you know Gershwin's *I Got Rhythm*?"

"Yes!"

Together, we started singing, making a pleasing sound.

I've got rhythm, I got music, I got my friends. Who could ask for anything more?

"My mother always sang it as she worked and would look at me every time she sang the next line." My voice hitched at the mention of Mamka, but I quickly added, "*I got daisies in green pastures. I got my friends. Who could ask for anything more?*"

"Girls!" Nelsy stuck her head in the door. "We've got people trying to nap here."

As soon as she disappeared, we giggled.

"We'll be good as gold, Daisy. Where you from anyway?"

I told her about Emery Township and my family.

"I'm from Middleton, not too far from here. My parents own a grocery store. It's just my brother Theo and me. I was a junior in high school. Sure hope I graduate."

"I never got beyond the eighth grade. We were needed on the farm. That's with most kids by us. I sure wish we could have kept going. I'm nineteen now."

"Lucky you. I wouldn't say I liked school, although now that I can't go…I miss my classmates, my teachers, and the home ec club. I can sew like nobody's business."

I chuckled at that and looked around the room. "I hope the days don't stretch out too long."

"I got here just over five months ago, and I'm finally up to two bloomin' pillows." She was not impressed.

"You've been in bed for five months?" A shiver skittered up my spine. "Will you be well enough to get out at six?"

"Six months? Where'd you come up with that?"

"That's what the doctor said back in Oak Park. Someone said it anyway."

"Good luck. Only the lucky few get out in six. It usually takes six to get the okay to get out of bed to use the bathroom."

"The doctor wouldn't have said that if he didn't think it was true." But, did he say that, or had I mistaken something else that had been said?

June shrugged. "Don't count on that. Some people have been here for years."

"Years? Why, I didn't plan for that. I have to get back to helping my parents." My heart plummeted. I felt tears gather, and my breathing came in gulps. No. I couldn't be here for more than six months.

"Oh, Daisy, I didn't mean to upset you." June reached across and put a hand on my arm. "We all go through this in our own way. Some heal faster than others. You'll see. Wait until you see the doctor."

I wiped away the tears. I was gathering a mental list of questions. We sat in silence for a moment. "Is it always so quiet here? Other than the coughing."

"Afternoons are quiet times for everyone to nap. You'll meet others who have been upgraded to walking around the building. And once you're upgraded from there, you can move into the cottages behind the hospital and walk the grounds. Poor Lily Stanley, on the second floor, has been back and forth here for five years. Shoot, I shouldn't have said that. I'm sorry, Daisy."

Five years? In the next five years, I had hoped to marry Harold, set up a house in Emery, a garden, and have babies. Giving that up for five years would put me into my mid-twenties. No, that could not, would not, happen to me.

June continued. "Once I get out, I am never coming back. They'll have to catch me and tie me up good." She began to cough and reached for a small green box on the metal chair near her bed. The cough became a great hacking and gurgling in her throat, making my stomach clench.

I sat up with my legs over the side of the bed.

"Can I get you something?"

June shook her head and spat into the box.

"Are you sure? A drink of water, maybe?"

The cough left her. After a moment, her breathing returned to normal, and she sank back onto her pillows.

"I'm okay. I haven't had a fever for a while now, but this cough is hanging on. The fever is the big thing. That determines so much of what you're allowed to do around here."

"They don't let you decide for yourself? When you are feeling better, you can't simply get up and walk around?"

"Heck no. Everything revolves around the sputum tests, which the box is for." She held up the box. "About the whole staying in bed thing, I cheat by sneaking out and prancing around the room when no one is looking. Just don't let them catch you." She grinned mischievously. "I hope old Nelsy didn't hear me say that."

"I heard you just fine," Nelsy said from the hall. "You're not fooling anyone, Miss June."

Nelsy stuck her head in the door.

"Miss Daisy, you must need a nap after your trip. Remember, rest and fresh air are the keys to getting back to that farm of yours. And you," she waggled a finger toward June, "go back to your book and zip that lip."

Eventually, we both took naps for the rest of the afternoon. At 5:30, a scrumptious dinner was served of roast beef, mashed potatoes, gravy, buttered carrots, rolls, fruit salad, and chocolate crème pie.

June said this was not unusual, as nutritious meals were as much a part of the treatment as anything else.

If only Mamka could have seen this feast before me, it would have eased her fears once she learned about my situation. I looked at the clock. By now, the family would be finishing supper, the girls cleaning up, and the boys milking cows. It broke my heart to think how upsetting this would be for them once our letters arrived.

Nelsy stopped to say goodbye as her shift ended at 6:00. The night nurse came in to introduce herself. Nurse Fromm was a tall, gray-haired lady who had a very limited sense of humor but was kind enough. June didn't care for her at all, which I assumed was Nurse Fromm's reluctance to June's mischief.

That evening, I wrote a letter to my dear family. I tried my best to reassure them and ease their worry. My letter focused on my room, the wonderful treatment I was receiving, and my new, fun roommate. I wrote another letter to Willa Grace, assuring her I'd made it safely and the hospital was far from scary. June also wrote to her family, and then we played a bedridden game of charades. Soon, it was lights out, and as darkness closed in, it brought with it the reality of my situation. I was nineteen, and my life was suddenly reduced to the confines of a bed.

Willa Grace

I'd received my first letter from Daisy in her new and temporary home. She seemed to be doing well. Her roommate sounded like a swell gal, the nurses were nice, and her room okay, although having windows open no matter the temp would take some getting used to. All in all, the first day went fine. I felt some relief at that, but I also knew dear Daisy would keep the unpleasant parts of her stay to herself. She was so like our mother in that. Me? There was never any mystery as to how I was feeling.

Thankfully, there was much at Thorpe's to keep me occupied.

Mrs. Thorpe's fiftieth birthday was coming up on April 24th, and Mr. Thorpe planned a huge party to celebrate, pulling out all the stops with no thought of a budget. The scuttlebutt around the estate was that this party was meant to cover his guilt over his many affairs. What a jerk.

The weekend of the party was mandatory duty for those of us on staff, as huge breakfasts and picnic lunches were planned for those staying overnight, with the highlight being the dinner party on Saturday night. I'd never seen anything like it. Excitement was all around.

For me I appreciated the distraction of all the preparations, but my worries over Daisy never left me. Not only her, but also our parents and siblings. I'd sent the letter informing them of Daisy's situation, and tried to be as encouraging as possible. I hated adding to Mamka's burdens, but there was no choice.

After three days, my Mantoux/skin test for TB was negative for disease. I shared the true nature of Daisy's illness with my new friends in the kitchen. I was met with nothing but support. Bonnie did her best to cheer me up, and as time went on, my sadness faded, only to be replaced by growing anger. I was short with people, impatient, and dissatisfied with everything around me. I cut out all unnecessary expenses, which was easier now that I no longer had Sundays with Daisy, and sent as much as I could to the family. Mamka wrote back that George had taken a job with the railroad, and I was to stop trying to compensate for Daisy.

My anger stemmed from one simple question. Why Daisy and not me?

As much as I hated being away from Daisy, I was grateful for my job and the friendship I found in Bonnie and Blanche, and really, everyone. They understood my moodiness and my need to keep busy.

On the night of the birthday party, an orchestra played on the veranda overlooking the giant lawn that sloped toward Shadow Lake. Balloons of pink and white decorated the largest tent I'd ever seen, birthday banners flapped in the breeze, and flowers, all in white, lined the tables and stage, as well as the back porch. Lanterns made it all seem magical. Even I, in my crusty mood, could appreciate what we'd all accomplished to make the evening special.

Even Mr. Thorpe, who was generally very hard to please, was impressed, while Mrs. Thorpe was over the moon. She went around to thank all the staff personally. Guests poured in from all over the place. Those of us in the kitchen were too busy to watch them arrive, but as soon as our chores were finished, Bonnie and I snuck out to see what we could. It was well after 10 pm.

Bonnie and I used the hedges along the lawn for cover as we made our way down to where a slight hole in the greenery offered us a peek. By that time, the tables had been cleared away for dancing. Women in fancy dresses with long, white gloves and jewels sparkling in the light danced with men in dapper tuxedos. Cigar smoke mixed with flowery perfume in the cooling night air.

I wish Daisy could see this.

"You know, if we get caught, our jobs will be over," Bonnie whispered, "so we'd better not get caught."

"Damn right," I nudged her.

It was foolish to take a chance with a job that I desperately needed. I suppose I still had some growing up to do, but right then, I didn't care. I needed a release from my worries over Daisy. Besides, my desire to see more of life was still strong, and before us was a sea of people who'd conquered Chicago. Maybe I could learn a thing or two from watching them.

Through our leafy cover, Bonnie and I watched. Prohibition had lifted, and alcohol flowed freely. Those who drank too much made fools of themselves. Women shrieked with laughter, the men spoke louder, and the dancing all the wilder.

With no one watching, Bonnie poked her skinny body through a break in the hedge and grabbed two glasses of punch that we assumed was safe.

"This tastes like it's got alcohol in it." Bonnie wrinkled her nose and then grinned.

I held my glass up and studied the reddish liquid. "I think it's yummy. Down the hatch!"

Bonnie and I threw the brew to the backs of our throats.

After stealing two more drinks each, lightheaded and so giddy, Bonnie and I kicked off our shoes and danced behind the hedges, feeling the coolness of the grass on our toes. We spun each other until we dissolved into a giggling heap, then returned to spy on the Thorpes and their guests.

Mr. Thorpe, a drink in one hand and a cigar hanging from his lips, sashayed up against the backside of a brunette with a shapely figure and a way-too-tight red dress. She eyed him over her shoulder as he pinched her bottom. She turned and grinned like a perfect tart as he ground his man parts against her hip. Meanwhile, Mrs. Thorpe visited with a circle of ladies and missed the whole thing.

"What do you think of that?" Bonnie's eyes were wide as the moon.

"He's a shit." I downed the last of my punch.

Just then, the band announced a short break. Bonnie and I heard a hoot and a holler coming from behind the barn. Keeping low, we ran toward the sound.

Rounding the corner of the barn, we found Jode and the other men who worked the grounds sitting on hay bales in a circle around a crackling fire built of sticks. They tipped bottles of beer to their mouths with empty bottles on the ground at their feet. Their cigarettes glowed in the dark of the night, melding with sparks from the fire.

Jode sat, long legs out at angles, a beer bottle in one hand, a cigarette in the other. The moon and the fire's light put shadows on the bones of his face. Seeing me, he pumped his chin and patted the bale, wanting me to sit next to him. His sly grin was hard to refuse.

The effects of the alcohol made me mellow as a lazy river. I was drunk and hoping no one would notice.

"Ladies!" Otto shouted. He was a thick-bodied German with a cheerful way about him and a head of messy brown hair. "Want a beer?" He held up two brown bottles.

"You bet!" Bonnie hurried in, took the bottle offered, sat on a hay bale next to him, taking a good-sized swig.

"Sure." I took the other and sat next to Jode. Colleen and Tilly from the kitchen were there as well. They waved, and we saw that each of them had a beer as well.

"What's your name again?" Jode asked.

"Do I have to tell you again?" I glanced at him sideways and sipped the beer. He laughed.

"I'm kidding, Willa Grace." He bumped me with his shoulder. I couldn't help but grin.

"There's quite the party going on in the yard," I said, not knowing what else to say.

"They don't know the real party is back here." His Adam's apple bobbed as he took a slug of his beer and wiped his mouth with the back of his hand. "' Course, it's a lot better now that you're here." A bead of beer was on his upper lip. I wanted to kiss it off, which was startling. Must be the beer.

He raised his lips in a half-smile, showing a dimple on his right cheek.

We listened as the others shared a few bawdy jokes and finished our beers.

"Want to go for a walk?" Jode angled his head toward the lake.

I looked around him to see Otto whispering in Bonnie's ear. She was giddy with the attention and the alcohol.

"Sure."

Jode grabbed my hand, and I could feel the strength of his grip and the calluses on his palm. We ran through the moonlit orchard, ducking under branches filled with buds soon to blossom pinky-white.

We continued along the hedge, staying low, past the party where the band struck up *April In Paris.*

"I want to show you something."

Hand in hand, I followed him to the shimmering lake.

"Over here," he pulled me to the left, where I could barely make out an overturned boat lying against a tree. Oars propped against it.

"This yours?" I asked.

"No," he answered, "but no one needs to know that."

"We won't get into trouble, will we?"

"Maybe." His eyes flashed with trouble.

Together, we flipped over the boat. It didn't seem very sturdy, but what the hell. I could swim. Jode pushed the boat toward the water, jumped in, found a seat in the bow, and steadied the boat. I hopped in, taking a seat, and he pushed us out with the oars.

The gentle tip of the boat sent moonlight skittering on the surface. I tipped my chin to see the stars smile down on us from a black velvet sky.

It was just the two of us, and I didn't feel awkward or self-conscious at all.

Jode told me of his family's blueberry farm near Lake Michigan, where they also raised Belgian horses. Jode was the oldest of six. The farm would have been his someday, but Jode wanted new opportunities, which royally pissed off his parents. He had ambitions to make something of himself in the city. The job at Thorpe's was only a stepping stone to something more. Of what, he wasn't sure.

"Oh, me too!" I blurted. Finally, a kindred spirit, someone with the same goals as me.

"I want more than working some old farm until I'm too old to move." He had a far-off look in his eye. "I want to get a job somewhere I can work my way up." His gaze locked on mine. "I'll work my ass off to get what I want. I will. I want to be the boss someday. Doesn't matter what I do, but I want to run the show. You know what I mean, Willa Grace?"

"I do." In that moment, I fell for Jode Swenson like a rock to the bottom of a quarry.

Just then, a loud bang shook the landscape. We looked up to see a burst of red and gold fireworks. The partygoers cheered in the distance. Jode pulled in the oars.

Our mouths formed perfect Os as we tipped our chins up and waited for the next. Within seconds, another, blue and green, followed by white and purple, then orange and red. One after another, they burst, bloomed, and faded into the night.

I looked at Jode, at the beauty of him, and of us gently bobbing on the water, fireflies dancing along the shore, and fireworks raining down from the black sky. I couldn't imagine a more perfect setting than this.

Jode returned my gaze with a lazy half-smile and a twinkle in his eye. He braced himself with his hands on each side of the boat and leaned toward me. I leaned toward him, and he kissed me right on the mouth. His lips were so soft, and when he pulled away, I kissed him right back. My heart was pounding so hard I was afraid he'd hear it.

His lips tasted of beer and cigarettes, and oh gosh, I wanted more. The sweet scent of hay lingered in his clothes. I put my hands on his shoulders, feeling the muscles beneath his cotton shirt as we kissed and kissed. His thumbs stroked just under my breasts, and my insides turned cartwheels down low. All too soon for me, the fireworks stopped, and so did he.

I grinned as Jode pushed back onto his seat. What happened to the girl who had no intention of being bothered by boys? That girl had never been kissed under moonlight and fireworks by Jode Swensen.

We drifted into shore, where Jode jumped out and pulled the boat back to its resting place.

"' Spose we should head back." He put his hands in his pockets.

"I suppose." I grinned and hooked his index finger with mine. We swung our joined fingers back and forth as we stared at each other.

"You're pretty, Willa Grace." He pushed a lock of hair off my forehead.

He said I'm pretty. My life was complete. I couldn't ask for one more thing, well, except for Daisy to regain her health, but for now, I was his.

He put a hand behind my neck and pulled me close, his lips pressed on mine. A powerful heat warmed my whole body.

"See ya, Willa Grace," he whispered, with a voice sweet as sugar.

NINE

Daisy

My doctor, Dr. Thompson, whom everyone referred to as "Doc," was a lovely man, probably in his forties, handsome, as far as I could tell under the mask, with shots of gray at his temples in his otherwise chestnut hair, and brown eyes. He always wore black trousers under his white doctor coat and a stethoscope around his neck. He listened to my breathing, both front and back, tested my reflexes, and examined my throat. Nelsy reported my temperature at 100 degrees. Unsatisfactory, Doc said, but not too bad.

My Mantoux test had clearly been positive for TB. I nearly vomited when I woke that morning and saw the bloom of color at the test site. There was no mistaking that I was truly infected with this awful disease. All my certainty in the days before, believing I would be one of the lucky ones, faltered.

I had done what I was told. I remained in bed, not enjoying the bedpan one bit, and collected my sputum, which was a tad pink. I didn't use a hankie when coughing as I'd been warned, although I didn't cough often, and shivered against the chill of the open windows at night. Whatever it took to get my life back was what I was going to do.

"Daisy, do you know much about tuberculosis?" Doc had asked.

"We saw some of it in our township, but I guess I don't know much."

"There are various stages of this disease, and different types. You have pulmonary tuberculosis and are in the active stage, meaning you have active symptoms—a cough, a trace of blood in your sputum, and a fever. Have you lost weight or not had an appetite?"

"My clothes have been looser lately, but I guess I didn't put much stock in that."

"Loss of appetite is a symptom. Any chest pain?"

"No, none of that."

"This is very important. I know you're aware, but we do not want you to use any kind of handkerchief. If you are given them as gifts, you can keep them, but if used, they will be destroyed. We cannot mix them with the laundry due to the contamination. It's good that you are using the collection box for your sputum. That will be collected daily and tested. Mobile patients must always carry them with them, although you have a way to go before that."

I nodded.

"Daisy, you must expectorate whatever you cough up. The tubercle bacillus can survive stomach acid and, from there, enter the intestines, which can travel through the body using the lymph system. That's when TB can affect other areas of the body."

"I'd never heard that before. I thought it was only a disease of the lungs."

He nodded.

"Primarily, it is a lung disease, but it can spread. We will do our best to ensure this doesn't happen to you. I promise."

Nelsy came in and stood at the end of the bed. She tweaked my big toe and gave me a grin.

"It's a lot to take in," she said, "but we're here to help you."

"Our goal is to get you to the quiescent stage. At that stage, your sputum tests negative, and X-rays will show that whatever lesions you have will not have grown. Once you get to this level and hold it for two months, you can take a half-hour walk twice daily."

"A half-hour walk isn't much of a goal. My legs will turn to mush." I thought of our active life on the farm. I'd give anything now to help clear the fields of rock, walk the cows in from the pasture for milking, and walk the few miles to Viola Villa to attend a dance.

"We will give you exercises you can do in bed to help your muscles," Doc said.

"Doctor Ferguson said I'd be here for only six months. It seems unlikely that it will take a few months to be upgraded to one more pillow, then two more months to get to only a half-hour walk. Do you think six months is possible?"

Nelsy's brows shot up, and Doc shook his head.

"I wouldn't count on that, although every patient is different. That is very unlikely. You are otherwise a healthy young lady. Most of our patients go much beyond six months. Nearer to a year." Doc put a hand on my shoulder.

"A year! Oh, no." My chin trembled. "I…I can't be gone that long. I just can't." My whole body trembled with fear.

"You will get there, Daisy." His blue eyes smiled above the mask. "We want to see you in the arrested stage before we send you home. There's no telling how long that will take."

"My parents need me." Tears rolled down my cheeks. "I have friends, my siblings, and a beau. I…oh, I…" I dissolved in a puddle of tears. June, who'd been listening all this time, turned away toward the windows.

Nelsy came forward with a hand on my other shoulder. "Oh, honey, once you start to improve, you can go home for short visits, and your family can come here to see you as well."

"They can't afford that. My younger siblings won't remember who I am."

"It's not so bad, Daisy. Please don't cry." June said from her bed. "We'll keep each other company." But she was crying as well.

Doc Thompson and Nelsy waited for me to calm down. "Have I given this to others?" This was the question I'd feared asking since my ambulance ride.

"TB isn't easily transmitted from one person to another," Doc said. "You haven't infected anyone unless you've coughed or expectorated on them with abandon. I don't think that would be you, as you only have a little cough as it is." I tried to think back if I'd shared a glass, an ice cream cone, a bottle of soda with Willa Grace or anyone. I couldn't recall that I had.

Nelsy patted my arm. "There is no doubt that you'll adjust to life here, and you will find many ways to pass the time and make new friends, especially once you are ambulatory. We have entertainment come in twice a week, classes offered to help you find work once you're on your own, and an art studio."

"An art studio?" I dried my eyes with my sheet. "I would like that." This was a small consolation to the mess TB caused in my life and that of my family. In one way or another, we were all infected.

"Focus on getting better, Daisy. Do all you can, and it will come. I promise. You'll get your life back." Doc looked at Nelsy. "Let's give Daisy some time to adjust to all this." Nelsy nodded left the room, and the doctor continued, "If you have any questions, the nurses or I will answer them as best we can. Now get some rest, dear."

He went out into the hall.

I looked at June, who pushed aside her covers and crossed over to take my hand.

"We're in this together. You're not alone."

I squeezed her hand as tight as any lifeline I'd ever needed. "I know. And I have so many people rooting for me back home."

June gave me a cross-eyed look.

"Daisy, you're going to break my hand."

"Oh, sorry."

Willa Grace

"Where have you been?" Horseface hid in the shadows of the kitchen as I snuck through after my evening in the boat with Jode.

I nearly fainted at the sound of her voice.

"Nowhere." My heart thumped, and I could barely breathe.

"You have been with a boy, haven't you?" Her wrinkled face hung before me in the dark like a ghost roaming a cemetery.

"No, ma'am." I took a step back.

She came forward a step. "You're guilty as sin. I saw you from the upstairs balcony. Did you think you wouldn't be seen on the water with the fireworks lighting the sky?"

"I…I was with Bonnie."

"Miss Bonnie came back long ago. She had no idea where you were."

Shit.

"I… I wanted to see the fireworks," I gulped. "I'm sorry."

"They were done long ago. I suppose you spread your legs for that stable boy as well."

"I did not!"

"I could fire you for this, you little whore."

"Please, don't. I like it here, and I need this job more than anything." Panic gripped me. How could I have been so careless? "It won't happen again. I promise."

"If we didn't have the dinner for the senator coming up, I'd get rid of you so fast. Next time, there will be no second chance."

I ran up the stairs, stripped off my clothes, and climbed into bed.

"Where've you been?" Bonnie whispered.

"I'll tell you tomorrow." I lay in bed that night, thankful I still had a job, vowing to pay more attention to my gut, which had told me I was playing with fire when it came to Jode.

But I couldn't help myself.

That next week, Jode and I stole kisses in the barn or the garage, behind the gardener's quarters, or anywhere else we could meet.

One evening, when I returned to my room, a letter lay on my bed from Henry.

"Another letter from your northern beau." Bonnie grinned and sat on her bed.

"He's not my northern beau." I sat on my bed, facing her, holding the letter, and was not at all excited to hear from him. I wrestled with telling him about Jode, but I knew that would hurt his feelings, and I didn't want that. Was I hurting him more by not saying anything?

Bonnie flicked the letter with a finger and grinned. "You should see how your face lights up every time you finish reading one of his letters."

"That was before I had Jode."

Bonnie kicked off her shoes and lay back on her bed, hands behind her head, her braid hanging over the side of the pillow. "So, what are you going to do?"

"I get this goofy flutter in my gut whenever I think of Jode, and seeing him makes me weak in the knees." My face was hot, and my heart skipped along happily. "I think I'm in love with him." I never thought I'd hear those words come from my mouth.

Bonnie shot up and gave my shoulder a little shove. "I knew it!" We giggled.

"What about you and Otto? You seem pretty hottsie-tottsie."

Her face was thoughtful. "I don't think so. I don't think I…I don't know."

"What?"

"I got enough of taking care of men and boys after my Ma died. No thanks. I don't mind fooling around a little, but nothing more than that."

"Otto's falling for you really hard. Everyone can see it."

"He can fall as far as he wants. Not me. Are you going to open that letter or not?"

I opened my letter.

Dear Willa Grace,

I was so sorry to hear about Daisy. You must be devastated. If there is anything I can do to help, please let me know. I ran into your Pa at the last meeting at Viola Villa. All of Emery is pulling for her and saying prayers.

I was accepted to the CCC camps and will start working there next week. If you haven't heard of it, it's called the Civilian Conservation

Corps. Old FDR started the program last year to create forestry jobs. A camp went up out in the Sheep Ranch area in Skookum Valley. I should earn a good $30 a month. We desperately need the money for the farm, so I'm happy to go. While I'm gone, my brother Frank will help out with the farm. Because of the dry conditions, we're working on building firebreaks throughout the forests. I'd sure hate to see a fire start. This is the driest spring I've seen.

We've got a few new calves, the finest we've seen yet. I miss spending quiet time milking and the satisfaction of seeing the crops and the garden take hold. It looks like we'll have a fine crop of corn this year. Hoping we'll be on track to be knee-high by the 4th of July. I'll sure miss it when I'm at the camp.

The Emery baseball team lost to the Viola Villa last Saturday night. I wish you could have been there. The VV team is unstoppable this year. Dover lost to East Highland last Sunday, so Dover is at the bottom of the league. Good for them! You should have seen Joe Jandacka run the bases. He sure can fly!

Well, Willa Grace, I'll sign off for now. You take care. Let me know what I can do for you, Daisy, or your family.

Sincerely,
Henry

I folded his letter in half and put it under my pillow for now. It was good to hear from him.

Soon, letters flew fast and furious between my parents and siblings, Daisy and me, and our friends in Emery. Everyone was concerned, frightened, and wanted to help as the news traveled through the township.

In return, I wrote him letters full of my concerns. I felt safe to share my sadness, anger, fear, and guilt. I could trust him to keep my words between the two of us. To everyone else, I accepted their much-needed support, and to them, I conveyed a sense of hope and complete trust in the care Daisy was receiving.

I wished I could believe it myself.

TEN

Daisy

At Statesan, or just the San, I'd met several young girls and women who could move about freely. They stopped to visit those of us on strict bed rest. Those visits were a lifeline to the world and beyond, and their mobility gave us something to strive for. The same could be said for the letters we received, but hearing new voices, seeing new faces, was golden.

Girls from the second floor came up to visit—Margaret from Racine, Dorothy from Kenosha, and Susan from DePere. It gave me great hope to see their smiling faces and to know that someday, that would be me.

I was becoming more aware of my body and how I was feeling. And I knew I was not improving. I had a fullness in my chest as though I couldn't fill my left lung, and the only way to describe it was as if a bag of grain was resting on my chest. My cough was worse, and I experienced some slight chest pain I hadn't noticed before. With so many hours in bed, I worried about how I would maintain what little muscle I had in my body despite doing the bed exercises. Napping, which I had rarely done before, was easy.

I also learned that there was more to come in the way of treatment than simple rest, fresh air, and nutritious food. Artificial pneumothorax treatment.

On a Thursday, I was taken in a wheelchair for my first treatment, of which I understood little. June said, 'It's not bad, just a big poke and then relief.' Still, I was anxious. Excited for the opportunity to leave the room that had become our whole world, but wary of the procedure.

My knees wouldn't stop shaking as I was wheeled down the hall and in the elevator to the first floor.

Once we arrived, I was relieved to see other residents in wheelchairs waiting for their turn before me. Two young men and a woman. They introduced themselves as Christina, who appeared to be in her late twenties, Leonard, a tall, lanky drink of water with sandy hair, and Rupert, short with auburn hair and mischievous blue eyes. The banter back and forth between them was easy-going and fun. Indeed, this procedure was nothing to worry about if they could joke this way while waiting.

Christina left three children and a husband in Green Bay. She had been in the San for five months now, and despite her illness, she had an infectious smile and black hair like mine. Christina's husband visited as often as possible, reassured her that he and the children were doing well, and brought pictures they'd made for her.

Len was from Door County, in his early thirties, and was a fruit farmer famous for his apples and blueberries, and promised to send us some when given the 'all clear' to resume his life.

Rupe was a very likable jokester from New Auburn. Just a year older than me, and was not having such great luck with treatment. His right lung was stubborn. Doc warned he might need thoracoplasty if he didn't respond to pneumo. Rupe explained that thoracoplasty involved the removal of ribs to force a lung to collapse and allow it to rest. After he told me, I had difficulty not staring at him, wondering how missing ribs could change a person's appearance. Maybe it didn't at all, but the whole procedure sounded terrible to me, and I hoped I'd never have to have that done.

The guys teased me that all the other guys in the San would be clamoring to visit me as soon as word got out that a pretty, single girl was new to the third floor.

They had me grinning and blushing something fierce.

Christina sat back and enjoyed the show. I felt so bad for her, leaving her babies, who'd all been farmed out to neighbors as her husband couldn't care for them and work. Still, Christina had a great attitude.

They were taken in one by one, Christina first, then Len, and finally Rupe. Rupe had a nickname for everyone. He decided mine was Dolly or just Doll.

"See ya, Doll," he said as he was wheeled in.

Once the door to the treatment room closed, there were no screams, no flailing to get away, so it couldn't be all that bad. And when wheeled out, they seemed just fine, although Rupe played dead as they wheeled him out. If I'd had something to throw at him, I would. As he passed me, he sat up, and we laughed. "Take care, Doll. I told Doc not to carve you up too bad."

"Rupert!" The nurse scolded him. We all chuckled.

Then it was my turn. The nurse wheeled me into a room painted light green, which resembled the emergency room where all this started. I was helped onto an examining table.

Doc Thompson spoke gently and explained the procedure. Artificial pneumothorax required a needle to be inserted into the area between the ribs to drain fluid and inject air between the lung's membranes. The purpose was to collapse the lung gradually over time so it may rest. I would need this treatment weekly until I showed improvement.

Weekly? Then, I saw the needle and syringes on a small metal table. My ears buzzed, and squiggly lines swam before my eyes. I thought I would faint. As if the nurse could read my mind, she touched my shoulder to reassure me.

"You'll feel much better when you leave this room. I promise," she said.

"She's right, Daisy," Doc said.

I had to lie on my right side with my left arm over my head and my pajama top pulled up to expose my rib cage. The room was cold, and I couldn't stop shivering. I wasn't sure if it was the temperature or fear.

I was instructed to take slow breaths and look away rather than watch.

Doc said, "Let's begin."

As June and the others had told me, a big poke of the needle, then nothing. Afterward, Doc showed me the cloudy liquid he'd been able to remove. It was no wonder I was feeling discomfort. Then, I was back in the wheelchair, heading to our room. Everyone was right. I immediately noticed an ease in my breathing. I was sore under my arm, but that was all.

That evening, two boys, Bobby and Chet, popped their heads into the room. June invited them in and made introductions. Both were farm boys: Bobby from Marshfield and Chet from LaCrosse. They shared hilarious tales of life in the San and titillating gossip. We laughed so hard that Nurse Fromm stuck her head in to glare at us. They only stayed an hour, but what an enjoyable hour it was.

Every night, once the lights went out, I lay in the dark and missed my family with every breath in my body. I wondered how little Rosalie was coming along. Was Issy still chasing the Jandusky boy? Was Tata working too hard? Was Mamka? George had said he wanted to work in the woods next summer as a lumberjack if they'd take a fifteen-year-old boy. Was that still his plan? Were the others doing well with their studies and chores?

Patience, always one of my best traits, was failing me.

I worried about Willa Grace. I hadn't been gone long, but I hoped she was not spending too much time moping over me. My sister had a way of jumping into situations without a second thought.

My chest tightened as I tried to hold back tears, but eventually, I had to let them fall. This yearning for home was nearly overpowering. The homesickness I'd felt when arriving in Berwyn didn't compare to this. Back then, I knew I'd be back on the farm before too long. Now, I wasn't sure of anything, no matter how hard I tried to convince myself I would recover quickly. I would be one of the lucky ones. But would I?

Once this lung of mine was back to normal, I would cherish every breath.

On Monday morning, Mr. Morgan, the mailman, stuck his head in the door and said, "You, Miss Maruska, have hit the jackpot with the mail today. Good thing it's not like this every day, or the seams of my bag might split."

Of course, he was joshing, but I got a nice stack.

"Look at you," Nelsy said as she entered, seeing the stack on my bed.

"She's making my two piddly letters seem pathetic," June said.

It was then that I realized there was nothing from Harold. Again.

I pushed that worry aside and focused on the letters I had, going through one at a time. There were letters from Mamka, Issy, and George with pictures drawn by Joey and Addie. Albert scribbled on a piece of paper, and someone outlined Rosalie's tiny hand. Joey drew a very unflattering picture of our dog, Ranger, pooping on a chicken. June and I giggled over that one. Mamka requested a list of anything I needed, as she always did, so that she could send it, as did everyone else. I received letters from neighbors, old classmates, and friends, the Havelka girls, Sissy and Edie. The last envelope was a letter from Willa Grace that I saved for last.

Mamka was busy sewing me new pajamas, Issy was knitting slippers, and Addie was crocheting an afghan for me. All would be sent shortly. George told of a girl he was dating. Tata added his signature to the bottom of Mamka's letters, which warmed my heart.

The letters did wonders to improve my mood. These first four days had been a reckoning of sorts. I was forced to admit I was sick. My symptoms could no longer be ignored.

Staying in bed all day, every day, was a challenge. I was too young to be so bedridden. I enjoyed visiting with June and others who popped in occasionally in the evening. Mornings and afternoons were busy with bed baths, vital checks, sputum collection, letter writing, and napping.

An aide came around offering books. I took *Topper* by Thorne Smith, a light-hearted, comical story that I thoroughly enjoyed. Willa Grace would have been so proud of me, a reader.

A week later, I received a care package from home, which included new pajamas, slippers, a word puzzle book, three ribbons for my hair in red, yellow, and blue, and two candy bars. As pleased as I was, I worried that this must have cost them a fortune to send.

While I waited to hear from Harold, I jotted down the names of the babies we'd have. If I had my way, we'd have an Isaac and a Josephine, named after Tata and Mamka. I had no idea the design of the house Harold purchased with the factory, so I designed one for us. I drew a floor plan with a large kitchen with enough room for baking Christmas cookies, allowing the children to help, and lots of windows to look out at my garden and watch the children play. If he were successful enough, maybe we could afford an indoor bathroom. That would be heaven. I wanted a dining room with a long table for family dinners, filled with laughter and storytelling, that would also serve as a creative space. I dreamt of sitting at an easel, painting a picture of our children in the orchard with apple blossoms blowing in the breeze as Harold and I cuddled together to watch. It was going to be so perfect.

Another week passed, and Harold still hadn't written, even after I had written to him several times. So, I wrote to Issy and asked her to stop by the cheese factory to see how he was doing. I waited on pins and needles until she wrote back.

She reported that Harold was fine and busy with his new enterprise. When she mentioned me, he said he wasn't much for writing now that he was so busy, but would get something in the post for me as soon as possible. I would have to accept that and wait.

Then, I received the most startling letter from Willa Grace. She was in love! Her letter spoke glowingly of her Jode and their shared dreams of city life. This was not the news I'd ever expected, but I was happy for her. With me away at the San, she would have someone to comfort her and keep her out of trouble.

Personally, my hopes for her were still pinned on Henry.

Willa Grace

I wasn't feeling like my old self. I missed my family. Daisy's illness was ever-present in my mind, and having my parents and siblings around me would help. We would share the sadness and fear of Daisy's illness. Our parents were grateful I was nearer to her, should her condition worsen. I was torn as I knew it was good to be where I was, but at times, I felt alone. I was not a praying type of person, but I prayed every day that I'd get that letter from her saying she was improving and would be released shortly. My prayers hadn't been answered yet. Maybe I was doing it all wrong. I had no history with prayer.

Thank goodness for Jode.

A part of me felt guilty for this unexpected joy with Jode, while Daisy lay in a sanitarium, but I needed all the distraction I could find. Besides, I was nuts over him.

In late August, as I was peeling apples for pies, Joanie from the laundry came into the kitchen to announce that she and her husband were expecting a child. There was a rule that a pregnant woman could no longer work in the household. Therefore, this was her last day in Thorpe's employ.

Joanie pulled her dress taut over her tummy and said, "Can you tell?"

Everyone nodded, but I could tell they couldn't see squat. I couldn't either.

"One nice thing is that I haven't had to deal with my monthlies since this happened."

A few of the other girls nodded, looking jealous. I had to stop for a moment and think.

My knees nearly gave way. When was my last flow? I steadied myself with a hand on the butcher block while the other gripped a serving dish, my brain desperately working.

"Shush with you," Blanche said to Joanie. "We don't need to discuss details. That's not proper talk for out in the open."

"Oh, Blanche," Joanie planted a smooch on Blanche's cheek, "this is 1934. These things need to be discussed." Blanche blushed.

I hadn't had my monthly in July, and August was nearly over. What about June? *Oh my word*!

Was I pregnant? Did Jode and I finally get caught, not by Horseface, but by doing what only married people should do?

My palms grew slick, and I dropped the serving dish. It shattered with a smash on the tiled floor.

"Willa Grace!"

"I'm so sorry. I don't know what happened to me."

Bonnie dropped down to her knees and helped me pick it up. She put her mouth close to my ear and asked, "Are you okay? You look a bit green."

"I'm fine." My hands shook terribly.

"Get that cleaned up before the old prune sees it," Blanche said. "She'll take it out of your paycheck."

We quickly cleaned the mess, and I followed Joanie into the hall.

"Joanie, can I ask you a question?"

"Sure can." Her peachy complexion glowed with happiness.

"I should know this considering how many children my Mamka had, but…." I felt so stupid.

"Out with it, girly." She stood before me, hands on her hips.

"How do you know for sure you're pregnant?"

"Who are you asking for?" Her green eyes narrowed.

"Just me. My mother never said how she always knew. I assumed there was some secret message her body sent her to say another one was coming." Mamka was never forthright with bodily functions. In fact, it had been painful for her to explain our monthlies to Daisy and me. So much so, she asked us to pass along the information when the time was right for Issy and Addie.

"Well, for one thing, your monthlies stop, and then the smell of food makes you want to vomit. It was the smell of onions in the beginning for me, but then it stopped at about three months. I've been fine ever since. I didn't want to announce my pregnancy unless I was sure. I could never have worked near the kitchen during those first three months, smelling all that food. It was hard enough being in the laundry." She leaned in closer. "The girls there had a bucket for me to vomit into that we kept hidden." She grinned.

Well, I hadn't been sick at all. However, I seemed to have an ongoing headache and was more tired than ever.

"Is there anything else?" I asked.

"Not really. Oh, wait. My boobs. They're huge and a bit tender. My hubby doesn't mind a bit." She giggled. "I knew I was pregnant almost immediately, but I kept it quiet. I wanted as many paychecks as possible before I had to leave."

Come to think of it, my boobs had been sore for the last week. I thought I was finally growing into a woman's body at eighteen. It appeared there might be another reason.

"What else?" I crossed my arms over my chest self-consciously.

"You feel the baby move around in the third or fourth month. My little sweetie just started," she patted her tummy.

"What's that like?" I was so light-headed I thought I might faint.

Joanie grinned. "Like having a tiny butterfly in your tummy. Just a little flutter. It's so sweet."

Nope, I didn't have that. Come to think of it, I had been slightly nauseous a few mornings, but never vomited. I thought I had a slight case of the flu, but it came and went.

Was I pregnant? Oh, holy hell!

"I have to go. My husband is picking me up." Joanie started to leave, then said, "Good luck to you, Willa Grace." She sent me a knowing wink.

I had to remind myself to breathe. I ran down the hall to the bathroom, where I wretched into the toilet. So *now I'm throwing up?*

When I was done, I stood before the mirror and washed my mouth with water. Before me, I saw a stupid girl who had gone too far for the love of a boy. How did I get so far off course?

With the palm of my hand, I smacked my forehead three times. *Think, think, Willa Grace*. What to do now? All my plans of walking the city streets of Chicago as a career girl, married or single, just slipped away like the water running through my fingers. What I, or Jode, wanted didn't matter anymore. We had to do right by the situation.

He'd see that, wouldn't he?

I couldn't predict his reaction. Although he hadn't said he loved me, I knew he did. A girl can tell those things. He'd be shocked at first, but then…but then.

And then, there were my parents. That was going to be the worst humiliation of all.

I knew how people talked about girls who got themselves into the family way without a husband. Tata and Mamka would be mortified. Not only were they dealing with a struggling farm, six children to feed, a daughter in a sanitarium, and an unwed daughter in the family way. They would be crushed.

I sat on the toilet seat and searched my brain for a solution.

Thankfully, I was far enough away from my family that if I stalled going home for a while, Jode and I could get married, and somehow, I could fudge the marriage or pregnancy dates.

That could work. Couldn't it? It would have to. I could see Daisy shaking her head at my foolish attempt at a solution. Daisy was another concern. She would be so disappointed in me. She had enough to think about, and I could not add to that.

For all my blathering on about my future in the city, I wanted Daisy to be proud of me.

I stood and took a deep breath. My hands shook, and my face was as red as a beet.

I thought of Mamka with all of us, one after another, never a free moment to herself. I vowed that would not be my life, and while I hadn't wanted children, this was just one. I could manage that, especially with Jode's help.

A light knock sounded at the door. "Willa Grace?" It was Joanie.

"Be right out." I splashed cold water on my face again and wiped it with a towel.

"I heard you slam the powder room door, so I waited," she said through the door.

I opened the door, and Joanie pushed inside and closed the door.

"You're going to have a baby, aren't you?" Joanie looked deeply into my eyes.

"What makes you say that?" I clasp my hands together to stop shaking.

"Willa Grace, look at you. You're as scared as a kitten in a busy street." She touched my arm.

I nodded. "I think I am." Then tears dripped down my face.

"Oh, honey." Joanie put an arm around me. "Is it Jode? You can't keep your eyes off him when the men come for a meal. And it's not a secret when you slip notes back and forth under the table."

"It's that obvious?"

"It is. What are you going to do?"

"I need to talk to Jode." Desperately, I tried to stay calm.

"That, you do." Joanie rubbed my arm.

"I don't know how he's going to take this. He's got such plans for his future."

"It will all work out. You'll see. I wish you the best." She gave me a quick squeeze, and then she slipped out the door.

I finished my day in the kitchen. Both Bonnie and Blanche commented that I was not my usual chatty self. My excuse was a headache, which wasn't a lie. All my dreams, the life I thought I'd have, sizzled and evaporated like a drop of water in a hot frying pan.

That night, I met Jode in our corner of the hay mow. He was waiting with that same light in his eyes he always had when he looked my way. How fortunate I was to find someone who loved me so deeply. The look in his eyes said it all. Yes, it would be okay.

I sat on the hay beside him. He pulled me close for a kiss. With arms wrapped around each other, I pushed back to see his face.

My stomach was in my throat, and it was hard to breathe. He kissed my neck.

"I have something to tell you. I need your attention." I dodged as he tried to kiss me again.

I held up a shaking palm to keep him at bay.

"I'm going to have a baby, Jode." I watechd his face.

"Ha," he grinned, "are you trying to tell me we need to be more careful?"

"Jode…"

"That's not funny." His eyes narrowed as the shadows of the hay mow played on his features.

"I'm serious. You and me. We're going to have a baby." I looked hard into his eyes to convey the seriousness of my news.

He shot up from the hay bale. "You're lyin'." His chin trembled, a severe set to his jaw. A tremor told hold in his hands. "What makes you think you're havin' a baby?"

"I didn't get my…well, my monthly. Look what we've been doing. It wasn't very smart of us." I stood as well, then sat back down for support. I couldn't read him right then.

He hung his head, rubbing the back of his neck. Silence tightened like a noose. I couldn't stand the quiet.

"We can get married now, Jode. We would have anyway, wouldn't we?"

"Married? I don't know–" He looked terrified.

"We have to, don't we?" Fear skittered up my spine. What if I had read him all wrong? No, je needed time to get used to the idea. That was all.

He wiped his palms on his trousers, his eyes darting every which way as though he were searching for an escape route.

"I…uh…not yet, though. I ain't got enough saved." He sat next to me.

"It's just a baby. We can handle that, Jode." It felt good to say his name. "We can, can't we?"

I put a hand on his thigh, and both of us were silent for a time.

"Please say something, Jode." I ran a hand across my sweating brow.

He breathed in deeply, nodded, then smiled. A shock of his blond hair fell across his forehead, and he pushed it back.

"Oh, Willsy. I guess this was bound to happen at some point. You aren't like the other girls, and I got caught up in how special you are."

I leaned into him and put my mouth up to his. He gave me a quick kiss.

"I'll be fired as soon as they find out about the baby. I can keep it a secret for a while and help save money. I won't tell my family just yet until we're settled. But I think we should marry as soon as possible to stop the rumors once I announce my condition."

"Got it all figured out, have you?" He licked his lips, breathed deeply, and turned toward me. "I suppose you're right. This is a shock, it is. Let me think about this. We'll do it real soon. I might have to put my plans on hold until we get settled in an apartment, but…anyway, we'll get married." He grinned and pulled me close. "Until then, it's our secret."

I nodded and kissed him hard. Joanie was right. All was going to work out fine.

That night was a long one. There was so much to think about. I wanted to talk to Daisy, but that would have to wait. I couldn't burden her with my troubles because of what she was going through. Not until Jode and I had solid plans so that she and Mamka wouldn't worry.

I wanted to reach over and wake Bonnie, but this wasn't the place. The other girls would surely hear, and I couldn't have that.

The following morning, I roused my weary self, the last into the kitchen. Bonnie and the others huddled in the corner, and when I entered, they broke apart, averting their eyes from mine. I had a feeling I had been the topic of their whispers.

I went to the long table, pulled out a large bowl from underneath, and went for the flour to make biscuits. I had the feeling that I was being stared at, and when I looked up, I was.

Did they know my secret? Jode and Joanie were the only two who knew, and I didn't think either would tell.

"Is my hair on fire?" I grinned, trying to appear calm.

"Did you hear the news?" Bonnie asked. Tilly and Colleen scattered to opposite corners of the kitchen, pretending they were busy.

"What news?" I measured the flour and put it into the bowl.

"About Jode?" Bonnie was serious as a judge. My heart skipped a beat, and my knees about gave out.

Blanche came into the kitchen.

"Most of the blueberries we got for the morning pancakes are rotten," she said as she bustled about. "We will have to change plans as we don't have enough. Bonnie, quit your gossiping there and see if we have raspberries."

Bonnie started to back away, but I grabbed her arm. "What about Jode?" I didn't care if the others could hear.

Bonnie's eyes shifted to Blanche, then back to me. She leaned in closer and said, "He left in the night. Packed his belongings and vanished. No one heard or saw a thing. Did you know he was going to do this?"

I shook my head, unable to speak or breathe.

"I'm sorry, Willa Grace. I know you liked him. No one knows why he left like he did."

I dropped the wooden spoon I held. It clattered on the tile floor alongside my heart.

"I'm sorry," Bonnie mouthed.

Blanche turned around. "The raspberries?"

"I'll get them," I said as I picked up the spoon. I needed air before I fainted.

"I'll finish the biscuits," said Bonnie.

At least none of them knew the whole truth.

Outside the back door, I leaned against the cool stone wall of the house. The ground tipped beneath my feet, and a ringing in my ears blocked all sound. I pinched my eyes together.

How could he?

I was truly on my own.

ELEVEN

Daisy

At Statesan, the friendships with my weekly pneumo buddies deepened. Christina, Len, Rupe, and I shared jokes, stories, and gossip from around the San. I looked forward to our time together, as it was the only time I was able to see beyond the four walls of our room. Rarely did we allow talk of illness into our conversations. TB was there, lurking in the shadows like a monster in the closet.

Sometimes, I thought of us as four comrades in arms, linked in our shared journey to better health and resuming our lives outside this place. June's treatments were on different days, and I suppose it was good for us to have some time with others. It gave us new things to talk about.

My sputum tests were still positive for an infection, and a tiny amount of blood was present, the fluid taken from my lung still cloudy, and my temp slightly high at one hundred. The doctor planned an X-ray for the following week.

June and I got on as best buddies. The Hewitts, June's parents, were very generous. They sent us a radio and earpieces to avoid disturbing the others. We giggled along to *The Jack Benny Program* and *Ma Perkins*. We sang along with *The Rudy Vallee Show* as quietly as we could. Willa Grace would be so proud of me if she saw the books June and I passed between us, which spurned great discussions about the stories, settings, and characters. We had competitions as to who could solve crossword puzzles the quickest. I usually won. Early evenings, if Chet, Bobby, Susan, Margaret, or Dorothy didn't stop by, June and I played cards. Old Maid or King's Corners.

Of course, I spent a lot of time writing letters. I received so many from family, friends, and Emery neighbors that mail delivery was often the highlight of the day.

My brother George sent me a disturbing letter.

Dear Daisy,

Hope you're doing good, kiddo!

Who was he to call me kiddo? I had five years on him. That made me smile.

I don't have much to tell. Hunting season is coming, and the hunters are all up in arms about that partly white deer. You know the one that shows up when someone is going to kick the bucket. I think it's bull, but lots believe it and are scared. They want the hunters to shoot it. Others say it would be bad luck. Some say it's rare and shouldn't be shot. A few of the guys got in a big to-do about it at the harvest dinner at the hall last Saturday. I think it would make a nice rug.

Anyway, that's all I got. Oh, I broke up with Patsy Mess. She was as crabby as Willa Grace told me she'd be. Take good care of yourself.

Love,
Georgie

Hunt that innocent deer? Despite the rumors of the deer and death, I couldn't forget its peaceful presence in the field as Willa Grace and I returned from Viola Villa that night so long ago. George was going to get a talking to in my next letter. A rug, my goodness. In the meantime, I would hope that the deer would survive another hunting season. Enough on that.

All in all, I was making the best of the current situation. Still, to be nineteen and confined to a small room with one other person could be depressing, but I wouldn't let it. I couldn't.

Death happened often here. So often. Then, one day, a terrible thing happened.

June and I heard a commotion sweep through our floor with a call for assistance. Nelsy and the other nurses went running. Word traveled fast that a young man, upset at his failure to improve, made his way to the roof and threatened to jump.

I lept from my bed, but my rubbery legs gave out. June came out of hers and helped me up, although she wasn't much better. We helped each other to the open window.

He was above us and to the left.

Doc Thompson was on the ground below, looking up. "Ned, please don't do this."

Ned, tall and thin with a shock of brown hair standing up in the wind, stood on the roof's edge, arms out to the sides, eyes to the sky. His blue pajamas blew against his bony body. Nurses and other patients had their heads out the windows, begging him to stop. Behind him, we saw the janitor inching across the roof to try to grab him.

"No, Ned, don't do it!" June and I screamed, coughed, and screamed some more.

I waved my arm, hoping he would see me. We weren't supposed to raise our arms for fear of disturbing any healing happening in our lungs, but right then, that was the least of our worries.

"Think of your family! Don't!"

But he did. He pitched himself over the side, falling stiff as a board, his shadow darkened our windows as he fell, landing with a sickening thud in the hydrangea bushes below, his arms and legs at impossible angles.

I screamed and dropped to the floor, as did June. We joined hands, and June said a prayer for his soul. I'd seen his face as he plummeted past. I'd looked into the eyes of a dead man. My mind was branded with the horror of it. For weeks, he was all I could see when I closed my eyes.

Then, Clarice Newsome, a nice girl from across the hall, died. She was such a sweet thing with auburn hair and a splash of freckles on her nose, only sixteen. We'd pass in the hall, coming and going to pneumo. Sometimes at night, just after lights out, she'd sing a song to ease us all into sleep, but as time passed, she coughed more than she could sing.

"I'll be good as new," Rupe said at our last pneumo before his thoracoplasty. "Won't be long now, and I'll be outta this place and back home working on my stock car. You'll all have to come to see me race. I'll be waving that checkered flag with every bit of muscle in me."

What a grand reunion that would be. I could picture Christina, Len, June, and me sitting together on the bleachers, cheering for all we were worth. Rupe's excitement was infectious.

"Hope losing some ribs doesn't hurt my driving."

"Aw, shucks, I don't think anything could stop you," Len said.

Rupe was thoughtful for a moment, his thumb hooked on his chin, "Yeah, I don't think anything could after all this. The ladies sure like a fella holding a trophy."

We all laughed.

"What do you say, Daisy. You gonna come watch?" I don't think it was a secret that Rupe had a thing for me. It was sweet, but I still held onto hope that I'd hear from Harold.

"Rupe," I said, "it would be an honor to watch you win a checkered flag. Maybe I'll bring June with me. You two might make a good couple." June was probably going to kill me for that.

"I'll hold you to that, Doll, but Junie's a bit young for me."

We wished him well for the surgery with pats on the back, hugs, and handshakes.

We heard later that the surgery went well, but Rupe developed an especially ruthless infection within a week. He died peacefully with his family at his bedside.

Suddenly, it seemed, death was all around us. But it had been all along. We simply chose to ignore it. With the tragic events of Ned and our Rupe, we were hearing dismal stories every day. Many of the residents housed in the cottages out back left for home, happy and healthy, but were forced to return as the disease reared its ugly head again.

Junebug, as I took to calling her, and she called me Daisy-do, together we made the best of life in our room. The days were growing colder, and I dreaded a winter with open windows.

Then, I received a letter from Issy.

Dear Daisy,

As always, dear sister, I hope you are recovering.

I will jump right in. Harold Smidl is engaged to Marion Radek. You won't believe it. She is a mail-order bride from Nebraska. He answered her ad in the Hlastel. They've been writing for a few months now, and last Tuesday, she arrived in Phillips on the bus. She's staying in town for now, but they plan to wed in two weeks.

I am so sorry to have to tell you this, as I know you had your hopes set on a future with him. I saw him at Viola Villa last Sunday for the township picnic. I confronted him, and when he fessed up, I tipped his plate of food onto his lap. I didn't think you'd mind.

Don't waste your time over a bum like him. Mamka says there's lots more fish in the sea, and Tata says the no-good cuss better watch out if he sees him.

Once you get back home, we'll go find you another beau. I'm kind of good at that.

Love you tons,
Isabelle

I stared at Issy's letter for an eternity. Numb was the only way to describe it. I suppose I'd known he was lost to me as soon as his letters stopped after I told him of my illness.

June looked up from her book. "Are you all right?"

"Seems I don't have a beau to go home to, after all, Junebug. He's getting married." I waved Issy's letter, then threw it down on the bed.

"What a crumb!"

I nodded, unable to speak. I tucked the letter under my pillow and rolled away to let the tears fall. Suddenly, I felt June's arms around me and her face resting beside mine. She held me while I cried. There was no more pretending that he was simply too busy to write.

Tuberculosis was robbing me of one dream at a time.

I gave in to my grief over Harold for a time. Junebug did her best to cheer me up, but I was

having none of it. Suddenly, my world was crushing me one breath at a time.

Willa Grace

I couldn't tell Daisy I was going to have a baby. I'd never kept a secret from her, but Issy told me about Harold marrying someone else, and I couldn't burden her with my stupid mistake. But I needed to tell someone, to get advice, to be comforted. I thought of telling Bonnie, but the girl was a terrible gossip, and a part of me feared I couldn't trust her. Joanie, who'd helped me see the reality of my situation, was gone now. Blanche?

She was responsible for the smooth running of the kitchen. Would her loyalty be to me or to Horseface? I always knew Blanche liked me, and we shared an easy-going banter while we worked, but this affected her job if it were found out that she knew and protected me. I had to trust someone.

I knocked on the door to Blanche's private room and waited. She answered immediately, her graying, auburn hair in pin curls and her body wrapped in a green robe, obviously getting ready for bed.

"You're going to hate me."

"Not a chance." Blanche indicated that I sit on an overstuffed chair in the corner with a pink floral design and a white afghan draped over one arm. She sat on her quilted bed. The room smelled of rose water.

I looked her in the eye, shoulders squared, my chin trembling. "I'm going to have a baby."

Blanche's eyes narrowed. "A baby?"

I nodded, feeling suddenly nauseous.

"A baby." Her round face reddened. "Good God, girl, tell me I heard ya wrong." I'd never seen a cross look on her face before, but I did then. Maybe I'd made a mistake, but she's all I had. Would she go to Horseface?

"I'm pregnant. All the signs are there."

"Jode?" The clock on her bedside table tick, tick, ticked.

I nodded, keeping my spine straight and chin up, ready for what would come. At this point, I had no choice but to be strong. "I thought he loved me. He said we'd plan a future. He said we'd get married."

"Jesus, Mary, and Joseph. How could ya be so daft?" Blanche raised her hands to her face. "Most boys, that's all they're wantin' is to get a girl to go that far."

It killed me to know I'd disappointed her. How could I have been so stupid?

With a pinched expression, Blanche stood and went to the window overlooking the gardens.

She let out a long sigh and then turned back. I expected to see disappointment, sadness, and worry on her face. But she was still angry.

"So, what is your plan now, lassie? Are ya going home? I'm guessing your folks have no idea." She rubbed her forehead with her fingertips. "What were you thinkin'? Were you thinkin' at all?"

"I honestly thought he loved me. Blanche, you've been like a second mother to me. I had to tell you."

"I'm wishin' I could be flattered that ya think ya should tell me, but I ain't. I counted on ya to help run the kitchen. I could tell ya weren't much for kitchen work, but you'd come a long way since ya started. Ya earned my respect, ya did. Now this. Are ya sure you're pregnant?"

"My monthly didn't come twice in a row, the smell of an egg makes me woozy, and my boobs are sore. I've only actually thrown up once." As if that were something to be grateful for, proud of.

"Ack…Willa Grace." She sat on the bed again. "So that's why the little coward left."

"Jode's scared. Once he gets a hold of himself, he'll come back. Then we'll get married." I was desperate to find some light in all this darkness.

"He's not coming back. You're on your own, girl." Her tone was cold as stone.

"He might. He's not a cruel person. He's not."

"He's been gone a week now. Wise up."

The disapproval in her eyes was nearly as painful as knowing in my heart that Jode was gone for good. And yet, Blanche's disappointment was a drop in the bucket compared to what my parents would feel.

"You don't need to tell me how stupid this is. I need your help, Blanche. Depending on how long I can keep it a secret, it'll be another month or two before I have to give up my job."

"What do ya expect me to do about this nonsense?"

"I guess…," What did I expect? "There's nothing you can do. I just…" It had been a mistake to tell her. "if Jode doesn't come back, I may have to put the baby up for adoption. What else can I do?"

"Oh, Willa Grace. I can't believe you were so foolish." Blanche put a hand on her forehead.

"Please don't tell Horseface. She'll fire me right then."

"Damn straight, she will." Blanche closed her eyes and shook her head.

"I need to work as long as I can and give myself some time to figure this out."

We sat in terrible silence for a few long minutes—tick, tick, tick.

"We'll keep it between you and me until there's no denying what's happening. Does Bonnie know?"

"No."

"That's good. I know she's your friend, but that girl has a big mouth. I don't know what you'll do, but if there's a way I can help, I will. I don't know what, though."

I leaned forward, my hands clasped. "Thank you, Blanche. I promise you won't be sorry."

"I already am." She looked away.

"And who knows, Jode may come back tomorrow. Then everything will be fine." It seemed I couldn't stop trying to find an optimistic solution.

"Willa Grace, grow up."

My eyes were watery for the first time, and I willed the tears to stay put.

"Ack, I don't mean to be so harsh. Matters of the heart are a tricky road to navigate. Me Ma told me that once, and I never forgot. Not that I had the boys fightin' to get at me. Oh, hells bells, Willa Grace. Get some rest if ya can tonight. We'll not say another word about it." She gave me a weak smile and looked away.

"Good night, Blanche." Good or bad, it was a relief to have someone know my secret.

My impulsive, reckless sense of adventure ruined everything. Daisy wouldn't be sick if she were still on the farm, I wouldn't be carrying a baby that I was unprepared for in any way, and I wouldn't have to fear the great disappointment I'd be to my family if they discovered my condition. I went to bed, curled into a ball, and wished the world would carry me away.

"Willa Grace?" Bonnie whispered and touched my arm. "What's wrong?"

"Nothing." I brushed her arm away.

"Jode was a bum. There'll be someone else someday."

"Yep." I rolled over. No, there wouldn't.

TWELVE

Daisy

I tried to take a deep breath of the autumn air wafting in from outside our window, but my cough was acting up with a vengeance. Over the last few mornings, my sputum box was nearly half full.

I blamed it on my mental state. Since Issy's letter about Harold, I'd been crabby. The Harold I knew would never have ended our relationship without a letter, without some warning. Yet, he did. There'd been nothing. I hadn't received one letter from him since I'd come to the San. That was my warning, and I'd acted like a stupid little girl pretending he was too busy.

Was this new woman, Marion, to blame? More likely, his rejection stemmed from my diagnosis, plain and simple. I was damaged. I knew of others who'd lost loved ones and friendships because of the disease. We were a group of unwanted people, diseased carriers of an illness that caused fear in so many.

I felt like such a fool. All the letters I'd sent him blathering on about all my dreams for the future. Of course, I didn't mention our marriage. I hadn't been asked yet. But I tried so hard to convey that I'd be back before he knew it.

I'd written to Willsy, who tried to talk some sense into me, but I wouldn't listen. She'd seen through Harold long ago. But not me. I couldn't let it go.

I'd been gone for nearly a year. Half of it in the San.

What's happened to my life? One moment, I was young and in love with so much of life ahead of me, and now, all those dreams were pushed to the side while I battled this disease that upended everything.

June was granted up to four privileges a day, including using the bathroom as needed, taking showers or tub baths, and attending shows in the auditorium four times a month. I had been upgraded to two lousy pillows, two trips to the bathroom a day, and a show in the auditorium twice a month in a wheelchair. This was my life at nineteen, almost twenty.

My dear Junebug had finally had enough of my sad-sack attitude. It was too easy to give in to despair and pull the covers over my head after I looked around me at nothing but sick people and medical staff. They tried to shield us from those nearing death by putting them on the lower floors, but we knew they were there. We noticed that when a cough worsened across or down the hall, that person was removed. Sometimes, death came before the nurses could act.

"Buck up, girlie. Isn't that what Willa Grace would say?" June tossed a pillow at me. I caught it, but didn't have the energy to throw it back. Instead, I handed it to her. Through the sharing of our letters, June and I felt we knew each other's families well. She often reminded me of my sister.

"You're right." She was, but something that morning wasn't right. I could feel it deep in my bones. Almost a 'knowing' that my fight was far from over.

A day later, when Nelsy came in for rounds, she removed the thermometer from my mouth and shook her head.

"Not good, Miss Daisy." She wiped it off with alcohol on a cotton ball. "You're at 101 and haven't touched your breakfast."

I felt so weak. It was a strain to raise my head from the pillow. "I can't. I don't know what's happened."

"She's still feeling all gooey over her love life," June said, and returned to her book.

"I'm sending Doc up to see you this afternoon." Nelsy put a rubber-gloved hand on my forehead, and I leaned into the coolness of it. "Don't you worry none. You'll be fine in no time."

Her eyes didn't match the words coming out of her masked mouth.

Shortly after lunch and another untouched meal, June hollered for Nelsy to return.

Nelsy came running across the hall and stuck a thermometer in my mouth.

"You're at 102," she said, reaching for my wrist to get my pulse. After a few seconds, she ran to the doorway and called for another nurse.

My eyes felt hot, and I could no longer lift my pounding head.

Nurse Carter bustled in and took my wrist. "Her heart rate is too fast. Call the doctor." Nelsy disappeared down the hall while Nurse Carter held my hand.

Within minutes, Doc Thompson came in, looked me over, ordered an X-ray, and I was quickly wheeled out. I had a powerful urge to fall asleep.

After the X-ray, Doc returned. His face was grave. He explained I now had lesions in my right lung as well. He suspected the bacteria were spreading through my body via my lymphatic system and causing infection.

I overheard Doc in the hall saying he would tell my family I'd taken a turn.

"No," I grabbed the sleeve of Nelsy's dress while hot tears ran down my cheeks. "Please don't let him tell my family. They'll worry so."

Nelsy patted my shoulder. "You just think about getting better."

Willa Grace was my nearest relative, but she was hours away. She couldn't afford to miss work and hover over me, and my parents would be worried sick.

Oh, how I hated this illness, but I was so sick I simply wanted relief.

Quickly I was moved to the critical care area on the first floor. The speed at which I was whisked down the hall on a gurney frightened me. Once there, in that white, sterile room, I felt a dramatic turn. My eyes burned with heat and it was a struggle to open them. Breathing became a chore, and my head pounded fiercely.

My temperature increased to 104 degrees. Attempts were made to bring the number down in a flurry, but I was only vaguely aware. I was later told that I had become delirious and somewhat combative. This was hard to believe, but I trusted what the doctor and nurses told me.

I coughed up great gobs of nasty-looking matter and some blood. The coughing fits left me as exhausted as I'd ever been. Eating was impossible, and I was being given fluids intravenously. My breathing was shallow, and half the time when I was spoken to, I only gave a slight nod, not knowing what was said. Every heartbeat pulsed in my neck.

Mostly, I drifted. My mind went back to the farm, the beauty of the wildflowers in the pasture, the smell of freshly cut hay, the bawl of the cows, the softness of baby chicks, Mamka singing in the kitchen, my brothers and sisters noisily gathering for a meal, Tata giving a stern warning for order, and Willa Grace next to me as we slept.

I was in deep trouble. For all my earlier self-assuredness that I would be one of the lucky ones upon arriving at San, I didn't feel lucky at all.

At the worst of it, I remembered looking to the door and seeing our lovely Mamka, watching over me, singing the lullaby I'd heard her sing to every baby that came into our family. She'd come to me. Hot tears streamed down my face. I tried to reach for her, but my hand remained empty.

Willa Grace

When Horseface said I had another telephone call, I nearly fainted with fright. I was right to feel that way as it was Dr. Thompson from Statesan. Daisy was not doing well. She was in critical care.

I said I would be on my way as soon as I could arrange travel, but the doctor said that wasn't possible. I would not be allowed to see her for fear of infecting anyone else. He asked that I call our parents to inform them. He or his staff would keep me informed.

My whole body shook with fear. I couldn't focus on anything before me. I thought I might faint and dropped into the chair before Horseface's desk.

"Your sister has TB?!" Horseface screeched when I hung up. "Why wasn't I informed we had a possible infestation in our midst?'

"You had nothing to worry over. I tested negative."

"You better have. You could have killed the entire household."

I closed my eyes and breathed through the urge to throttle her. Exhaustion, fear, and helplessness weighed over me. "Please, may I use your phone to call my parents?"

To my surprise, she let me without another word. I called Havelka's to relay the news of Daisy's setback to my parents and to let them know that I would call with any further updates. I silently cussed Tata for not allowing a telephone in the house.

Daisy was worse. The doctor said to pray. I'd prayed Jode would return, but it hadn't worked so far. Did prayer require particular words in a specific order, or did people say what was on their minds and let God figure it out? Did a person need to say a prayer over and over for it to work? Was someone like me, who hadn't been to church except for a wedding or a funeral, worthy of God listening? I hoped so. Daisy was worthy of answered prayers.

I stood in the long, dark hallway outside Horseface's office, tipped my head back, and whispered, "Please help my sister." I listened to the silence.

I returned to the kitchen, my heart banging as I knew how upsetting that information was going to be for Mamka and Tata. I knew my parents well enough to know they'd walk to be there for Daisy if they had to, but I stressed to Mrs. Havelka that the doctor said they couldn't.

I pulled up a seat next to Bonnie to chop carrots for beef stew. My hands shook terribly, and I promptly sliced my index finger. "Ow!"

"Are you okay?" Bonnie jumped up.

"Let's see," Blanche came over and took a look.

I shook my head. "Daisy's taken a turn."

"Oh, no. How bad?" Blanche asked as she bandaged my finger.

"It's bad enough that the doctor had me call my parents."

"Oh my word, girl, I'm so sorry," Blanche wrapped her arms around me. Bonnie came over and hugged us as well. The other girls came, and we made a great glob of sadness in the middle of the kitchen.

Suddenly, it was all too much, and I pushed free from them.

"I don't feel well," I blurted, running from the room. In the bathroom down the hall, I vomited.

Blanche stuck her head in the bathroom and told me to lie down for a while.

The long room of beds was silent and semi-dark as rain spattered the windows. I lay down on my bed with a hand on my tummy. Tears streamed down my face. Would Daisy survive? I couldn't live without her. I couldn't. She was my safe place, my best friend, my strength.

I wanted to be there for my sister. Of all people, Daisy, the kindest, sweetest person outside of our mother, gets this damned disease. Life was so unfair. Thinking of Daisy suffering with no family to comfort her made me want to hit something. I pounded my fist on my bed, but it did no good. I was terrified for her. All I could do was focus on what I could control. Or try to.

Soon, my ears, hair, and pillow were soaking. I rolled to the side and pulled my knees up. On top of it, I was going to be a mother. I wasn't a good daughter or sister, so how in the world could I be someone's mother? How could Jode leave me to deal with this on my own?

I was upset with myself for selfishly turning from her troubles to mine. My trouble would pass, and my life would go on, either with a baby or not.

Oh, how I longed for the simple, uncomplicated life we had on the farm. What a mess we had found ourselves in.

THIRTEEN

Daisy

I had a strange dream about Teddy. We were swimming at the creek as Mamka often took us on hot summer days. We splashed and giggled so happily. Then, without warning, I was pulled under by an unseen hand gripping my ankle. No one noticed but Teddy, little as he was. He reached for my hand, but only our fingertips touched. When I gave up all hope, his tiny hand found mine, and he pulled me to shore. I woke with a start.

"Well, look who's back." One of the nurses said.

It was then that my body started to respond to treatment. Taking air in and out was no longer as difficult. My temperature eased, and I was able to take in liquids. Doc warned that I still had a long road to recovery. This had been a huge setback. I was back to one pillow.

"Welcome home!" June sat up in bed, clapped, and cheered as I was wheeled into our room. She had cut paper hearts and spread them over my bed. Each one had a message that read, 'Get well,' 'Love you,' 'Hello sunshine,' 'Smile,' among many others. It was good to see her smiling face. A stack of mail waited on the nightstand.

Nelsy helped me to bed. "You're weak as a newborn calf, my girl. We'll get you all fattened up in no time. Why, I hear the cooks made you your favorite dessert for tonight. Lemon meringue pie."

"I can't hardly wait." And I honestly couldn't.

After Nelsy left, June jumped out of bed and hugged me. I wanted to hold on to her forever. What good luck I'd had in getting her for a roommate.

"You scared me half to death. Nelsy checked on you every day before her shift because she knew I'd be asking. Even old Nurse Fromm was concerned. Gosh, I've got so much gossip to catch you up on. Ruthie Guthrey from down the hall got caught sneaking out to meet a fella from the cottages in the chapel. In the chapel for heavens sake. Oh, and Percy Marstan was released only to find another man in bed with his wife when he got home. He wrote one of the fellas here all about it. He's in big trouble for the pounding he gave the other guy. Lillian from the housekeeping crew is engaged, and Paulie from the grounds crew came to work drunk and was promptly fired." She stopped for a breath. "Are you sure you're okay? If you're not, I'll call Nelsy toot-sweet."

"Oh gosh, Junebug, I missed you. I must look like an old dishrag after all that," I said, picking up my mail and looking through the letters.

"Well…you look a bit gray, and goodness, you've lost so much weight."

"Maybe they'll bring me two desserts tonight." I grinned. It was so good to be back.

I wasn't cured, but I was grateful to be alive.

Tuberculosis still had a hold on me. The lesions were still present, and the possibility of thoracoplasty, the removal of ribs, hung over me. I had no idea if I would ever be free of this disease, and I'd just had a good show of how mean and nasty it could be. I wondered, might everyone have been better off if I had died, if that's my outcome anyway?

The thought caused a shiver that cut through me, and I knew that kind of thinking was more destructive than anything. I needed to make use of this second chance.

The day after I'd returned to my room from critical care, Nelsy came by with a young woman named Faye. She was twenty-one and studied to be a beautician before contracting TB from a coworker. Faye offered to wash, cut, and curl my hair for free. What a treat.

"Oh, thank you!"

A small tub was brought in, and Nelsy helped me angle my neck over the edge while Faye washed my hair and June supervised. I tired easily and had a hard time keeping up with the conversation, but Faye and June chatted easily enough. The simple touch of Faye's gentle hands on my scalp was heaven. Then she put a mirror before me, and I was stunned.

While the bob she gave my black hair was stylish, especially with the carefully crimped curls along one side, I was white as a sheet, with dark-rimmed eyes. My cheekbones stuck right out. A tremble started in my chin and my eyes watered.

"Oh, Daisy, don't cry," June said. "You're beautiful."

I caught my tears with a finger and sniffled.

Faye dug into her bag. "I brought some makeup with me as well. How about we get your face all gussied up to match your hair?"

By the time she finished with powder, rouge, mascara, and lipstick, I felt like my old self again, but secretly, I thought I looked like a movie star—a younger version of Claudette Colbert. How vain of me, but how delightful.

"After what you've been through, honey, this is the least I can do," Faye said as she finished primping. "Otherwise, I charge a small amount to earn spending money."

I turned my head this way and that. It was remarkable how she powdered away the dark circles and rouged color into my cheeks and lips. I looked alive.

"Too bad you're stuck in this old room and can't show it off," June said.

Too bad Harold wouldn't see this—his loss.

"Now," Faye turned to June, "let's give you a little makeup too."

"Yippee!" June bounced on her mattress like a little child waiting for candy.

"Miss Hewitt!" Nelsy stuck her head in the room and pointed a finger. "Down, girl."

June faked a frown and sat still against her pillows as Faye got to work.

"Why, June-bug, you look just like Jean Harlow," I said when Faye was through with her. And it was true. With her blond curls, luscious lips, and blue eyes set off by black lashes.

"What do you say we wait until lights out, sneak down, and visit the boys in the cottages?" June was feeling full of herself.

"I wouldn't make it two feet."

"I tell you what, ladies," Faye grinned, "I have a camera. I'll take a picture of the two of you."

Faye pulled out a Brownie Box camera from her bag. June and I leaned in together, and Faye snapped the picture, promising to send it to us as soon as it was developed.

When Faye left, we looked into her hand-held mirror, admiring ourselves for quite some time.

"Maybe others will stop in tonight for a visit," As tired as I was, I hoped. And they did.

Our old friends Bobby and Chet stopped in that evening and brought someone new. His name was Emmett from Madison.

Emmett had the bluest eyes. He was of average height, slim, with deep, brown hair. He smiled at June and me, and I thought I would faint because of how handsome he was. He had a dimple on his chin and a glint in his eye that spoke of kindness, respect, and a sense of humor.

Oh, gosh, he was just so darned cute, and here I was all made up.

The boys fawned over our movie-star looks until I told them to stop. We were the same two gals we had always been.

"But why stop?" June had a mischievous grin on her pretty face. I couldn't help but laugh at her. By now, thanks to Faye, I was feeling more energetic, but I knew I had to pace myself.

"Old Emmett here, just got his wings to be ambulatory," Chet said. "We're taking him around to meet our friends."

The boys all brought folding chairs, so they set them up at the ends of our beds. Emmett was closest to me. Lucky me. He leaned his elbows on his knees with his hands clasped before him. Whenever we exchanged a glance, I felt a kinship with him that I'd never quite felt with a boy. Not even Harold.

I have never been more grateful for hair and makeup in my life.

The boys shared stories and jokes, taking turns to make us laugh. Nurse Fromm yelled at us twice, but it was worth it. I was having the best time, and here I was, stuck in a bed in a sanitarium. Life was just wild sometimes.

Before too long, the boys had to leave. Emmett asked if he could write to me. It was common practice for residents to write to each other, as conversations were rarely private, and visitors weren't always permitted. When they were, it was limited to one hour.

"Oh, yes," I gushed, then blushed with embarrassment.

After they left, June pumped her brows at me, and we giggled. That night, I barely slept a wink.

Willa Grace

The door to our attic room creaked, and Bonnie stuck her head in. I was wallowing in self-pity over my situation and had a hell of a headache. Daisy was better, thank goodness, but I still had decisions to make, and make them soon.

"How are you?" she asked gently. "Blanche wanted me to check on you."

I rolled over. Bonnie was startled at my red, swollen face, confused by my appearance.

"Are you that worried about Daisy? I thought she was better." Bonnie sat across from me on her bed, leaning forward, elbows on her knees, hands clasped, and her long braid draped over one shoulder.

"She is." I swung my legs over the edge of the bed and sat.

"Are you still missing Jode on top of this?" Bonnie frowned. "He was awful pretty but I didn't think he was a good egg. He thought he was too good for his britches."

"I feel so stupid."

"I'm sorry." Bonnie switched to my side and put an arm over my shoulders.

"Daisy and I came here with such dreams. At least I did. And now it's all gone to shit, and I feel so responsible." I slumped forward with my face in my hands. "There's more."

I had to tell her.

"I'm pregnant." I straightened up and looked her in the eye. "Jode."

"Oh." She took her arm from my shoulders and stared at me. I waited for her disappointment. After a moment, she shrugged and said, "There's an easy fix for that."

I pulled in my chin and stared. "What?"

"You can lose it on purpose."

"What? I never heard of such a thing."

"It's not pleasant, but you can do it."

"How? And how do you know?"

"They go up inside you and pull it out." Bonnie averted her gaze and smoothed her uniform skirt over her knees. "Doesn't take long at all."

I put my hands on my belly, considering the size of something that would go inside me to take it away. The thought made me lightheaded and nauseous.

"That's horrible. It must hurt something awful."

"You get over it."

"You've had this done?"

Bonnie bit her lower lip.

"Before I ran away from home."

Ever since I'd met Bonnie, I sensed there was a secret, a mystery about her. I took her hand, not knowing what to say at first.

"Well, then, you know just how I feel. Left by a boyfriend to fend for yourself."

Bonnie shook her head and took a long, shaky breath. "It was my Pa. After Ma died, he had me take her place."

Her words took a moment to sink in. Then I gasped and put a hand to my chest, the other tightening around her hand. I'd heard whisperings of such happenings, but I was staring at proof that such horror is out there. "Oh, dear. I…I'm so sorry."

"My oldest brother came after me, too, but I never let him. That's when I left. Rolled what little clothes I had into a blanket and took off in the middle of the night."

We sat silently for a time. I felt small in the face of what Daisy and Bonnie endured.

"I wish there was something I could do for you, Bon."

"There's not, but I can help you. I know where you can go to get rid of it."

"You do?" I wasn't sure I wanted to hear more. "I'd never thought there was a choice in the matter or any hope of getting past this."

"I didn't have a choice. Pa said I had to. He also made Ma get one years ago. Poor Ma." Bonnie ran her hands up and down her arms like she was cold. "There's a cost. I can find out how much. Pa paid for mine with his poker money."

"I'm scared," I whispered.

"You'll survive. I couldn't wait to get rid of it."

Neither of us could look at the other.

"Miss Bonnie." We both turned slowly, fearing the familiar voice.

Horseface stood in the doorway, "You have a job to do, right? You know better than to be loitering up here."

How much did she hear?

"Yes, ma'am." Bonnie stood and started to leave, but Horseface stopped her with a hand on her arm.

"On second thought, you might as well stay for this. You'll learn a few things." Horseface looked down at me. "You," she said with a hateful glare, "pack your things. You're done."

"What!" I jumped up, but dizziness forced me back down onto the mattress.

"No!" Bonnie glared at the woman.

"I've been waiting to do this since you first entered my office." She stood over me with arms crossed, her skinny body straight as an arrow. "You rubbed me wrong from the get-go. You're too cocky for your own good. And, you brought the threat of TB into this house."

"Why? You've got no reason, Hor... um, Miss Mulchaey. I've been a good worker." This can't happen on top of everything else.

"You've been indecent with that boy who worked in the barn, and now I have proof."

"Proof? You have no cause to say that." Had she overheard? Had Jode and I not been as careful to hide as we thought?

"I have ears."

"But why? I deserve an explanation." Did she know I was pregnant? I wanted to hear her say it. Only Joannie, Blanche and now Bonnie knew. Did she hear us talking?

"You know why. Do I have to spell it out for you? You're a whore. Now, get your things and go." I'd never seen a more evil person in my life.

"Please don't do this. I need this job. Especially now." I rose from the bed.

"Especially now?" Horseface's beady eyes narrowed into slits, and she chewed the inside of her cheek as she studied me. "Why, especially now? What are you hiding? Is that why the boy suddenly disappeared? I couldn't blame him if it's what I think I just overheard." Her gaze slithered up and down my body. "You're pregnant, aren't you?"

"No! I'm not." I vigorously shook my head. "I don't know what you heard, but I'm not."

"Oh yes, you are."

"I need this job to help my family all the more now that Daisy can't. Please."

"Oh, boo-hoo," she spat the words at me. "Go on, get." Then she turned to Bonnie. "You want to be fired as well?"

Bonnie shook her head and backed against the wall.

"No, Miss Mulchaey, please. I will do anything if you let me stay." My stomach churned.

She put her hands on her hips and leaned toward me. "Get. Your. Things. And. Go."

My jaw trembled. I could barely get the words out. "Where? Where will I go?"

"Who cares?" She shrieked with her palms up and a smug look on her pinched face.

While the old bag continued to rant, Bonnie ran to her nightstand, rummaged in the drawer and grabbed a notebook from the writing table across from our beds and began writing. I didn't know what she was doing, but I kept my eyes on Horseface.

"You have no idea how much information I have on the comings and goings of this place. I could ruin nearly everyone here, including Mister Thorpe and his side dalliances—even your dear Blanche. You can't tell me she isn't taking food from the pantry for her own use. I could make trouble for her just like that." She snapped her bony fingers.

Without thinking, I brought my foot back and kicked her hard in the shin. With a yelp, she doubled over, grabbing her leg. Bonnie hollered, "Oh," and put her hand over her mouth, eyes wide.

I stood over Horseface, knowing there was a good chance she'd find some way to make me pay for what I'd just done, but it was worth it.

"There's a little something to remember me by," I said, shaking like flower petals in a storm.

Horseface looked up at me with a face as red as a beet. "You little witch!"

Through gritted teeth, I hissed, "You dried up, old prune."

With that, Horseface limped through the door and out into the hall, where she turned and opened her mouth to issue a threat, but I slammed the door in her face.

"I'm calling the authorities," she yelled.

I opened the door and yelled, "You do and I tell Mister Thorpe what you just said about him." Then, I slammed the door.

Bonnie was wide-eyed, her mouth a perfect circle, as I listened for Horseface on the stairs. When I heard her go down, I quickly knelt before my bed and pulled out my suitcase.

"Willa Grace, you are my hero." Bonnie knelt next to me and wrapped me in her arms. "You better get the hell out of here. I wrote down the name and address of a woman who can help you. Good luck."

"Thanks." I stuffed the folded note in my pocket. "I hope you don't get fired as well."

"I don't care. That was worth it." Bonnie looked at me with raised brows.

All at once, we realized we would not see each other again. I threw my arms around her. "I'll send you a letter when I'm settled. I will think about what you suggested. I love you, Bonnie."

"Love you, too, Willa Grace. Now git!" Bonnie slipped out the door and was gone.

I only had a moment, so I stuffed my things in my suitcase, checking to make sure the money from my last paycheck was still hidden in the lining. I shoved in as many books as possible and left the rest for the others. I found a bar of wrapped chocolate I'd pilfered from Thorpe's last dinner party and stuck it under Bonnie's pillow for her love of chocolate.

Remembering the memories and friendships made in that room, I turned and ran down the staircase to the second floor. Then, as they would never think to look for me there, I made my way from the service staircase, along the hallway past the family bed chambers, and down the grand central staircase of the house, the luxury around me a blur. With a finger to my lips, I hurried past Mr. Sebastian, the butler, who looked at me with astonishment. I ran out the front door and down the driveway toward the front gate.

"Whatcha doin', Willa Grace?" Otto called out as I ran past him.

"See ya, Otto!" I called over my shoulder. "Got myself sacked."

"Well, shit. Take care, girl."

At the gate, conveniently open, I darted around the stone pillar and came to a stop. Now what? Hmm.

I looked back at the house to see that I wasn't being followed. I looked down the street one way and then the other. I wish I could have said goodbye to Blanche. I was going to miss her. I hoped Bonnie would warn her of Horseface's threats.

With a deep breath of freedom and a healthy amount of fear, I turned right.

Afraid Horseface sent a posse after me, I kept running down the tree-lined street. After a few blocks, I missed a heave on the sidewalk, spiraled out of control, and landed on my knees, my garments and books in a heap from my open suitcase.

What a sorry state I was in. I brought my knees up, picked out a few tiny stones from the scrapes, and pushed my hair away from my eyes. No home, no job, no sister, little money, and a baby on the way.

I sat on the heaved and cracked sidewalk, knees up, not caring how unladylike I appeared. I had more important problems.

A few cars whizzed by.

I wiped my wet face with my hands just as a white milk truck pulled up along the curb.

Derby Dairy was painted in red on the side. The passenger-side door swung open, and a gentleman dressed in a white shirt and pants, black shoes and belt, and a white hat on his white hair leaned forward. With all the white, I thought this might be an angel sent to help me. It was just my luck that my angel would appear as a milkman.

"Are you okay there, Missy? Do you need a ride?" He smiled, stretching his white mustache.

From my seat on the sidewalk, I looked up at him, surrounded by a wreath of mussed clothing and open books.

"I…I was just fired from my job. I have nowhere to go. I don't know anyone here, and I'd have no one to call if I could find a telephone. My sister is in a sanitarium in Wisconsin. She's the closest relative I've got, but," I shrugged, "she can't help me. I guess I'm homeless." I'd heard of homeless people and even saw some as our cab driver took us through the city, but I never thought that could be me. But it was, and it happened so fast, like a comet streaking through the sky.

Where would I spend the night? Where was my next meal to come from? Suddenly, the fact that I was pregnant didn't seem so urgent, as silly as that sounded.

The man got out of his truck and came around the front. For all I knew, he could be a murderer disguised as a milkman, but at that point, I didn't care.

His rotund form stood over me. The black belt holding his trousers up was stretched to the limit. "Those knees of yours don't look too pleasant. Let's get you up." He extended a hand, which I accepted. He then handed me the handkerchief from his breast pocket. Of course, it was white "Wipe yourself as best you can, and I'll help with your clothes."

"I can get those," I said as I spit into the handkerchief, wiped furiously on my stinging knees, and looked at my undergarments littering the sidewalk. How humiliating.

"Oh, let me help." He bent over and picked up a few of my dresses, rolling them into balls.

I would have to iron every piece, but that was the least of my worries.

I handed the bloodied, dirt-smeared handkerchief back to him as I grabbed at a brassiere and panties. Once my things were back in the suitcase. I thanked him.

"I suppose you're wondering what I did to get fired. I'm a good person and a good worker. I am, but I wasn't good at following the rules." I smoothed my dress in front, grateful I wasn't showing my pregnancy, and realized I'd just stolen a uniform.

"That's none of my business. You're clearly in need. Where can I take you?"

I shrugged, looking up and down the street as though a boarding house, and a job would magically appear. "I need a place to stay. Do you know of anywhere? I have very little money to start, but I'll work for my keep. I'm strong, and I have lots of energy. I can do anything." Of course, I dare not mention my current condition. I might have confessed that to a woman, but not this kindly gentleman.

"Well, now, my sister-in-law Gladys owns a boarding house just west of the downtown. She just lost a girl. The room might still be available."

Before crawling into the truck, I took one last look back down the street toward Thorpes—no posse in sight.

"Need a hand?"

"Nope, I'm good." I hoisted myself up into the passenger seat.

Mr. Bartley, the milkman, left his route to drive me to Gladys Voss's boarding house, a large two-story house in green with red and beige trim on the windows and a large front porch. I followed Mr. Barkley across the porch and waited while he knocked on the door. A pleasant enough-looking elderly lady came to answer. She had silver hair pulled into a bun on top, a fleshy body, and a kind face. I liked her at once. I think it was her smile that reminded me of Mamka.

"Found another stray, Archie?" She pulled in her chins with fake sternness.

"This here," he said, "is Miss Willa Grace Maruska. She needs a room, and last we talked, you had openings."

"I now have two."

Mrs. Voss ushered us into the entry, with green wallpaper with brown scrolls. The staircase to the second floor was had a carved wood railing and a green and pink floral runner on the risers. To the left was the parlor with a fireplace and comfortable furniture in shades of gold and maroon, and to the right was a dining room in shades of green. If I could stay there, I'd feel very lucky. Provided I could afford it.

Mrs. Voss looked me up and down. "Do you have a job?"

"Not yet, but I plan to get up bright and early tomorrow morning, and I promise to have a job before I return." I reminded myself to stand up straight, as Mamka always said, and look her in the eyes, as Tata would say. "What do you charge?" I held my breath.

"Ten dollars a week."

"I can do that." I couldn't have been more grateful.

Mrs. Voss looked over the tops of her glasses at Mr. Barkley. "Good luck with the job hunt."

"I vouch for her, Gladdy. I feel like I got to know this gal pretty well on the way here. She's good Czech stock. A farm girl."

"Hmph. Well, these aren't good times for needing work, but I'll do this for this brother-in-law of mine." Mrs. Voss patted her hips and winked, "I will show you the room and see what you think." Then she turned to Mr. Barkley. "Archie, you best get back to work."

He laughed and put his cap back on his balding head. "Good luck to you, Miss Maruska."

"Thank you, Mister Barkley." I set my suitcase down and gave him a good hug.

I followed Mrs. Voss up the stairs, to the left, and down the hall into a room at the far end. I felt at home right away.

My new room had light blue wallpaper with tiny pink flowers, two long windows with lacy curtains, and white shades rolled up at the top. Two single beds were covered in colorful patchwork quilts and paired with blue pillows, all set against black metal headboards. Each bed had a bedside stand with a lamp. Two tall dressers stood against the opposite wall, and a wooden chair sat between the windows. A door to a small closet stood open.

For now, the room was mine alone until another boarder was found.

Mrs. Voss took me through the rest of the house and explained the rules: no boys, in by nine weeknights and eleven on weekends, rent due every Friday, no loud radios, and phone calls are ten cents each for a half-hour. I gave Mrs. Voss the money for the first week's rent.

That evening, I met the other four boarders over dinner. They were all nice gals with jobs ranging from waitress to stenographer, sales clerk, and secretary.

Once settled in my new room, I wrote short letters to Daisy, Statesan, and my parents to inform them of the change of address and phone number. The reason was a new job opportunity, for which I didn't share any details. Not even to Daisy. She didn't need the worry.

Then, I sat on my bed and took out Bonnie's note with Mrs. Pearl Frisk's address and phone number, and out dropped twenty dollars. Tears welled up. I knew how long she worked for that money. Somehow, I would pay her back.

I think I stared at the name and address for at least an hour. Could I? Should I?

FOURTEEN

Daisy

I received my first letter from Emmett the next day. He was housed in the cottages behind the main hospital, where I was housed. His was the Chippewa Cottage, which contained a small common area with two long wings extending on either side. My hands were shaking with excitement as I opened his letter.

"Hurry up," June leaned forward as though I'd let her see it.

I put it to my chest and said, "A little nosey, are we?"

"Hey, I feel responsible for this turn of events. You can't leave me out."

"Responsible how?" I pulled in my chin and studied her.

"I was friends with Bobby and Chet before you came. If it weren't for me, you wouldn't know them, thus, meeting Emmett with the blue eyes." She batted her eyes at me.

"That's a shoddy excuse, but I will tell you the highlights. Maybe." I scrunched up my nose at her and giggled. Gosh, I felt so good.

"Oh, go read your love letter." She picked up the latest book she was reading. "I'll just sit over here and read all by my lonesome self."

I laughed and slipped the letter from the envelope.

Dear Daisy,

It was nice meeting you. You're very pretty, but I'm sure everyone tells you that. I'd like to hear about your home up north.

You spoke about it so lovingly that it must be a special place. I'll tell you about me.

I am from Madison, where I studied to be a pharmacist at the university. It seems complicated to reconcile that I studied the use of drugs, but there's not one to cure this darned disease. I've been in the San for almost two years now, and I finally feel like I'm beating this thing. I've been able to go home to visit my folks for a few days, and they've been here to see me. I think you'd like them, and they'd like you.

Perhaps that's too forward of me to say, as we hardly know each other, but I hope we do get to know each other well. I have a younger sister named Mary. She's a sweetheart and plays the flute in the high school band. My father is a physician, and my mother is a homemaker. They are very active in The First Congregational Church.

Outside of the San, I like to collect stamps, play some football, and look forward to playing the saxophone when my poor old lungs are in the clear.

Well, that's a little about me.

Sincerely,
Emmett Brandenberg

I reread the letter, held it to my chest, and couldn't stop grinning.

"Well?" June looked over the top of her book. "Did he express his undying love?"

"If you must know, no, he did not. We hardly know each other. Now, stop bothering me. I've got a letter to write." I giggled while June rolled her eyes playfully.

Dear Emmett,

It was wonderful to receive your letter. Collecting stamps is a fine hobby. There are so many letters that flow through this place, you must have tons of them. A woman on our floor receives letters from an aunt in Czechoslovakia, and another who has relatives in France. I will have the nurses ask them to share for your collection.

I come from a large family up north, Emery Township, east of Phillips. My parents own a dairy farm that has been hit hard by lower milk prices. My sister, Willa Grace, and I went to the Chicago area to earn money to help them. Unfortunately, I'm not being very helpful at present.

I have three other sisters back home, Isabelle, Adeline, and little Rosalie, who's just a baby. She's the most beautiful baby I've ever seen, although I haven't seen her in a year. I also have three brothers, George, Joey, and Albert. My father is a hard worker, and my mother is a saint. I miss them all terribly. Sadly, we lost a brother, Teddy, when he was four.

In my spare time, I've always enjoyed anything artistic. I enjoy painting, embroidery, quilting, and sketching. Oh, and all spring and summer back home, I arranged bouquets of wildflowers and put them in every room of the house.

It's close to lights out here, so I will close. Thank you for writing.

Sincerely,
Daisy Jane Maruska

Letters flew back and forth between Emmett and me, even though we saw each other often. Romances between patients were looked down upon, but not forbidden. Heaven knows we needed something to give us hope for a life after the San. Every day, because of Emmett and my growing love for Junebug, I felt stronger. I was going to live.

Willa Grace wrote to me about her change of address, mentioning that Horseface fired her over a misunderstanding. I felt so sorry for her, as I knew she'd made some wonderful friends there, despite being thrown over by that boy named Jode. She assured me she was done with him for good, calling him a no-account jerk. Oh well, this was just the first of many beaus for her. I was certain of that and told her so, although secretly, I would continue to root for Henry.

June was a bit jealous of me and Emmett, so we always included her in our conversations when he came to visit. Sometimes, the three of us listened to a radio show, read aloud from a book, or played cards. Chet had been released, but Bobby came with Emmett occasionally, and we'd have such lively conversations or games that Nurse Fromm treated us to her glares. Too bad Bobby was too old for June.

All in all, life was going well.

One fine morning, Doc Thompson upgraded me to four privileges a day. I was allowed to walk to the bathroom whenever I wanted and attend a show in the auditorium four times a month, in a wheelchair. What a relief to say goodbye to the old bedpan. June was ahead of me on privileges and had already given up her bedpan, but we sent mine off with a silly song we made up. Even Nelsy joined in. We had the whole wing laughing, and unfortunately, coughing. But it was a little thing to give the others hope.

I was utterly smitten by Emmett. Every time our eyes met, we blushed, and I felt my heart pity-patter so strongly I thought he might hear. I wished for more than simple glances when June wasn't looking. I wanted to stroll the grounds hand in hand, sneak off into the surrounding forest, and steal kisses in the moonlight. Soon, we would make that happen.

Another piece of good news was that one of my drawings of a sparrow outside our window was chosen for the cover of the Beacon, a newsletter that circulated in the San. Every month, the Beacon announced those who'd gotten the okay to leave, introduced the newcomers, included crossword puzzles, poetry, cartoons, shows coming to the San in the form of live entertainment or movies, and updates on the latest advances in TB treatment, along with periodic explanations of the disease itself.

I was so honored to have my drawing chosen, and I immediately fired off letters to my family and friends, receiving many letters of congratulations in return. The only thing missing in this journey of mine was my freedom.

Willa Grace

The day after losing my job and finding a new home with Mrs. Voss, I returned to the streets looking for work. I went from shop to shop, restaurant to café. No one was hiring. Thanks to the high unemployment, no one asked why I wasn't currently employed. If they had, I would have lied anyway. No one needed to know I was practically thrown out of Thorpe's.

Walking down Twenty-Second Street in downtown Berwyn, my stomach started to rumble. I hadn't eaten since breakfast, and it was nearly three o'clock. The weight of not finding work was oppressive. I only had enough money for the first week at the boarding house. Beyond that, I would have to take to the streets to live if I didn't have a job. Of course, I could go back to Emery Township, but my pride wouldn't allow me to give up on my dreams just yet, and going back would put me even farther away from Daisy.

I stopped at the window of Marlenga's Czech Bakery, enjoying the beautiful display of sweets all arranged on fancy plates over white paper doilies—and oh, the aromas coming through the screen door. I had to go inside.

Just then, a little boy nearly bowled me over as he barreled out the door carrying a cupcake. A woman followed, presumably his mother, and called, "Frankie, wait till we get home to eat that cupcake, or I'll whop you a good one." She nearly bumped into me. "Oh, that boy of mine." Frankie's mother shook her head, rolled her eyes, and took off after him.

I watched him go and thought, 'Run, Frankie, run!'

A tiny bell over the door announced my presence. Immediately, I was hit with the most delicious scents since being in Mamka's kitchen. Inside, the small bakery was painted a pleasing pink with a white ceiling and a black and white tile floor. A large glass case across from the door held the fanciest cakes I'd ever seen, some with piping in great swells like waves around the bottom, others with frosting flowers running down the sides and spilling over the tops. Along the other wall, the long counter had shelves holding cupcakes, kolache with every kind of fruit and filling I could think of, and cookies. The wall behind the counter had shelves with bread in many shapes and sizes, houska, and puffy golden dinner rolls.

"May I help you?" A girl slightly older than me with brown braids wound tight around her head, tightening a pink apron over her slender middle, with a blue gingham blouse and brown slacks, came from the back.

I didn't answer right away.

"Tough choice, huh?" The girl grinned widely, pushing her freckles back.

"Very, but I will take just one poppyseed kolache." Then thought better of it. I didn't need my teeth full of seeds when job hunting. "Make that cherry instead."

The girl, whose name tag read "Varina," wrapped the small pastry in white paper and handed it to me. I ate the whole thing in two unladylike bites, enjoying the buttery, cakey base and the sweet and tart filling.

Varina chuckled as I handed over the coins.

"You're a fan of kolache."

"My favorites. I haven't had one since I left home."

"You must be thirsty." Varina reached for a pitcher of water sitting on the back counter, poured some into a cup, and then handed it to me with a napkin.

"Thank you." I drank it all and wiped my mouth before returning it to her. "I've been looking for a new job all day and hadn't bothered to eat lunch."

"You're looking? Hmm. Can you bake?"

I wiped the corner of my mouth and lied. "Sure can. You should see my houskas." What was I doing?

Over her shoulder, Varina called, "Mamka, come here."

From a door in the back, a large, fleshy woman pushed through. She had salt and pepper hair wound around her head in braids like Varina's, round wire glasses perched on her nose, and a welcoming smile.

"She's looking for work," Varina said to the woman. "This is my mother, Rose."

Rose put her hands on her generous hips. Her white apron smudged with dough and frosting, and her green floral dress hung just below her knees, revealing ample lower legs, short white socks, and black slip-on shoes. Rose looked me up and down with a scrutinizing gaze.

"Varina is leaving me to marry a bum across town," Rose said in a clipped Bohemian accent.

"Mamka! Benny is not a bum." Varina's face reddened, and she glared at her mother.

"She knows I'm kidding." Rose stepped forward. "A little, anyway."

"Do I?" Varina's brows arched.

Rose grinned. "Her Benny plays a squeeze box in a polka band. He's good, but you can't put much bread on the table with only that."

"He lost his job in the shoe factory. He'll find something else. I'm going in the back," Varina said. "Nice to meet you…"

"Willa Grace Maruska."

"Good luck with this one, Willa Grace." Varina indicated her mother with a sideways glance, grinned, and went through the door to the kitchen.

"There's plenty of dishes to do," Rose called after her, then turned to me. "So, you bake? I need an extra hand around here, but it's got to be someone who knows their way around a kitchen. Where you from?"

"Northern Wisconsin. I grew up on a farm in Emery Township." I now appreciated the value of being raised on a farm and the good work ethic it inspired.

"Hmm." She stared me down, then said, "I specialize in Czech bakery mostly." She narrowed her eyes and said in Czech, "Jaká je nejlepší chute kolache?"

She'd asked me, 'What is the best flavor of kolache?'

I responded, "Mák samozřejmě, i když moje matka udělala chutnou borůvku." 'Poppyseed, although my mother made a tasty blueberry.' Right then, I could have kissed Tata if he'd been there for insisting we learn the Czech language.

Rose grinned widely, pushing her face into a round plate. "Very good. I was starting a batch of houska. You know of houska?"

"I sure do. Mamka always said mine was better than hers." Oh my, if Mamka were here, I'd get the devil's eye from her. Although I was fairly sure I could pull off a decent houska, considering how many I'd witnessed Mamka making and how many times she tried to teach me. My mouth watered at the thought of houska again, that braided bread with apricots and raisins.

"Good, come with me, and I will watch you finish it." Oh, boy.

I followed Rose into the back. Varina was at the sink, swishing and clinking dishes. I was handed an apron from a hook on the wall. I put my purse on the counter, wrapped the apron around my middle, and deftly continued kneading where Rose had finished. The bread dough was then divided into thirds, and I made a braid with the dough.

"Do you ever soak the raisins in brandy?" I asked.

Rose pulled in her double chins and raised her eyebrows, "No."

"Back home, we did that on special occasions. My Tata kept a bottle of brandy in the back of a cupboard in the barn." I grinned, thinking Tata never seemed to mind if it was used for a houska. Of course, I allowed myself a little nip as well. "Once the dough rises again, I brush it with egg white and water."

"Job is yours. I'm picky, mind you." Rose waggled a finger at me.

"Thank you!" I threw my floury hands in the air and whooped, doing a little dance. In the back of my mind, guilt over keeping my pregnancy secret worried me, but these were desperate times. I would deal with that another day.

Rose chuckled. "Start on Monday. I pay forty-five cents an hour, and you'll work a ten-hour day, from five in the morning to three in the afternoon. I give a half-hour break for lunch. You can eat in the back."

"I can do that. I will be here bright and early next Monday morning."

"Welcome, Willa Grace."

"See ya, Missus Marlenga! See ya, Varina!"

"It's Rose," I heard behind me. "I like you, but you didn't fool me with that houska. We'll get you trained proper in no time."

I made up my mind to be the best baker yet.

FIFTEEN

Daisy

The following Saturday, Emmet came by at six thirty to escort me to my very first movie without a wheelchair. Yes, without that darned chair. I'd gotten some strength back in my legs by walking around our room a few times on my return from the bathroom. Nelsy warned me to take it slow, but it felt so good to be up and about. I also gained five pounds.

The movie was *Duck Soup* with the Marx Brothers. Oh, we laughed ourselves silly.

At one point, in the darkened auditorium, Emmett reached for my hand, entwined his fingers with mine, and stroked my hand with his thumb. I could barely breathe, much less follow the movie. I caught him staring at me several times, and we'd smile. I couldn't believe my good luck in finding him.

And, my luck continued.

The following week, Olga, the new manager of the art studio, stopped in. She was a mid-thirties gal with long, straight chestnut hair that hung down her back and a wildly colored floral dress that stood out from the nurses we were used to seeing.

After introductions, Olga invited both June and me to grow our artistic interests. June was uninterested, but I was elated.

Olga said there was a need for tally cards for the card games in the dining hall between meals. She'd provide the paper and other necessary materials if I came up with a suitable decoration for the outside of the cards. Inspired by Emmett's stamp collection, I experimented with creating pictures using canceled stamps by cutting out the shapes and colors needed for the picture I wanted to create. I'd seen the work a former resident had done. There was a ton of mail coming and going out of the San, and it seemed a shame to throw the stamps away, as some were so pretty. Therefore, I had Nelsy put out the word for patients to save their stamps for me.

Soon, I started making greeting cards with pictures on them using stamps. I was nearly overwhelmed with orders for all kinds of cards, including thank-you and get-well cards, but especially for the upcoming Christmas season.

Nelsy brought in stacks of used envelopes with stamps, while Olga brought over a ream of heavier paper. She also brought me a set of watercolors, a few brushes, and a pen for sketching. June was a whiz at coming up with sentiments for the inside, so we formed a sort of business between us.

Nelsy's husband made me a tilted bed table, which was helpful because I still needed to spend some time in bed every day. Olga advertised my creations to all those in the dining hall, and before long, June and I could hardly keep up.

It was great to earn money and pay for my toiletries and whatever else I wanted. It was humiliating to have to ask my parents for items when the whole point of my leaving was to help them. Even so, Mamka knitted me slippers and a shawl, and sewed me new pajamas, all while sending me many letters and cards. Tata whittled me a sparrow out of curly maple, which I proudly displayed on my bedside table. Our room was heavily papered with pictures drawn by my siblings, along with cards wishing us well. I heard from Willsy every week. She sent comics clipped from newspapers and photographs from magazines. Her letters were very wordy, but she always made me laugh. Gosh, I missed her with a longing so deep it was crushing. The only consolation was that she was thriving in Berwyn with her plans for Chicago growing closer every day.

Willa Grace

I now had a job and a room at the boarding house, so I made an appointment from the information Bonnie had given me to take care of my other problem. Rose gave me the afternoon off. Of course, she had no idea of my plans.

It was a drizzly, gray day when I took the bus to Tally's Tavern on 22nd Street, a seedy-looking place painted brown with peeling green paint around the doors and windows. A half-lit neon sign screamed Tally's in red. As I was told, I went between the buildings to the back, where a pot of pink geraniums sat on the stoop by a blue door, entirely out of place in this sad, run-down alley.

I stopped short of knocking. Could I really do this? What other option did I have? I took a deep breath, wiped my sweaty palms on my old, brown dress, then knocked.

A short, stocky woman answered. Gray curls wreathed her cheerful face. She had a generous bosom for hugging grandchildren, and wire-rimmed glasses over kind hazel eyes. Her blue floral dress was covered with a green apron.

"May I help you?" Her voice was as sweet as pie. This couldn't be the woman I was scheduled to meet, could it? Honestly, I expected a painted-up barfly.

"Hello, I'm Willa Grace."

"Hello, sweetheart. I'm Pearl." Then Pearl looked up and down the alley and opened the door wide. "Right this way."

I followed through a room filled with puffy floral furniture in shades of cream and pink. Pearl led me into a clean, yellow kitchen with a large metal table at its center. Sunshine streamed in through the window over the sink, creating a bright and cheerful atmosphere in the room. She took a towel and wiped the tabletop down. For some reason, my gaze was drawn to a green cookie jar with pink flowers. It made me think of Mamka, but my dear mother would never do what this woman offered.

"Is this safe?" I shifted my gaze to Pearl.

"It is, the way I do it. Not a thing to worry about." Pearl took a folded sheet, shook it, and spread it over the table. "This probably wasn't what you thought would greet you. Most girls expect a barmaid or a madam, but this is me. My son runs the tavern and lives upstairs. This," she indicated the apartment with the sweep of her arm, "is where I live." She smiled warmly, each cheek a little rose.

I set my purse holding the precious $20.00 fee on a chair along the wall.

On the floor, Pearl put down newspapers and a chair at the end of the table. She wheeled over a small table with scissors and a few long, sharp instruments, one of which resembled a long spoon, that sparkled in the sunlight.

I was struck with a sudden sense of panic. I pulled my shoulders, chin trembling, and hugged myself, feeling gooseflesh prick my skin.

Pearl noticed my fear.

"There's nothing to worry about. I've done this many times." Pearl patted the sheet-covered table. "Up you go." She sat in the wooden chair at the end.

I smoothed the front of my dress, but my feet wouldn't move. It was hard to breathe.

Pearl sat back in her chair. "Let me tell you why I do this. I was a midwife by profession. My husband was a terrible alcoholic, and I had seven children. I told my husband, 'Enough.' You know what he did? He forced himself on me, and I had number eight. As a midwife, I witnessed babies being born, cherished with every breath they took. Then I saw women have children that I knew would not be loved, and even abused. The women felt they had no choice but to have them." Pearl sat forward and held up a finger. "No one has the right to tell a woman what happens with her body. Especially a man. That's when I started this. Of course, I divorced my husband first." She crossed her arms over her bosom. "Unless this pregnancy is too far along, I will help. You said you are under three months. That's within my guidelines. You," she pointed a finger at me, "decide what you want for your future."

"I don't know," I said, feeling slightly faint. I put a hand on my stomach, feeling sweat beading on my brow and under my arms. My breakfast roiled inside me.

"Honey, I have another appointment after yours, so we need to get busy."

I pulled myself up onto the table and swung my legs toward Pearl.

"You need to remove your panties, sweetheart." Pearl gave me a grin.

"Oh, sure." I hopped off, removed my panties, put them next to my purse, and repositioned myself, keeping my legs together.

Pearl pushed my knees apart, and a rush of cool air hit my privates. I'd never been so exposed. Despite the sheet covering the table, it was cold and hard against my back, the light above harsh and unforgiving.

"Have you had anyone die?" I craned my face to look between my bent legs.

"Of course not. I'm meticulous with disinfecting. I must remind you, this is highly illegal, and you mustn't breathe a word. You do promise me, don't you?" It was then that Pearl's warm smile faded into a glower. "That's why I only take referrals, and I remembered your Bonnie. Poor little thing."

I took a deep breath and thought of all the children who came from Mamka. Aside from Daisy, I'd seen them all directly after they were born, most red-faced and crying or quiet and angelic. I thought of Mamka screaming and straining to bring the new life into the world. It never occurred to me that she might not have wanted so many children, although you'd never know it by the love and care she bestowed on us all. Every new baby was treated as a gift.

"No, I don't think so." I squared my shoulders, brought my legs together, and swung off the table.

"Willa Grace! Think about what you're doing to your life." Pearl was angry.

"I got myself into this. I will figure it out."

Pearl quickly stood and grabbed my elbow. "You'll be on your own. You've no idea how cruel people can be toward unwed mothers. No one will hire you or be willing to put a roof over your head. And what of this child? What kind of life can you give it?"

"I…I will go to one of those homes for girls waiting to have their babies. I've heard of those. They will take me. If not, I will swallow my pride and go home. I won't rely on my parents to raise this baby, but I know they will be there to help. I'm eighteen. I can do this."

"You're a baby yourself."

"I know you say you've never killed or hurt anyone, but you're cutting into people. There must be a risk of infection, and what about future babies? I might want one someday." That last comment brought me up short.

"I am a clean woman. Don't you go saying otherwise." She shook a warning finger at me.

I could hear Bonnie reminding me that I didn't want children, but then I thought of Daisy. My sister would be so disappointed in me for ending a pregnancy that she would die to have.

With that, I grabbed my purse in one hand, my panties in the other, and stormed out of Pearl's home behind the tavern.

"I was counting on that payment," Pearl called behind me. "You owe me for my time!"

Sparks nearly flew from my feet, hitting the concrete as I left.

SIXTEEN

Daisy

October 1934 arrived with cooler nights, and with our open windows, a reminder to toughen up before winter. Thankfully, we had a few months to go before that.

Doc Thompson and the nurses couldn't believe my progress. Although still positive, my weekly aspirations were clearing, and my X-rays showed marked improvement. I could now walk outside for 30 minutes a day. Emmett and I were elated.

Woodsy autumn scents filled the air, the sky was a brilliant azure blue, and the leaves began to wear their fall colors. Emmett and I met at 2 pm for our daily trek around the grounds. We chatted about nearly every aspect of our lives and agreed on almost everything. Although he hated tomatoes, I loved them. He loved liver, one meat I refused to put near my mouth. He vowed to cook me liver someday and promised I'd come to appreciate it. I promised he'd love my homegrown tomatoes.

"Oh, Daisy, our half-hour walks are not nearly enough," he said one sunny Wednesday.

"The way I'm improving, it won't be long, and that will be lifted." I looked up at him and grinned, feeling the familiar swell of my heart. Some days, it was nearly painful how much I wanted the freedom to spend all my time however I wanted, and I wanted to spend it with him.

He'd just returned from a long weekend with his family to celebrate his parents' thirtieth anniversary. His sister Mary sent me a red hair ribbon, which I wore nearly every day. I listened as he described his parents and their devotion to one another, his extended family, and his friends.

Before long, our half-hour was up, and I was supremely sad.

"Daisy, what's wrong?" Emmett angled his face over mine and touched my chin with his finger.

"I want more of us than a short walk, supervised visits, and a show once a week." I felt tears gather. "I'm sorry. I enjoy our time, and it's hard to be told this is all we get. Oh, I know it's not as if we're in prison. I could stay with you longer if I wanted. After all, you have that privilege, but I don't."

"You need to get better so we both can be free of this place."

I often wondered what our future held once we were healed and out on our own. I longed for my family and the farm, but I loved Emmett. Would I be happy to settle with him in Madison? It was so far from Emery Township, but I believed I would, for Emmett. Would he consider moving north? Pharmacists were needed there as well.

I also worried that if Emmett were released before me, I'd be a distant memory, easily forgotten, like I was with Harold. Emmett would never hurt me that way, but I hadn't thought Harold would, either.

I calmed my anxious heart, knowing that Emmett and I knew each other better than Harold and I had. Emmett was a kind, gentle, loving man. Of that, I was certain. Still, I worried.

For now, I had to bide my time, follow my treatment plan, and get better.

"I'm a little impatient, is all." I intertwined my fingers with his.

Emmett looked around to make sure we were alone and grinned mischievously. "Come here," he tugged on my hand, and I let him pull me around the corner of the brick boiler house.

"Emmett, what are you doing?" I laughed.

"What I've wanted to do for as long as I've known you."

"Oh, really?" The mischief in his eyes was contagious.

He whirled me around so that my back was against the building on the side facing the woods. Then, he wrapped his arms around me, and we were nose to nose.

"Daisy, I'm going to kiss you." His breath was warm on my face.

"Emmett, I'm going to let you." I raised my face.

His lips lightly touched mine. Then, I pulled him into me as our mouths opened, and we kissed with a hunger from deep inside. We moved our mouths this way and that. Neither of us wanted to stop. His hands cupped my face while mine ran up his back. We finally drew apart, but his lips were on my neck, and I was melting with desire.

It was then that his hands went to my sides, and his thumbs brushed my breasts.

I could feel his need as much as I could feel my own. He shook his head and stepped back.

"We can't." He was breathless.

"I know." My heart thrummed, and my knees were weak.

He again pulled me close, and I clung to him, both of us breathing in and out, ragged and raw.

I was past my curfew and knew Nelsy would be looking for me. For once, I hated the idea of seeing her.

Within minutes—delicious minutes, I might add—we regained our composure and slipped back onto the walking trail, pretending nothing had happened, but both of us were red as Macintoshes. He walked me to the entrance of the San, and we went our separate ways. Inside, I went to the nearest window and watched as he walked toward his cottage.

I felt a presence at my side. It was Nelsy.

She glanced sideways and said, "You've got it bad, Miss Daisy." Then she nudged me, and we chuckled as we walked down the corridor to the stairs.

At my next appointment with Doc Thompson, I was upgraded to eating in the dining hall.

I whooped and cheered as Nelsy ran in with a stern warning to shush. Doc just laughed, and I took this as a sign that I was finally, blessedly, getting better. I was one step nearer to being upgraded to live in the cottages, nearer Emmett.

One Saturday night, the movie in the auditorium was *Morocco,* starring Marlene Dietrich and Gary Cooper. Everyone was excited, and it was expected that the auditorium would be filled to capacity. The rumor was that Marlene played a character straddling the line between male and female. It was very titillating and surprising that Statesan would show a film so shocking. When it first came out, it was the talk of 1930. By now, in 1934, it was old news, but still, it was a bold choice in a film, one many of us hadn't seen, and those who had wanted to see it again.

I also wanted to see the movie, but I had a better offer.

That afternoon, as Emmett and I walked the trail around the grounds, we stopped under a large maple tree nearly out of leaves. Around the backside of the wide trunk, we kissed and held hands.

"I know you wanted to see the movie tonight, Daisy, but…" he blushed. "I thought, since so many would be there, they wouldn't notice us missing, we could have some time to ourselves," he shrugged nervously. "That's if you want to."

"What do you have in mind?"

"You leave that up to me."

"Hmm, a bit of mystery." Whatever he was planning, this mischief was absolutely delicious and just what the doctor ordered. Well, maybe not quite. I couldn't wait.

For this night together, I had curled my hair, dabbed on powder, and applied a light touch of red lipstick. Then, wore my best dress, a blue floral that accented my eyes. June teased me mercilessly. I was almost sorry I'd let her in on our secret. The evening was warm for fall, so all I needed was a warm sweater.

As planned, we met at the auditorium, visited with friends, and held back as everyone took their seats. Then, as the lights went down, we scooted out the door and into the darkness of the night. Our hands joined, and we snuck around to the backside of the building.

"I found a break in the fence," Emmett whispered next to my ear.

I was intrigued.

There was a sizable hole in the fence surrounding the campus grounds, located at the edge of the lawn. We stepped through and into the cover of the forest, silver from the half-moon. I followed him through the trees and up a rise, our shoes crunching over dead leaves.

At the top, the lights of the town of Wales beyond the surrounding dark forest, twinkled. The inky sky was cloudless, and stars peeked out one by one.

"What do you think?" Emmett asked, still holding my hand.

"It's gorgeous. How did you find this place?"

"Wish I could take credit, but one of my buddies brings his girl up here." Emmett kissed me. "I've got a surprise."

At a downed log a few feet away, Emmett picked up a bundle and a small bucket and returned.

"I have a blanket for us to sit on and watch the stars, along with two bottles of Pabst beer smuggled in to me by my best buddy from home." He showed me the bottles sitting in water with a few ice cubes floating on top. Are you game?"

"You bet!" Oh, this was such fun.

Emmett spread the blanket out, and we sat next to each other. He opened the bottles with an opener from his pocket.

"To us," he said, holding up his bottle.

"To us," I repeated. We clinked our bottles and drank. I was never one for alcohol, but this was a celebration of freedom, what little we had, without prying eyes.

We sipped our beers and watched the night shadows.

"Whoa!" We shouted as a falling star jetted across the sky with a brilliant tail.

"It's a sign that we're meant to be, don't you think?" I looked up into his face.

Emmett set his empty bottle aside and put a finger under my chin. His hand came around to my waist. I absently set my half-drunk bottle alongside the blanket, where it tipped and emptied.

His lips were on mine, and mine on his. We kissed and kissed for the longest of time. Then, I pulled him down on top of me, and under the cover of an October night, I finally found out what it meant to be a woman.

Willa Grace

Twilight was settling as I left the bakery. Rose had taken on a catering job, and I stayed late to help with the cream puffs. I'd bought an old bicycle off a roomy at the boarding house, but it had a flat tire, and while I could have taken a bus, I decided to walk through the chilly night.

We'd had a busy day, and honestly, the walk would do me good. I had so much on my mind, a future to plan, decisions to make. How I wished I could talk this all through with Daisy. I would have to tell her eventually, but she was so happy right now, so in love, and so hopeful.

Just the day before, Jenny at the boarding house commented on my loose-fitting dresses, suggesting I wear clothes that better suit my figure. I joked that working at the bakery wasn't doing my figure any favors. I thought that was a damn good response.

A plan had been slowly forming.

When I could no longer hide my condition from Rose and Mrs. Voss, I would go to the Foundling Home in Chicago to have my baby. The only fly in the soup was hiding my pregnancy from my family, once I had no income. I hoped beyond hope that a solution would show itself soon. It had to. Milk prices were slowly rebounding. Mamka said they'd been able to hold off the bank from taking the farm and would be fully self-sustaining soon.

Once I had the baby, I would offer my child up for adoption and, hopefully, a better life than I could give. I worried that the decision would be more difficult once I felt that telltale flutter of life.

I briefly considered keeping the baby. No matter the hardship, I knew Mamka would welcome another into their home, but I couldn't face the shame I'd bring upon them. This child would go to a loving home in the city with all the opportunities I'd dreamed of, and still did. Then, I could go home for a visit.

I walked as far as Proksa Park and sat on a swing using my feet to gently push back and forth while savoring a chocolate chip cookie I'd hidden in my coat pocket as I left the bakery earlier. I didn't do that kind of thing often, but I couldn't resist. Rose would have given me one if I'd asked. *Why do I do these things?*

Children chased a large, red ball in a game of kickball in the early evening dusk. A young mother pushed a buggy, and three boys barreled through on bicycles, probably heading home for supper.

Soon, I was alone except for an elderly man walking a small terrier. Darkness pushed the sunset farther to the west, and streetlights blinked on.

I'd stayed too late and had a long way to go. Mrs. Voss would not be happy if I were late for supper.

The wind kicked up, blowing leaves over and around my shoes. I hurried out of the park, a few blocks down 22nd Street, and then crossed a parking lot to pass along a large black building with dark windows.

A loud bang caused me to nearly jump out of my skin. I whirled around, holding my purse tight against me, knees knocking. A tabby cat ran from a garbage can lid.

I bent over, breathing deeply, trying to steady my nerves. I was sure to get a lecture from Mrs. Voss on the dangers of being out alone after dark.

I tilted my chin, stood tall, and confidently swung my purse as I walked along. Experience taught me that a scary animal generally backs down when faced with a confident foe. When I came upon a bear a few years ago, I carried my head high and continued as though I didn't have a care in the world, though inside, I was a trembling fool. The bear let me live.

I wasn't sure what would work for human prey.

I turned up Ridgeland Boulevard—only five more blocks to go.

I thought about Mamka again, hoping little Rosalie didn't give her fits like Albert. That boy cried nonstop for what seemed like months. No one could calm him except Ranger, our cocker spaniel, who would stick his snout in the cradle, after which Albert would quiet. It seemed the whole house gave a sigh of relief, but unfortunately, Ranger had no interest in standing by the cradle all day and night.

And now, here I was, carrying a baby of my own. *What in hell was I thinking to let Jode put himself inside me?*

I quickened my steps.

Suddenly, and without warning, two dirty hands grabbed me from behind. I let out a screech and was pulled into an alley between two vacant buildings.

At first, I was so shocked I couldn't breathe. My head smacked the brick wall along with my right shoulder. Then I looked down into the smudged, greasy face of a man with wild hair. A distant streetlamp showed the whites of his angry eyes. It was a vagrant I'd seen occasionally along this street. His filthy hands bunched in my coat as I tried to pull away. With a dangerous look in his eyes and a twisted mouth, he whispered, "Don't scream, or I'll hurt ya. I promise I will."

I found my voice and screamed.

"Goddamn it!" He growled.

He pulled me toward him, then shoved me up against the brick wall. Once more, the back of my head smacked the bricks, and this time, I learned what it was when people said they saw stars.

"Please, don't hurt me." My voice was hoarse and shaky. I could smell liquor on his breath, making my stomach churn. His jacket oozed the awful smell of vomit and the lack of a bath.

I then realized my purse held my week's pay. I'd worked hard for that money and was damned if I gave it up to this bum.

"Don't fight me, missy, or you'll be a sorry one," he said in a gravelly voice, his face so close I could feel the heat of his breath.

"I…I…please let me go." I heard the terror in my voice terrified me even more.

"Oh, I ain't lettin' you go." He pulled at my purse, but I held on.

When he couldn't get the purse, he threw me against two trash cans that exploded into the alley. I almost fell to the ground, but used the wall for balance and screamed again.

Still, no one came.

We stood facing each other. Then, he moved. His hands went to my waist, inside my coat, and he bunched up my skirt as he pushed me harder against the wall. I knew what he had in mind, and if I had any say, he wasn't getting that either.

"Maybe you got more for me'n that there purse." The snarl of his mouth reminded me of the little black snakes that slithered among the hay bales back home. The hate in his eyes was like nothing I'd ever seen before.

"No!" I struck at him, and my purse fell to the ground.

He grunted as he pulled at my coat, his hands rough on my body. I kicked and pushed at him with all my might.

Then he punched the side of my head. It felt like an explosion in my left ear, and I couldn't catch my breath. He followed that with a knee to my midsection. I stumbled against the downed trash cans, trying to stay upright. I fell to the ground onto my hands and knees. He pulled me up by the arm, grabbed my coat, and raised his fist again.

Hell's bells, I knew what to do.

I shoved him to get some space between us, then raised my knee and went for his man parts with all the force I could muster. He went down like a sack of feed dropped from the barn loft.

As he curled up, holding his crotch, I kicked him in the chest.

"You bitch!" The words came out of his mouth in a high-pitched whine for lack of air.

I stood over him, smoothed my clothing, and secured my purse in the crook of my elbow.

Then I bent over him and said, "Don't mess with a farm girl."

I shook like a leaf holding on through a tornado.

"Watch your back, missy," he ground out through clenched teeth, spat at me, but missed.

It was tempting to give him another kick, but the evil coming from him scared the dickens out of me, and I ran.

I ran as fast as I could, looking over my shoulder every few steps. What if there were more of them hiding in the shadows?

I ran past houses lit up as families gathered around the dinner table or around the radio. I ran past the elementary school and the public library, then took a shortcut through a vacant lot and a backyard where children played kick-the-can under the porch light and onto our street—two blocks to go.

I kept running even though I wanted to lie down and give in to the pain, fear, and embarrassment.

I arrived at the boarding house, ready to collapse on the front stoop. My time walking alone after dark in the city was over. Back on the farm, it was nothing to walk miles through the forest after a party at the Villa, through woods filled with animals looking for dinner.

Under the yellow glow of the light, I could see my knees were scraped red, my hose ripped, my palms roughed up and bleeding. I picked the gravel out of them and tried to pull my stockings up to hide the scrapes. My head hurt something awful.

Mrs. Voss came through the door.

"Where in blue blazes have you been, girl? You're never late coming from work. I didn't know if I should send for the police or ask the neighbor to take me in his car to have a look for you." Then she looked me up and down. "My Lord, what's happened to you?"

"A vagrant jumped me in an alley," I went from angry to weepy in two seconds. "He nearly took my pay."

"I told you, did I not, to be careful when you're alone in the dark? These are desperate times, my dear, and folks are hungry, some without homes. You're lucky you weren't jumped by more than one." She put a comforting arm around me and squeezed. "Willa Grace, have you learned nothing by living in the city?"

"I know." I wiped my tears away and realized I must have dirt smudged across my cheeks. "He…oh, never mind."

Mrs. Voss stared at me for a moment. "Your skirt is torn. Did he do more than try to rob you?"

"No. He didn't." Sure enough, my new skirt was torn. "He wanted to but didn't."

"How in the world did you get away?"

"I kicked him in the…you know."

At that, Mrs. Voss burst into laughter and quickly covered her mouth. I realized what I'd just said and started to laugh as well.

"This isn't funny," she said, trying to stifle her laugh.

"I know, but you should have seen him crying like a baby." I couldn't help it. I laughed out loud. I was more relieved than anything.

"Come inside, my little prize fighter. We'll get you a bath. You stink."

"Thanks." The chewing out I expected hadn't amounted to much. I suppose she figured I'd learned my lesson in spades.

After a long bath and a bowl of Mrs. Voss's chicken soup, the girls gathered around to hear what had happened. They were frightened for me and sympathetic, but when I told them what I'd done to get away, we laughed until tears ran down our faces. I laughed so hard that I doubled over and felt a stab deep in my belly that took my breath away.

SEVENTEEN

Daisy

My life was complete, which sounded silly since I lived in a sanitarium, but it was true. The love Emmett and I had for each other only grew, even though it had only been a week since we got to know each other in the way couples do. I had no doubt Emmett and I had a future together, and I didn't care where we ended up as long as we were together. I remembered how Mamka said she'd have followed Tata anywhere. That's how I felt.

I could now spend afternoons in the art studio when I wasn't taking my strolls with Emmett. I'd started a regular correspondence with his mother, Constance, and his sister, Mary.

Besides Emmett, the art studio also gave me peace of mind. Tables were set up in front of long windows to take advantage of the light. Shelves held any art supply needed: paints of different mediums, jars of brushes, and stacks of paper and canvases. There was a throwing wheel for clay and a kiln for ceramics. June and I continued with the tally and greeting cards.

Emmett worked in the campus leather shop, where he learned to make wallets, belts, and other items to pass the time. The San had several programs for both men and women to teach skills that could be taken with them.

The Christmas season was inching closer, and I challenged myself to copy the year's Christmas Seal using the stamps I collected. It depicted three children caroling with a banner underneath offering Christmas Greetings. The sale of Christmas Seals earned money for the Wisconsin Anti-Tuberculosis Association, a cause we all supported and encouraged others to support as well.

One sunny day, Olga asked me to stay after the others had left.

"Oh, Daisy dear, I have news for you. I hope you don't mind, but I did something." Her eyes gleamed behind her chunky black glasses.

"Do I need to be afraid?" I teased as I brushed paper scraps into a trash can.

"Remember the poster you did with the stamps you'd collected? The copy of the Red Cross Christmas Seal?"

"Sure." Olga had it hanging on the studio wall.

"As you know, I thought it was just wonderful, so… I contacted the Red Cross about it. I have a friend who works for them as a publicist. She'd like to feature a picture of you with it for a full-page ad in the Milwaukee Journal."

I held my breath. This had to be a joke.

"It's true, Daisy. You'll be famous. For a week at least."

Slowly, Olga's words sank in. I brought my hands to my chest. "Oh, my goodness. Me? Are you sure? If you're lying, it's not funny."

"The Milwaukee Journal, Daisy! Can you believe it? They want to feature you and your wonderful picture."

"No. I…no. I'm at a loss for words." I felt a bit faint.

Olga came around her desk. "Do you realize what this will do to advertise Red Cross fund-raising to fight TB, not to mention positive publicity for Statesan? This is big. Huge!"

"Me. They want a picture of me?" This was unbelievable.

"Your picture will be seen all over Wisconsin and the Midwest."

"I'm going to be sick." The room started to spin as I put a hand on my stomach. I'd never wanted to leave Price County, and now my likeness would be all over the Midwest.

Olga laughed. "Nonsense. You're nervous, is all. It's time you realize the talent you have."

"What will I wear? I don't have any fancy dresses."

"Don't you worry. We'll fix you up just fine."

"I need to put on some weight and get a haircut, Olga. I look like a TB patient."

Olga took my chin between her finger and thumb. "You are a TB patient. A beautiful one."

I could feel myself blush.

"Doc Thompson wants to congratulate you. He's just as excited as I am. He'll visit you tomorrow."

I dropped down hard on a stool.

"I don't believe this. It was just one of my little projects."

"Girlie, stop talking like that. Your art is amazing. How many times must I tell you that?"

"I think I need to lie down for a bit."

By dinner time, it was all over campus. I mentioned it to June just as she left for a book club meeting. I should have known she'd spread it all over creation. I didn't mind. This was so exciting, and seeing the pride in Emmett's eyes was the topper.

A few days later, the photographer from the Milwaukee Journal, a lovely young man named Tim, came for the picture. Right from the start, he made me feel at ease. Nelsy and Olga helped me find an outfit the day before, but seeing that I was patient, Tim suggested a robe. Ultimately, they chose a gorgeous red silk robe with puckered sleeves borrowed from Vi Duncan in the cottages. The robe was fancier than anything I owned. Vi even had a matching ribbon for my hair.

"Oh my, Daisy," Olga said, standing back. "The red with your black hair and those blue eyes—you are stunning."

"You clean up well." Nelsy nudged me and grinned. Olga took me to the studio.

Tim sat me in a regular folding chair, holding the portrait at an angle, with an open box of stamps on my lap. I looked slightly back over my right shoulder at the camera. He took dozens of photos. The issue was scheduled to be released on December 1st.

Goodness, they made me feel like a movie star.

My first letter was to Mamka to tell her all about the photo session. She wrote back immediately, with all of them signing at the bottom, Tata too. They were thrilled and very proud. The next letters were to Willa Grace at her new boarding house, and then to Sissie and Edie, my good friends back home. Willa Grace's response was a letter filled with exclamation points, so overly enthusiastic that it made me laugh.

It didn't go unnoticed that only a few months before, I was fighting for my life. I had no idea what brought on the good fortune I was experiencing, but I was mighty grateful and not about to take it for granted.

Willa Grace

I didn't let on when that first pain struck while laughing with the girls.

That night, at three in the morning, the cramps started. I sat on the side of the bed until a horrible pain sizzled through my belly. I stumbled to the toilet down the hall as quietly as I could. Sweat poured from my skin, making my hand slick as I tried the doorknob.

Once inside, I sat on the toilet with my head on the cool porcelain of the sink. My body was doing something awful, and I was grateful that no one was awake.

The pain was terrible, and blood dripped out of me. I prayed I wouldn't die sitting on a toilet.

And then, I realized…my baby was dying. He or she was leaving me, pushed from my body. The vagrant was stealing something more precious than a lousy paycheck.

I was gripped with terror and grief so deep and unexpected. My baby, in its dying, was finally real to me. This little person I'd pretended not to know was slipping away. I cried and cried. How I wanted my mother to hold me, talk me through this.

With a great, searing stab and a gush, the baby was gone. I sat weak, sweaty, and nauseated over what Jode and I created through his need and my childish love. In a moment so strong and clear, I knew it was a girl. My daughter was gone.

Did I deserve to feel this loss? I hadn't wanted this baby, yet, given a chance, I might have decided to keep her. The choice had now been stolen.

I wiped down the toilet and the floor.

This child and I might have had a chance if it hadn't been for Jode's leaving. God, I hated him at that moment. I cried until I could cry no more. I stood looking down at what had once been inside me with a hole in my heart, I hoped I would never know again. Covering my eyes, I flushed away the evidence. Then, I vomited and had to clean again.

Afterward, I sat on the covered toilet seat and found another sea of tears.

After losing the baby, I spent a lot of time alone, not wanting to join in conversations, and ate little. Mrs.Voss and the girls in the house chalked it up to the aftermath of being attacked. They had no idea I'd been pregnant.

I was sad for the baby I hadn't wanted until it was too late. Nearly every night, I had nightmares and, as always, I worried about Daisy, no matter how she was doing. I knew she'd never come back to Berwyn. I didn't want her to.

She wrote me about her Emmett. Daisy was in love, and I was so happy for her. And who knew, maybe she'd marry Emmett, and they'd live near his family. Although I found that hard to see. Daisy always said she'd live her life on a farm in Emery and have oodles of babies, but only time would tell what life had in store for us all.

The house girls invited me to the Sokol for a dance, but I wasn't interested. I'd enjoyed dances and social gatherings until then and knew I would again. Still, I needed time to face the guilt over the situation my decisions had put Daisy and me in.

But you know, life can be so surprising at times. You never know what will step into your path when you least expect it.

Mrs. Voss and I were listening to the radio while the girls were out. A knock on the front door startled us. I opened the door without peeking through the window to see who it was.

"Yes?"

Then my eyes met his, and I nearly leaped into his arms. It was Henry. I threw the door open and hugged him tight.

"Hello, Willa Grace." He wore a brown tweed jacket, trousers, a dark brown vest over a white button-down shirt, and a blue tie. Pretty spiffy for a farm boy from up north. With a nod, he removed his hat and held it before him.

"My goodness, Henry! How did you get here? What are you doing here?" I brought my hands up to my mouth. What a shock, and what a welcome surprise.

"I came with my sister Marian to meet her new beau."

"Her beau?"

"She's been writing this fella who's worked in the stockyards for quite some time. He invited her to come to the city so they could meet. She's going to stay with his family as they get to know each other."

"Willa Grace?" Mrs. Voss called from the parlor. "Is everything all right?"

"An old friend has stopped by to visit. We'll sit out on the porch."

We sat side by side on the wooden swing that creaked back and forth. It was a chilly night, and I was happy to have grabbed a coat.

"How long will you be here, and why didn't you let me know?" I poked his arm.

He grinned. "Marian was supposed to travel down with Anna Marek, our cousin from Catawba. Two days ago, Anna broke her leg in a fall from a hay wagon. Marian howled like a stuck pig, thinking she couldn't go. Ma said she couldn't go alone, and there wasn't time to get a letter off to you. I hope it's okay I showed up like this."

I turned toward him and put my hand on his sleeve. "Of course it is, Henry. You've no idea how I needed to see a face from home. So much has happened in the last few months. I needed to see an old friend."

"When did you arrive?"

"Just yesterday, we took the train and went straightaway to her fella, Jim's parents' house. They're nice folks and seemed happy to meet her. The house is very comfortable, and Jim is a likable guy. I think Marian will be happy there."

"I hope so. Maybe she and I can meet for lunch one of these days."

"She'd love that." Henry shifted in his seat. "I heard Daisy went through a bad bout. How's she faring since your last letter to me?"

"Better all the time. She used old stamps to create a copy of the Christmas Seals that's going to be featured in the Milwaukee Journal. Can you believe it? The Milwaukee Journal! I am so proud. And," I grinned, "she has a crush on a fella at the San."

Henry chuckled and slapped his knee. "Well, good for her. By golly, it's time her luck changed for the better."

"Yes. Nice to have good news for a change."

He turned the hat over in his hands. "You said, 'so much going on,' is there more?"

He was fishing to see if I had a beau. I could tell Henry still cared for me. How could I tell him I'd given myself to someone else? That I'd been pregnant. Henry surely wouldn't take that well. I could tell by the tone of his letters that he still hoped for something more from me someday. I hastily decided to share one thing with him.

"There is one other thing," I looked him square in the eyes, "I don't want you worrying, but I was attacked one evening on my way home from work."

Henry's eyes grew wide, and he abruptly turned toward me. His hat fell to the floor, and he took my hands. "My God, Willa Grace, were you hurt?"

"No, and don't you tell anyone back home. I didn't even tell Daisy. My bicycle had a flat tire, so I was walking home from work in the dark. I'm no worse for wear. Skinned knees and a torn skirt were all. My attacker will think twice before doing it again. Of that, you can be sure."

Henry's face softened. "I take it you made him pay."

"Yes, I did, and you don't need the details."

At that, he laughed out loud, and I joined in.

Henry picked up his hat and sat back in the swing. "You are a spitfire, Willa Grace." Then, he grew serious. "That attack could have gone much worse. Do you realize that?"

"I do, and it didn't, so end of discussion. And remember, not a word. My mother would come undone, and Tata would make me come home. I can't leave Daisy. I just can't be that far away from her if she needs me."

"I understand. Promise me you'll not go out in the dark alone anymore."

"I promise. Besides, my bicycle is fixed, and I never work that late. It was a set of circumstances that won't happen again."

"I should hope not."

"Whose taking care of the farm?"

The evening air was crisp and sweet, with the smells of late autumn, although when the air stirred from the west, I caught a whiff of his spicy cologne.

"My brother will go over every morning and night to give Ma a hand. I'll only be here for a few days. I have always wondered what a big city is like. Now, I'll know. Do you have plans for the weekend?"

"What do you have in mind?" I was grinning, happy, and excited for the first time in ages.

"I thought you and I could take in the World's Fair."

"Oh, Henry, I would love that!" I clapped my hands. The 1933 Chicago World's Fair was the talk of the town, and so successful that it was extended into November of '34. Henry had gotten here just in time. I'd hoped Daisy would get out of the San so we could go, but that wasn't to be. We should have gone shortly after arriving the year before.

"Well, hunky-dory!" He jumped up from the swing. "We'll do it up right."

"Thank you, Henry. You're a dear." A bit of fun was just what I needed. Leave it to Henry to save the day. "Now, let's dig into some gossip."

EIGHTEEN

Daisy

"What's up, buttercup?" I whispered in the dark. The harvest moon lent a buttery sheen to the night outside our open window. I couldn't sleep and noticed June staring at the ceiling.

"A lot on my mind," June said.

"Care to talk about it?"

When she turned to face me, I saw a seriousness on her face I'd never seen before. "Doc says I've plateaued and is looking at thoracoplasty before the end of the year if nothing changes."

"Oh, no." I looked for Nurse Fromm. She was nowhere in sight, so I stumbled to June's bed and took her hands. "It's worked for lots of people, Junebug. Doc wouldn't want to do it if he didn't think it would help."

"I know all that." She splayed her hands out under her breasts, her fingers covering her ribs. "What will I look like with two ribs gone on one side, maybe more? I'll be lopsided."

"You'll look just fine. Who will know?"

We both studied her body for a moment, trying to picture the aftermath of the operation.

June raised a tearful gaze at me. "I don't want to have it."

"But if Doc thinks...."

"That's not it. I have a bad feeling about it. We're talking surgery, Daisy. I've never had surgery before. I've heard it's a painful recovery. Doc says I will be put to sleep so I won't feel a thing. I'm not afraid of the pain, but I can't see being asleep while they cut into me. I don't think it'll work. What if I wake up during surgery? Can you imagine?"

"Oh, Junebug, they won't let that happen. They do these operations every week. When have you ever heard of someone waking during surgery?"

"Well…"

"And look at our friend Dorothy. She had it done and is doing great. Bobby, too. He wrote last week to say he's taken up his life on the farm again as though he'd never been sick."

"What about Rupe?"

"Doc said Rupe had heart problems that no one knew about."

"I know." June squeezed my hand. "I have a bad feeling about it, is all, but it's probably the fear of going under the knife."

"Please don't say it that way, under the knife. Look at it as the next step toward going home." I was energized for her, "Yes, that's it. Keep your eye on what's to come after. I bet it won't be long, and you'll be back at school, playing your flute in the band, working at the grocery store with your family, and finding a new beau." I squeezed her hands.

"Maybe you're right. That's how I need to see it." She squared her shoulders, took a deep breath. "Wouldn't it be wonderful to be home with my family for Christmas?"

"It will be!" I took her hands in mine. Everything was going so well, there was no room for anything else. "We'll get you through this together."

The orderlies came for June on a cold day with overcast skies threatening the first snow flurries.

"It's a perfect day for a new beginning." I gave her a confident smile.

June was helped into a wheelchair, and before they left, she reached for me.

I jumped up and hugged her, holding her tightly to my chest, and she hugged me back.

Nelsy stuck her head in, "Miss Daisy! Back in bed."

"Yes, Mistress Fromm." I giggled, trying to remain light-hearted for June's sake.

She gave me a weary smile with teary eyes.

"Nothing to worry about. Right?" I squeezed her hands tightly. "You're going to be just fine. Now, what do you say?"

June bobbed her head once in confidence. "Yes! Nothing to worry over."

"See ya later, Junebug." I kissed the top of her head and settled back in bed, listening to the one squeaky wheel of the chair as they went down the hall.

I placed my arms over my chest and, for a time, held onto the feeling I had when I'd held her close, her heart beating against mine. June was like a sister to me now.

June's surgery was scheduled for ten o'clock that morning. I wasn't sure how long it would take, so I busied myself in the art studio, making tally cards to pass the time.

Olga shooed me out to lunch at noon. Emmett and I sat together over our chicken soup, fruit cups, bread, and apple pie for dessert.

I tried to think of anything I could to distract myself from what was happening with June. After lunch, Emmett walked me to our building.

I'd asked Nelsy if she'd heard anything, but she hadn't, so I pulled out a book, *The Thin Man*, by Dashiell Hammett, but I couldn't concentrate.

At two o'clock, I was sure something wasn't right. Just then, Nelsy came into our room with a somber look.

"What's happening?" I sat up straight.

"We lost her," Nelsy said, dropping onto June's bed like a sack of wet laundry.

"No!" I shook my head. My book fell to the floor. "No. That's not true! What do you mean?"

Nelsy reached back for the stuffed rabbit June kept on her bed and held it in her lap.

"I'm going to miss that girl." Tears ran down onto her mask.

"Nelsy, no! She's not dead. Stop saying that." I thought I would faint.

"It's the God's truth, Daisy."

Panic choked me, my stomach roiled, and my hands shook. Suddenly, I was so angry.

"What happened? What did they do to her?" My voice was between a scream and a raw, heart-ripping moan.

Nelsy reached for me, and we joined hands. Regardless of the rules, I pushed off my bed and stood before her.

"Everything was going well, but she had a massive stroke. No matter how hard they worked on her, it wasn't enough. She's gone."

"NO!" My knees gave out, and I crumpled to the floor. I reached for the pink spread on June's bed and buried my face into it. Nelsy reached down and rubbed my shoulders.

"I think I'm going to be sick." I could taste the acid.

Nelsy reached for the metal waste can between our beds and pushed it at me. I vomited until there was nothing left.

Nelsy helped me up into bed with a hand on my shoulder as I cried.

"How do you do this?" I asked her. "How do you continue to work amid so much death?"

Nelsy pursed her lips and blew out a breath. "For the love of those suffering." She gave me June's rabbit, which I hugged close. "Say a prayer for her, Daisy. That's all you can do now."

"I'd like her parents' address. I want to write them. Tell them about our time together and…how much I loved her."

Nelsy nodded. "I'll give you some time before we gather her things."

On the wall along her bed, she'd taped photos of her family and friends. All happy faces about to be shattered. This young girl, a woman really, with so much ahead of her. Why?

The next afternoon, I went to the chapel on the grounds and stood outside the large wooden doors. Vines clung to the brick surrounding the door and the stained-glass windows on the south side.

Cautiously, I put my hand on the door and pulled the iron handle. Inside, the sanctuary was quiet, and the afternoon sun streamed through the stained-glass windows in golden beams. It reminded me of the forest before the sun drifted to the west, when every leaf and branch was dusted in gold. It was a holiness that always calmed me.

I raised my eyes to the wooden beams overhead and then to the colorful windows that seemed to reach toward the heavens. In front was a pulpit from which I could almost hear the flow of comforting words. I needed to listen to those words now. I needed to understand this taking of innocent young souls.

A large cross with a statue of Jesus hung behind the pulpit. He looked so sad, like all the world's ills were on his shoulders. What an awful burden for a person to bear.

The floor creaked quietly as I walked forward. About halfway up to the front, I sat in a pew, resting a hand on the back of the bench before me.

I sat like that, listening to the silence, watching the dust motes dance on the beams of light, before resting my gaze on the man and the cross up front.

'Let your heart be still.'

I was unsure if I heard those words with my ears or my heart, but they didn't help. It would be a long time before my heart would ever be still in the face of this tragedy.

I wanted to ask this God how he could allow my sweet June and dear Teddy to die when they'd done nothing wrong? Anger built within me. What kind of God was this?

"Why!" I pounded my fists on the pew as my words echoed. I wanted to kick and scream. Why did this have to happen? It was too much. I bent forward and sobbed.

A hand softly touched my back. I gasped and sat up straight. I hadn't heard anyone enter. Slowly, I turned.

No one was there. I know I was touched. My skin prickled. I looked from side to side, then stood. I was most certainly alone. I wrapped my arms around myself and sat again, staring at the altar. Should I be frightened? I wasn't.

After some time, I folded my hands under my chin and prayed. I had seen June do it when she thought I was not paying attention. Sitting in that pew, I prayed for June, my family, and for release from tuberculosis for the many who struggled with it. I didn't pray for myself. I didn't need to. I was going to be fine.

The light from the windows darkened, and the sanctuary lost its golden glow.

On the third day after June died, I agreed to take my meals in the dining hall with a group of girls. I still hadn't found my appetite, but I promised Nelsy I'd try. Emmett came in a little late and sat with his friends. He wore a somber expression when he saw me and nodded, his hand on his heart. He'd tried to comfort me when he visited in the evenings, but I wasn't up for company. He motioned for me to meet him outside after the meal.

I finished, eating little. We met behind the boiler house by the trail circling the grounds.

"How are you holding up?"

Tears dripped off my nose. "I miss my Junebug. This is so unfair. She had so much life to live." I stopped walking, my heart thumping. "I'm so damn angry, Emmett. I don't know what to do with it all. I hate that I'm here and not with Willa Grace helping our family, and I hate that Mamka worries about me. And I hate having a little sister I don't know. I've never been able to put that little girl on my knee and sing her songs and watch her grow. I've never really hated before, but I hate TB."

"You're allowed, Daisy."

"I hate this goddamned disease!" I whirled to face him. "You and I should be out there," I swung my arm toward the front gate, "We should be going to movies and dancing, meeting each other's families, planning a future, but look at us. We're caged up here like rabid animals." I was scaring myself with the hysteria in my voice.

"We aren't caged."

"We might as well be. All the healthy people living their lives don't want any part of us. We're stained with disease. We always will be. If we make it out of here, no one will want to hire us. If they find out, they won't want to live near us. They won't want to walk on the same side of the street as us. And it can come back, you know. Once you have TB, it can hide in your body until it decides to attack again."

Emmett tried to take my hand, but I pulled it back. I didn't want his voice of reason.

"I had dreams, Emmett. I wanted a husband, babies, and a home to raise them in. I should never have followed Willa Grace to the city. I knew I shouldn't come, but I wanted to help my family, and the jobs up north don't pay squat. Did you know that some women can't have babies after they have had TB? Did you?" I slapped my belly with both hands and held out my palms. "If you stick with me, you may never know what it's like to have a baby of your own."

A cardinal alighted on a poplar branch near us.

"Please..." Emmett was crying now as well.

A sob thrust from my throat, and my body shook. "I hate this. I hate it so much that I don't know what to do with all the hate inside me. I...I just..."

Emmett grabbed my arms and shook me. "Stop it, Daisy." He then tugged me toward him.

My body went to his as naturally as a seed to the soil. His arms held me tight while I buried my face against his shoulder and wept bitterly, my knees barely able to hold me up.

I don't know how long we stayed that way, but his shirt was plenty wet when I pulled myself together.

"I made a mess of your shirt." I stepped back, wiped my wet face with my hands, then wiped my hands on my skirt, and wondered what he must think of me after such an outburst.

"It's only tears, Daisy. They dry and they disappear." His smile warmed my heart. "You're looking pale. You need to take care of yourself."

I waved a hand in front of my face. "Oh, I know. I'm still not sleeping well, and it's a chore to eat. The room is so empty without her."

"Let's walk." He reached for my hand.

We walked along in the deepening shadows of a gray day. The cardinal was still in the trees alongside us, branch to branch, as though keeping us company.

"I'm sorry to have put you through that. So many things anger me right now." I looked up at him. "Since June, I'm so tired. I'm tired of everything. Except you, of course." I nudged him with my shoulder.

"You still have your picture coming out in the paper before too long. That's a big deal."

I shrugged and kept walking.

"I still love you, even if you're a sniveling mess." He nudged me with his shoulder, and I elbowed him back. "Tell me what you can of your little sister."

"Rosalie is a gorgeous baby with pink cheeks and blond curls. Other than that, I can only tell you what has been told to me in letters. She loves to dance when Mamka sings to her. My sister Addie says Rosalie giggles like crazy when my brothers make faces at her and often begs my sisters to read her books and take her for walks. Oh, and animals. She loves the animals on the farm, especially our dog Ranger. Mamka said one day, when weeding in the garden, she looked behind her to see Rosalie pulling out all the beets that had just poked through the soil."

"I'm with Rosalie. All beets should be pulled out and never replanted." I loved the way his eyes crinkled in the corners when he smiled.

"Not a lover of beets?"

"Not even a smidge."

"Good to know."

Emmett pulled me to him. I looked into his eyes as he wrapped me tightly in his arms. We kissed again for what seemed an eternity.

He cupped my face in his hands, his thumbs brushing my temples. Our gazes locked, lost in the depths of our souls. I placed my hands on his chest.

"You've become the light of my life, Daisy."

"And you for me." We embraced, and he rested his cheek on my forehead, his arms around me. I could have remained in the safety of his arms forever.

But then, he stepped back and touched my forehead. "You're very warm, Daisy. Have you checked your temp lately?"

Willa Grace

I wore my best blue shirtwaist dress for my day with Henry, crimped my brunette locks and newly trimmed bangs, and borrowed a navy cloche hat with a white ribbon with a matching white purse to complement my white sling-back shoes. I didn't think I looked half bad. In fact, in the mirror I saw the city girl I'd hoped to be.

Henry, who looked dapper in a belted gray tweed jacket over gray trousers and black fedora, picked me up in a taxi. For a country boy with no interest in the city, he was about to fit right in. Just maybe I could change his mind and get him away from the farm. It would be wonderful to have such a good friend living close by.

I feared I might explode with excitement before we arrived.

Henry and I were dropped off at the Avenue of Flags. I was awestruck and had to keep reminding myself to close my gaping mouth. The fair's theme, "A Century of Progress," was well on display, with exhibitions showing the latest and greatest for nearly every aspect of life. The Sears Building greeted us right away, so tall and sleek. There was color everywhere, and the level of excitement in the crowd of visitors pushed us along.

Strolling through the Meet Me In Paris building, I thought I was right there, taking my time along the streets of Gay Paree!

"I'm going there one day, Henry."

Henry laughed.

"I mean it. Someday, I'll be eating pastries and sipping wine in a sidewalk café. Mark my words."

He nodded, grinning, but I could tell he thought there was a good chance that would never happen. 'You just watch,' I thought to myself.

Then, oh my, a rollercoaster. I goaded Henry into taking me. Daisy would have loved it. My heart thudded like our old tractor as we ascended the track, but then I screamed like a banshee as I held my hat with one hand and Henry's arm with the other. My fingers dug into his sleeve so hard I was afraid I was hurting him, but I couldn't let go. Henry also held onto his hat, whooped, and laughed the whole time. I liked hearing him laugh.

We enjoyed the Czechoslovakia Pavilion immensely and learned more about our shared heritage. I thought of how Mamka and Tata would have been so impressed. The music and food were simply the best. We gorged ourselves on cabbage rolls and kolache. I was experiencing it for my whole family and couldn't wait to tell them.

With full bellies, we then went to see Admiral Byrd's Polar Ship, which he took to the Antarctic. It was a wonder to see a piece of history and think of the spirit of adventure in every person aboard that ship. The Goodyear blimp was also at the fair. Aside from skyscrapers, I'd never seen anything so massive. I couldn't imagine that big lug floating in the sky, light as a feather.

Henry enjoyed the automobile pavilions best. Packard, then Ford, and General Motors, where we saw an actual production line. At the Chrysler Building, a real track was built to show the testing involved for their products. We cheered and clapped as Plymouths raced around the circle, over hills, skidding around corners, and reaching speeds over fifty miles per hour. It's all Henry could talk about for the rest of the afternoon.

After a while, our feet were killing us, and we found ourselves at the Skyride, transporting people up and over, from one end of the fair to the other. Why, it was taller than any buildings in Chicago, all of which we could see in the distance.

"I will, if you will," I grinned at Henry.

He took a deep breath and bobbed his head. "Okay, Willa Grace, but I won't forgive you if we die."

"Sure you will." I nudged him playfully.

The view from the Skyride was spectacular. I didn't know where to look first. Chicago stretched out below and beyond. Berwyn was off in the distance in one direction, and the great lake of Michigan shimmered blue and sparkling in the other. At one point, I pointed out the Chicago Board of Trade Building, and when I looked back at Henry, he was smiling at me, not following the point of my finger at all.

At the end of the day, we took our time walking out. Henry bought us each an Official World's Fair in Pictures booklet as souvenirs.

"To remember our special day," he said, then he offered me the crook of his arm, which I gratefully accepted. I held the booklet tight to my chest, looking forward to showing it off to everyone I knew.

"Oh, Henry, I can't wait to tell Daisy about our day. Now, do you see why I love the city?"

The smile slid off his face, and I knew his plan, if that's what the day was, had backfired for him. Despite Daisy's illness and Jode's betrayal, I still saw my life in the city.

The ride back to the boarding house was quiet, both of us exhausted. Still, I invited him to visit on the porch if he had time.

Henry excused the taxi.

"It's been a glorious day, hasn't it?" I swung my purse with my right hand, my left in the crook of his arm. He held onto both of our booklets.

"Uh, huh." He looked up at the stars above. "Look at the Milky Way up there so high."

I followed his eyes. "Sure is a miracle."

"Saw lots of those today." His gaze met mine. He indicated the bench under the maple tree in the front yard rather than the porch. "Let's take a seat." We sat, and he handed me my booklet.

The evening was warm for October, and the trees had passed their peak in terms of color. Brown, dried leaves crunched underfoot and drifted down around us. A full moon made a milky glow around us.

"This was so nice of you, Henry. It was just what I needed. You have no idea." We sat shoulder to shoulder, arm to arm, thigh to thigh.

I wanted to lean my head on his shoulder, but that couldn't happen. He would take it all wrong.

"I was happy to do it, Willa Grace. Emery hasn't been the same without you."

I looked down at the book, unable to look him in the eye. I knew what was coming. I had felt it when he let the cabbie go, and was sorry I'd invited him to stay. While my feelings for him had grown in just these past few hours, he and I could never be.

Henry was an honorable man with a deep sense of right and wrong. He would not want a woman who had lost her innocence to someone else, a girl who'd been pregnant, never mind the outcome of that pregnancy, and I couldn't blame him for that.

And I couldn't lie to him. Henry may not know of my mistake with Jode, but I would. He deserved better than lies. He deserved better than me.

"Willa Grace, I…"

"Henry, wait," I looked down at the booklet in my hands. Considering that I was about to tell him everything, I worried he'd feel I'd used him to go to the fair when I could have told him much earlier. I'd pulled him along by not telling him. It was childish of me to take his gift of a trip to the fair, knowing how he felt about me. I didn't like myself much at that moment. And in a few moments, he wouldn't either.

"Let me say my piece. Please?" He gazed at me with those puppy-dog eyes.

My heart raced and my knees felt weak. I was glad to be sitting. "No, Henry, I can't let you go any further. There's something…"

"Willa Grace?" Mrs. Voss had stepped out onto the porch.

"Yes, Missus Voss. We're right over here. I'll be in shortly."

"You had an urgent phone call, dear."

NINETEEN

Daisy

Everything had been going so well.

I had an ideal roommate in my Junebug. My time at the San would have been torture without her. She was younger than I, but that never seemed to matter. Then, just like water to a flame, her life was snuffed out. June was gone. Life could be so unfair.

And I was in love. I had never known the depths of true love until Emmett. He made me feel as though nothing could ever spoil what we had, and the future was ours. We'd get clean bills of health, I'd meet his family and he'd meet mine, we'd plan a wedding, and the rest would unfold in the easy joy of a home of our own and babies we'd spoil.

I don't really know when my health started to slide downhill.

I'd suffered night sweats here and there for a few weeks. Those mornings, my temperature spiked when I checked, but only for a bit, not enough to alert Nelsy. The rest of the day, I felt normal enough. Although looking back, I wasn't eating or sleeping well, but in my defense, I was in love and then in mourning.

Since June's death, I had the room to myself, and that was for the best. I cried buckets every night, and I'm afraid I would have been terribly unfriendly to whoever they put in her bed. Thankfully, her things were cleared out while I was out for a walk with Emmett. June's family left me the pink rabbit she'd kept on her bed.

The nurses were sympathetic, as were the friends June and I had made at the San. I tried to accept all the kindness shown to me, but I was angry and so, so sad.

Emmett took me right to Doc's office after he suspected I had a fever. I was run through all the usual tests, an exam, a sputum smear, and X-rays. The next morning, Doc came to see me, closing the door behind him.

He took a deep breath before he began.

I now had tiny nodules throughout both lungs, my spleen and liver were enlarged, and he detected a slight crackling in my breathing. I knew this was bad. I'd learned a lot about TB in the last two years.

"Miliary Tuberculosis," he said, then waited for the words to sink in.

I'd never heard of that. "I don't understand. I…"

"Miliary TB travels through the bloodstream to attack other organs, Daisy." He cleared his throat. "As it turns out, your kidneys are the battleground of the disease."

"My kidneys? How could that be? How do we fix that?"

As gently as he could, he continued. "There's nothing to be done." He put a hand on mine. "Your kidneys would eventually give in to the disease."

I was terrified to ask. "Then wh…then…,"

"Daisy, I'm afraid there is no cure."

"But, what about fresh air and good food?"

He shook his head, then explained the progression of the disease.

My ears buzzed, my lungs refused air, and I fell back onto my pillows. I needed my mother, and I needed Willa Grace.

I was going to die. My God, he was telling me I was going to die.

I looked around my, our, room. Soon, it would be empty of the both of us, June and me.

Death had always been hiding in the background of our lives at the San. Rarely talked about, but it's there in the shadows, around every corner. Someone quietly dies, and someone new is quietly brought in. We don't usually dwell on the deaths because the next one might be our own. TB, I just learned, can turn its ugly face your way when you least expect it.

June and I had spoken of her version of heaven. She had a strong belief in God and was sure what awaited was a place of light, love, and all good things. I hoped she was right, but I wasn't so sure.

What God would take another child from two such wonderful parents as Mamka and Tata? I didn't know of a sweeter mother than the one I could call mine. Causing her such pain was unthinkable. Tata worked so hard to take care of us all. His gruffness hid a tender heart, and watching him try to be strong after losing Teddy was heartbreaking. Now, it was my turn to be his heartbreak.

And Willa Grace—she was the strongest person I knew. She would help them all move on, without a doubt. But I could tell by her letters that she blamed herself for my illness. No matter what I say, I know she will never forgive herself.

Emmett.

After Doc left that day and gave me the diagnosis, I sent a message to Emmett, asking him to meet me under the oak tree behind the cottages where we usually met when we were able.

Emmett jogged up, smiling, and planted a kiss on my cheek. I pulled him to me with my fingers curled into the material of his shirt. My face pressed into his chest. After a moment, he put his hands on my upper arms and held me away from him. The moonlight played off the planes of his face. I ran my gaze over his features, memorizing every detail.

He angled his head with concern in his eyes. "What's wrong?"

I put my hands on either side of his face.

"I have something to tell you," I whispered.

He lightly kissed my neck and put his arms around me. "Tell me."

I told him of my diagnosis, and as soon as the words left my mouth, he dropped down onto the cold ground. I put a hand on the back of his head. He slammed his fists into the grass before abruptly standing.

"NO! This can't be, Daisy. It can't." He paced back and forth, sheer terror on his face.

I hugged myself hard as the tears came.

Emmett grabbed me by the arms. "We'll leave, just like that. They can't stop us. This isn't a jail. We'll have that life we talked about."

"But Emmett, that won't matter. We can't. We won't."

He hugged me briefly, then held me at arm's length. "Let's get married. Tonight. I've got money. We'll pack up our things and get the hell out of here."

"Emmett, no." I shook my head as tears continued to flow. "It's no use."

"Don't say that. We love each other so much, we can outrun anything."

"Not this. Doc knows what he's talking about. I don't know how long I have, but I'm going back to my family. I need to be with them. You're not out of the woods with TB yourself, Emmett. You need to do what Doc tells you, get better, and live your life."

"What life do I have without you?"

"You'll find a life. You will. You've got so much to live for."

"I'll go to the farm with you."

"NO, Emmett. Please don't make this harder for me. I don't want to see you before I go. I want this to be our goodbye."

That hurt him, and I was sorry, but there was more to come.

"I don't want us writing, either. It will be too hard." I felt cold to say that, but I couldn't bear to think of his seeing me die letter by letter, and I couldn't say I was fine when we both knew I wouldn't be.

He turned away from me, shoulders slumped in surrender, his arms around his middle.

I'd never considered life cruel, but as I walked away from Emmett, the sound of his sobs following me, I knew life could be a son of a bitch.

Willa Grace

I raced across the lawn, up the porch stairs, and down the hall to the phone, leaving Henry to wait on the porch. Mrs. Voss followed me to the hall table with the phone. The message she'd written down said 'call right away' with the phone number of Statesan.

I stood there shaking. I'd expected to see a message from Missus Havelka asking me to call her as something was wrong back home, but it was the sanitarium.

Oh God, no.

Mrs. Voss took the receiver from my shaking hand, dialed, handed it back, and went to the kitchen, where I could see her waiting inside the entry.

After two rings, a nurse answered.

"It's Willa Grace Maruska," I said, my voice shaking. "I'm returning a call. My sister, Daisy, is in room 302 and…"

"I am one of the night assistants. I will transfer you to her floor."

"Well then, can I speak with a nurse?"

"Yes, I'll put you through to the nurse on that floor. Hold on."

Those were the longest minutes of my short life.

"Nurse Fromm."

"I'm calling about Daisy Maruska. I'm her sister."

"Doctor Thompson needs to speak to you, but is unavailable this evening. He tried you earlier."

"What's happened?" My voice was a shrill form of itself.

"You will have to speak with Doctor Thompson. Your sister is resting now on the critical care floor, and I cannot disturb her."

"Let me talk to my sister!"

"I can't do that, Miss."

I looked down the hall to Henry and shook my head. He came to stand at my side.

"I will come right away," I choked out the words.

"No, that's not advisable until you speak with the doctor."

"Is she going to be okay?"

"That's for the doctor to discuss with you. You can be sure he will call again tomorrow morning."

"I…I have to work. I will give you my number there."

Once I replaced the receiver, I looked up into Henry's eyes.

"She's in critical care again." I could barely get the words out and collapsed into Henry's arms. He held me tight. Mrs. Voss brought a chair.

Poor Henry. He so wanted to help, but all he could do was calm me down as best he could before leaving for the night. I lay in my bed and shook all night.

The next day, I was afraid to focus on anything other than work, so I poured every bit of myself into baking, willing the phone to ring, yet terrified of hearing it.

"My, you are a ball of energy this morning," Rose said, standing over me as I scrubbed at a dime-sized bit of tar on the white linoleum. My hand was sore, so I sat back on my haunches and massaged my aching bones.

"Are you complaining, Boss?"

Rose chuckled and put a hand under my chin. "What's wrong?"

"Daisy's sick again. I'm waiting for a call."

Rose drew her lips into a thin line and nodded. "Not good."

At ten o'clock, the phone finally rang. I held back while Rose answered. It was Dr. Thompson.

"Hello, Doctor."

"Unfortunately, Miss Maruska, Daisy is not doing well."

The doctor went on about tests and X-rays. All I wanted to know was if she was going to be okay. To hell with his doctor-talk.

"Daisy's tuberculosis has spread to her kidneys through her bloodstream. We've done all we can for her here. It is her wish to return home. Back to her parents."

"Are you saying she's going to…," I couldn't say it.

"Most likely, she will. I'm so sorry to have to tell you this. Daisy has been a ray of sunshine here. Beloved by everyone. Her replica of the Christmas Seal poster will bring much-needed attention to Statesan and raise a lot of money for the Wisconsin Anti-Tuberculosis Association. We will always be grateful to her."

"No, Daisy will beat this. She has to." Panic, such as I'd never experienced, ripped through my heart. I could barely hold the receiver from shaking.

"We can't stop tuberculosis once it invades the rest of the body. I wish we could, and maybe someday we will. For now…there's no good response to this. She's asked to go home, and we are honoring that request. She is weak but able to travel."

"This is so unfair. She's only twenty." An awful sob broke from my lips. Rose came behind me with a hand on my shoulder. My face was a wash of tears.

The doctor continued. "She needs you to be strong, Willa Grace. All of you need to be strong for her. I will send your parents a letter explaining what has happened, what precautions will be needed, and what they can expect."

The doctor allowed me to cry and catch my breath.

"Is she contagious?"

"Daisy has been schooled in the sanitary measures needed to avoid the spread. Contrary to what most people think, tuberculosis is not easily spread from one person to another. For that to happen, Daisy would need to have more than casual contact with someone for an extended period. She knows how to take care of herself. Take your cues from her."

"How are we to transport her?"

"You or your family will have to make arrangements, but she can travel by bus, car, or train as long as she can rest. She is welcome to stay here at Statesan as long as she needs until you can transport her. We will help in any way we can."

I thanked him and we ended the call.

Rose quickly put out the 'Closed' sign as I rocked back and forth on the chair while the gravity of the situation took hold.

Suddenly, I jumped up and screamed. I dug my fingers into my hair and pulled.

"This can't be, Rose. It can't be." I shook my head from side to side as though I could dislodge the words I'd heard the doctor say.

Rose reached out, but my anger couldn't, and wouldn't, be contained by an embrace. I had enough wits to avoid destroying Rose's shop, but it wasn't easy.

Then I stopped.

"I have to tell my parents. How in the world do I do that? How do I tell my mother she will lose another child?" I shook. I gasped for air. I fought the urge to run down the street screaming.

"I don't know." Rose started to cry, and Varina, who'd stopped in to decorate cakes, came running and put her arms around me.

I sat on another chair in the corner of the shop by the front window and looked up at her. My heart was banging so hard in my chest, I feared it would explode.

"I have to take Daisy home, Rose. I have to take her home to die."

With balled fists to my mouth, and tears running down my arms, all I could see was the vision of my sister lying in a sanitarium. Was she in pain? Was she afraid? Was she cursing me and my big dreams? Of course, she was.

A knock on the glass had the three of us turn toward the door. There stood Henry. He hadn't left. I ran to the door, yanked it open, and flew into his arms.

TWENTY

Daisy

"They're here." Nelsy came into the room with the saddest of eyes. She stood by the door behind a wheelchair. We were back in the room that June and I shared so I could pack my things. What didn't fit in my suitcase, I gave to others.

Our gazes met, and an unspoken love passed between us.

"I'd love to see your face." I tried to smile.

Nelsy took off her mask, showing me her pretty brown eyes, with a dusting of freckles across her creamy skin, her short red hair neatly curled. I wanted to remember her face.

Nelsy replaced her mask, wheeled the chair around, and helped me into it. It had only been two days since my diagnosis, but my body responded to the illness quickly. Maybe it was the shock of it taking its toll. It took some effort to pull myself up and pivot into the chair.

My temperature wasn't all that high, but I was weak. I knew I'd lost weight, notably when I put on the same dress I had worn the day I arrived at Statesan. It seemed fitting to wear the same on my way out.

It was a cold November day, so Nelsy helped me into my brown coat, a blue knit hat on my head, and white gloves on my hands. And, of course, a white mask to cover my mouth and nose.

I saw Willa Grace and Henry waiting outside the front door as we reached the reception area. I hadn't seen my sister in over a year. She looked different somehow. Grown up. She waited next to Henry, who came forward and held the door.

Willa Grace and I locked eyes. "It's good to see you, Willsy."

"Oh, Daisy-do."

My eyes blurred from tears building. Willa Grace faltered against Henry a moment, then came forward and bent over me, circling me in her arms. We clung together for a short time until Henry came forward with a hand on my shoulder.

"The cabbie needs to leave," he whispered. "I'm sorry."

"Hello, Henry." I looked up at him as Willa Grace stepped back.

Henry nodded. "Hello, Daisy."

Nelsy put her hands on my shoulders from behind and kissed the top of my head.

"Goodbye, Miss Daisy. I'm going to miss you. God bless."

"I love you, Nelsy. Thank you for everything." I leaned my head against her hand and covered her other hand with my own.

"I love..." I heard her sniffle, and then she left.

Henry wheeled me to the taxi he'd hired to get us to the train. He purchased our train tickets home. If Willa Grace didn't marry him, I'd kick her across Price County if I could.

Just as Willa Grace was about to help me to stand, I heard my name called and turned.

Emmett stood at the corner of the sanitarium, masked, handsome as ever. My heart nearly split in two.

"Emmett." I barely got his name out. Is it possible for a heart to soar and crash at the same time? He came forward holding a small, pink rectangular box tied with a red ribbon.

"I know you didn't want to see me before you left, Daisy, but I couldn't help it." He stood before me. "I couldn't." I sat back down.

"Willsy, Henry, this is Emmett."

My heart broke that this, this awful circumstance, was how I introduced him to my sister and Henry. No one shook hands. No one hugged. Goddamned TB.

He knelt before my chair and handed me the box. I held the weightless box in my gloved hands as though it were a precious jewel.

"I bought this for you on my last visit to see my parents. I was waiting for a special time to give it to you." His mask was thoroughly soaked. He removed it from his beautiful face.

I stared at him, tracing his face with my eyes, never wanting to forget this man I loved so. I touched the side of his face. He covered my hand with his own and kissed it.

He put his other hand on my knee. "Are you going to open it?"

"Oh, Emmett." I closed my eyes and held the box to my heart. With a deep breath and a clearing of my throat, I tugged the ribbon, opened the box, and gasped. It was a tiny gold locket in the shape of a heart on a gold chain. I ran my finger over the filigree covering the heart.

"It's beautiful. I will treasure this…always."

"Open it. Open the heart."

Inside was a small picture of him on the left and me on the right, both of us smiling as though all was right in the world. As though nothing but joy were ahead for us.

"Here," Willa Grace said, "let me help you." She put it around my neck while Henry and Emmett exchanged hellos.

I looked up at Emmett, and we locked eyes. So much passed between us. The life we could have had, the babies we'd have made, the old age we'd enjoy surrounded by love.

He took my hand, and I brought it to my masked, moist cheek, feeling his strong hand against my warm face.

Finally, it was time to say goodbye so we would not miss our train.

Emmett bent over me, pulled my mask down, and kissed me sweetly on the lips. My soul drank him in, his musky smell, and how his nose brushed mine. My heart shattered.

Willa Grace

Watching Daisy say goodbye to her Emmett was the most heartwrenching scene I'd ever witnessed. As we loaded Daisy into the taxi, Emmett caught my gaze and motioned for me to step aside. When I did, he slipped a piece of paper into my hand without Daisy seeing. He asked me to write and keep him abreast of her condition. I promised I would. Daisy had asked him not to write, which I thought was wrong of her. Maybe his letters would keep her spirits up in the months ahead. But we had to respect her wishes.

The trip home was long and hard on her. We sat in the back of the train car to avoid attention and make others wary of Daisy's presence. Her mask caused the stares of others. People were terrified of TB.

I leaned my forehead against the window and watched the world pass. I felt like I was in a fog. Henry and I were bringing Daisy home to die. That thought repeated throughout my brain until I thought I would go crazy with it. I sat alongside Daisy and, when she wasn't dozing with her head on my shoulder, we held hands. Henry sat in front of us and would turn now and then to check on us.

I was so grateful for Henry. I don't know how I'd have managed without him.

The sweet twitter of a toddler's giggle caught my attention. A mother with her young daughter sat a few rows ahead of us and across the aisle. The mother entertained the girl with a chubby baby doll. Her mother called her Shelly.

Shelly peeked at me over the top of the seat. I put my hands to my face and played peek-a-boo with her. Shelly bounced on the seat and giggled at me. Then her mother turned her head to see what was amusing her daughter so. The woman smiled at me, saw Daisy's mask, and abruptly pulled Shelly down.

Tears stung, but I understood. If I ever had the chance to have a perfect baby girl like Shelly, I would protect her with everything in me.

The thought was startling. I didn't want children, did I? Something inside me was shifting. I couldn't put a name to it, but it was.

I looked back at Henry, who had his nose buried in a newspaper. What would he think if he knew my awful secret? I should have told him before we spent the day together at the fair, but I selfishly wanted that time to enjoy life, to shed the worry over Daisy, to shed my sadness and shame over the pregnancy. I also knew I wanted to be with him. I needed it. Needed his friendship, his nonjudgment, and… was there more?

Shelly's mother quietly sang her to sleep. Daisy should be singing to her own little one. Daisy would never know what it was like to be a mother.

Finally, the train pulled into the Phillips station, so different from where we'd come. Our brother George was waiting for us, looking tall now at sixteen with his brown hair slicked back. It seemed so strange that it had been so long since we'd seen him. We'd left to help our parents through a downturn in the milk market, which was now past, and stayed because of Daisy's illness.

George couldn't hide the shock on his face when he saw Daisy.

Big, strong George looked at me with watery eyes. I nodded in encouragement for him to come forward, that it was all right, she wasn't going to break.

"Daisy," George gingerly moved nearer, "can I hug you?"

"You better." Daisy opened her arms wide. She and George embraced. "You're taller than me now, Georgie."

George stepped back, wiping a tear from his eye. "I'm taller than Tata, too. I don't think he likes that none." He quickly swiped at a tear that slipped down his cheek.

Daisy looked around at what she could see of Phillips. "Why look at the old town. Not a thing has changed." Along Lake Street, people came and went. Shop doors opened and shut. Automobiles sputtered. No one was aware that our world had just stopped.

I stepped forward, hugged George firmly, and whispered in his ear, "Strength, Georgie." He nodded against my shoulder, then stepped back and extended a hand to Henry. They exchanged a few words while Daisy's eyes drank it all in.

"Well, hey," George said with a wide grin. "Wait till you see the jalopy I bought." George angled his head to the side and turned.

Waiting on the other side of the train station, a brown automobile with a few hard miles on it, as Tata would say, waited to take us home.

George proudly held out an arm. "What do you think?"

"A Ford Model A Coupe. That's slick," Henry said. Daisy and I oohed and ahhed.

"It's a '29. I bought 'er off a guy over in Lugerville. Got a good deal, of course it's five years old, but I have been working on it. You girls will have to crawl into the rumble seat." His eyes widened. "Oh, Daisy, I don't think you'll be able to climb into that. Shit! I'm sorry."

"I'd rather sit up front so I can keep an eye on your driving." Daisy grinned.

George relaxed. "Probably a good idea." With a hand, he helped her into the seat.

"I'd rather sit next to Willa Grace any day," Henry said and offered me a hand up and in.

George handed us our bags to hold on our laps. "I've been tweaking on the motor, Henry. Took 'er out on County D a few days ago and nearly got it up to sixty."

"No kidding!" Henry was impressed.

"Sixty? I don't believe it," I said. "Think you can do it again?" Daisy's head shot around.

"Willa Grace! No! Georgie, don't you dare." Daisy said, but I could see a bit of excitement in her eyes. "Oh, okay."

"Nah, I can't do that with you two in the rear."

Henry laughed. "What kind of horsepower you got?

"Forty. If I keep working her, I think I can get the speed up to sixty-five." He got in the driver's seat.

"Holy smokes, Georgie." I reached around through the driver's side window and patted him on the shoulder. "Better not let Mamka know that. She'll have Tata tan your hide for being so reckless."

"Hell no," George called back. "This is our secret."

"Looks like a fine vehicle. I may have to get myself one." Henry winked at me, and a blush warmed my neck.

With a whoop and a holler, we were off. Henry and I held onto our hats.

George delivered us safely, being careful to slow down once he reached Hickory Road. We pulled into the barnyard, and the whole family came rushing out. George parked in front of the porch. Ranger circled the group, leaping and barking, not wanting to be left out.

Henry and George helped me, then Daisy, down. Our younger brothers and sisters rushed forward, wrapping us all in their love and welcome, everyone happy and talking at once. Mamka must have told them to put on their happy faces to greet us because there wasn't a sad frown in the bunch. Or, I wondered, maybe Mamka hadn't told the others the gravity of the situation.

Mamka came through, held her arms wide, and wrapped them around Daisy. At first, Mamka's eyes were closed, tears seeping out the sides, then she looked behind Daisy at me. I nodded, sharing the pain she felt.

Tata came to stand before me, holding out a hand for a shake. A shake! To hell with that. I grabbed him, and slowly, his arms came around me. Loosely, but that was our father. He nodded as we parted, unable to look me in the eye, and swallowing hard the tears he would never let us see. "Řad tě m'am doma." Good to have you home.

Mamka held out an arm to me, and I joined the embrace.

Tata stood behind the others who still peppered us with questions.

I stood back and watched, trying hard not to sink to the ground with emotion. It was so wonderful to see everyone, but we were here for Daisy, and my heart was breaking. Henry put an arm around me, and I let him keep it there.

Everyone had changed somewhat. Mamka's hair was completely white now at forty. Tata still held himself tall and proud, but with a few extra pounds around the middle. George looked thicker, more like a man. Addie, now a teenager with little boobs poking out behind her blouse. Joey had grown so I hardly recognized him. Then he stuck his tongue out at me. It made me laugh. Albert ran about the yard on his own. He was nearly four, after all, and no longer hanging on Mamka's skirt. And Rosalie tottered after Ranger. She was a beauty at two with cherries for cheeks and a halo of blonde curls.

Mamka pulled me close and whispered in my ear. "I missed you, my strong girl. Thank you for bringing her home."

"It's good to be here, Mamka." I meant that with all my heart.

She held me at arm's length. "My city girl's come back and I am happy for that." Then her chin trembled. I squeezed her hand, knowing the bitter sweetness of that sentiment.

"You both look so different," Addie said. "You look like city girls with your hair short."

Tata looked us over. "Hmph. Adeline, you're keeping yours long. Not all my girls need to look like boys."

Addie's smile dropped into a frown, and she shook her head. Everyone laughed.

"Where's Issy?" I asked.

"Uh, oh," Addie's freckled face drew back, and she rolled her eyes.

Mamka and Tata shared a look of disapproval.

"She ran off and got married. Her new husband took a job in the mines on the Iron Range." Mamka shook her head. "This only happened last week, before we received the news of your coming. She didn't tell either of you what she was planning?"

We both answered her no. I looked at Daisy, and she was clearly disappointed, which flared the flame of anger in me. Issy could be so selfish.

"No, she didn't. She's only seventeen." I fumed. Issy had always been a challenge.

"Is it the Janko boy? She'd mentioned him in her letters," Daisy said.

Mamka nodded.

"The mines are a good place for that bum," Tata said, kicking the dirt.

"Now, Isaac," Mamka admonished. "We barely know him, so seeing her go has been hard."

"Maybe she'll come for a visit soon," Daisy said.

She'd better, I thought. *Little shit.*

"Let's go in," Mamka said. "You too, Henry. Come." Mamka shooed us all inside. Everything looked the same as the day we'd left. I found that comforting. I know Daisy did.

Addie piped up, "We have a surprise for you, Daisy."

"You do?"

"Come on!" Addie grabbed her hand and pulled her forward toward a new door off the kitchen.

"Careful, Addie," I said and hurried forward in case Daisy would lose her balance.

"I'm fine," Daisy said, her eyes telling me to ease up. "What's this?"

Mamka put an arm around Tata, a show of affection we rarely saw.

To Daisy, Mamka said, "Your Tata and brothers built a bedroom for you."

"You don't want to be going up those stairs all day and night," Tata said, trying to sound gruff and matter-of-fact but not succeeding.

Daisy opened the door and stuck her head in. "It's beautiful."

Tata blustered, then said, "Wasn't me alone."

"Half the men in the neighborhood came to help us," Georgie said.

"I even helped," Joey said.

"I don't believe that." I mussed his hair, and he took a swipe at me. As the others gathered outside the door, I followed Daisy into her new bedroom.

"Thank you," Daisy's voice hitched. The walls were unfinished, but a small window faced south with pink floral curtains gathered on either side. A single bed was against the wall with a pink chenille spread in a floral pattern, a white pillowcase with embroidered wildflowers along the edge, a dark wood dresser along one wall, and Mamka's rocking chair in the corner.

As I went to inspect the window, and I turned back, with Daisy's back to our family, her gaze met mine, and I knew she was thinking, *'This will be where I die.'*

I closed my eyes, turned back to the window, quickly composed myself, and followed Daisy out of the room.

"It's perfect." Daisy embraced our father. Tata faltered at the emotion of it all as he hugged her back.

Mamka quietly moved to the back of everyone and put a hanky to her eyes.

George said, "It went up in just one day. Got me thinking I'll build my own house someday."

Addie pushed forward. "Patsy Cummings brought the spread for your bed, I made the pillowcase, Sissy and Edie sewed the curtains, and Brendel's brought a bed they no longer use,"

Mamka slipped away into their room.

"The inside walls will be finished shortly," Tata said.

"Thank you all." Daisy suddenly looked very tired. I looked for Henry. He'd stepped outside.

"I'll put your things away," I said to Daisy, then to our siblings, "Give Daisy some time to get situated. Scoot." I flapped my hands at them, and they drifted away. Then Daisy reached for my hand.

"We'll do this together. I promise," I squeezed her hand.

"What about your life in the city? I won't have you give that up for me."

"To hell with the city. Too goddamn many people, and it stinks. Give me good country air any day." I grinned.

"You're a shitty liar, Willa Grace." Her eyes crinkled at the corners.

"Cussing like a sailor, are we?"

"Get used to it." She sighed, slumping her shoulders. "I need some time." She took a ragged breath, and her eyes got watery.

"Lie down, take a nap. I may do that, too." I hugged her and gently shut the door.

Mamka was weeping quietly in their bedroom, holding Rosalie on her lap. Everyone else had gone outside. I put my arms around them and squeezed, then took Rosalie outside, giving Mamka time as well.

I bounced Rosalie on my hip, loving the feel of her against me. I went to Henry, who was outside visiting with Tata. As I approached, Tata left for the barn.

"After all this, I bet you'll think twice about going to the city again," I teased.

Henry reached out and offered Rosalie a finger, which she grabbed. I bounced her a few times and kissed her downy, golden curls.

"I'd do it all again," Henry said. "You know I would."

"Yes, I do."

Rosalie wiggled from my hold, and I put her down. Ranger came up, and she wrapped her chubby arms around his neck.

"You saved the day, Henry. Thank you."

"You've got a tough time ahead. Let me know what I can do." His gaze held mine until I looked away. "I would do anything for you. For you all."

"I know."

Mamka came out just then and invited Henry to stay for supper. He was anxious to check on his farm, so George drove him home.

The family did their best to keep the mood light at supper that night. Daisy and I heard the latest gossip and township news. Everyone spoke at once while platters of chicken and dumplings, bowls of gravy, and cooked carrots rounded the table. Laughter was plentiful, and Mamka treated us to a raspberry cobbler with fresh cream.

Finally, Daisy had to beg off to get some sleep. Tata, the boys, and Addie went to do the milking. Mamka and I cleaned up and then put Albert and Rosalie down for the night.

Mamka quietly crept into Daisy's room. She was still awake, and I could hear them talking. I stood just outside the door, my back against the wall, eavesdropping.

Mamka offered to close the curtains for Daisy.

"Please leave them open. I'd like to see the moon and stars if I can. Also, could you open the window? I'm so used to fresh air now. I feel stuffy otherwise."

There was a short silence, and then Mamka said, "Would you like me to sing you a song like I did when you were little?"

"I would love that," Daisy replied.

I heard the springs of the bed squeak and knew Mamka had sat down beside her.

Then, our beautiful Mamka quietly sang a Czech lullaby.

> Sleep, little baby, sleep,
> Close your eyes,
> When you wake in the morning,
> Your Mamka will be here.

I sank to the floor, head to my chest, and quietly sobbed.

TWENTY-ONE

Daisy

"Is there something I can do for you? Anything?" Willa Grace sat with me in the yard. November blew in cold and gray. We had a light dusting of snow, and the leaves had been whipped from their branches with the bluster.

"I'm fine." I pulled a woolen lap blanket over my legs and tightened my coat.

"What I mean is, is there anything you always wanted to do that you haven't?"

I tilted my head and thought. "I always wanted to learn to drive a car."

Willa Grace pulled in her chin, brows furrowed. "What? Drive a car? That's right, you never have, have you? You know how to drive the tractor. Won't be much different."

"I suppose not, but learning would have been nice. To have the freedom to take off down the road. I wish I could have done that."

"Hmm, you still could." Willa Grace's eyes lit up. I could see the gears turning in her head.

"I'm not sure I have the strength to press the pedals." I shrugged and held my palms up.

Willa Grace stood and held out her hand. "Come on. We'll figure something out."

Luckily, George was home from working in the woods. "You betcha, Daisy!" He was excited to have something he could do for me. We crossed the barnyard, and they loaded me in the passenger seat.

From the driver's seat, George showed me how to work the pedals and the shift. I didn't think I could do it, but I had more strength than I thought. When he felt I was ready, he drove Willa Grace and me down the road and back to watch him. Double-clutching was tricky, but I managed to do well enough. Willa Grace drove up and down a few times as well.

Then, the real test. George slid into the middle, I took the driver's seat, and Willa Grace squished into the passenger side.

"You can do it, Daisy. Just concentrate," George said.

After a quick review, I released the handbrake, hit the clutch, performed a herky-jerky shift from neutral to first, and we were off down Hickory Lane. In moments, I shifted into second, then third, and we cruised at twenty-five down the dirt road, dust billowing behind.

Oh, the wind in my hair, the adventure the open road offered, and the feeling of freedom tugged at my weary heart. I wanted to drive down that road so far and so fast that TB could never catch up to me.

I whooped and put a fist of triumph out the window as the last surviving purple asters, white yarrow, and yellow goldenrod swished and bowed at our passing.

"Keep your hands on the wheel," George advised.

"You're doing great, Daisy!" Willa Grace shouted.

Suddenly, a partridge flew up from the ditch, startling me. I jerked the wheel, and the car veered to the road's edge. I screamed as we clipped Mrs. Schmidlekofer's mailbox. With a smash and a crunch, the metal box flew through the air as the wooden post cracked and splintered into pieces.

"Pull 'er back on the road!" George hollered. "Push in the brake!"

When the Ford finally stopped in a swirl of dust, we sat silently for a few seconds before Willa Grace said, "Well, shit, that was something."

George looked at us both. "Old biddy Schmidlkofer's going to dirty her unders when she sees this." We all looked out the back window to see the old woman's rusty mailbox crumpled and what was left of the post alongside, then turned to face each other.

I was the first to break into a giggle, and then they joined me, and we laughed uproariously.

Oh, this was the most glorious bit of trouble. Then I thought better of it.

"Georgie, I hope I didn't ruin your car."

"Naw." George waved a hand. "Ain't no damn worse than I'll do sooner or later."

Willa Grace angled a thumb over her shoulder. "Who's going to fess up and tell her what we did?"

I cleared my throat and swung my gaze to my siblings. We stared at each other, waiting for one of us to offer to come clean to crabby Mrs. Schmidlkofer.

I squared my shoulders, raised my brows, and said, "I will. What's the worst she could do to me?"

Dead silence followed. Georgie was red as a beet until Willa Grace started to giggle. Once again, we broke out in laughter. The three of us laughed until we cried. It was a memory I knew I would cherish for as long as I could.

On December 1st, the Milwaukee Journal published my picture—for heaven's sake, it took up an entire page. Neighbors stopped by in droves to congratulate me. Most remained out in the barnyard as they feared my disease, but it was nice of them to come. Cards and letters flowed in from all the little communities in our area.

I was made to feel like a celebrity, and I did my best to put on a good masked face and accept it all. A reporter from the Phillips Bee came out to the house to do a story on me. Of course, I stayed on the porch, and he sat outside the window. It was just another cruel twist of fate that I received all this attention, but it did give me something else to think about. I wished fate would take the knife out of my heart and leave me be.

Doc Thompson sent a card of thanks for bringing attention to the plight of the Statesan patients and the influx of donations it was sure to generate. I also heard from Olga, Nelsy, and Nurse Carter. Emmett sent a gorgeous card of congratulations with a long letter. I hadn't written to him once.

Willa Grace

The rest of 1934 finished fine. We Maruska's settled into the routine of farm life. At first, Daisy's condition seemed to remain on an even keel, or so it seemed. She was often exhausted, but on most days, she was up and about between naps. Our Bohemian diet put a little weight on her for a time.

Tata and the boys hunted and harvested two deer. Thanksgiving came, and we put on a meal to beat all. Except for the absence of Issy and her new husband, having the family under one roof was comforting for us all.

I was so angry with Issy for her selfishness in marrying so young and giving our parents another reason to worry. But most of all, Issy wasn't making an effort to visit her dying sister. Her selfishness was hard to ignore. Mamka, Daisy, and Addie sent letters to her every week, but not me. Issy reciprocated with a letter once every two weeks.

Christmas that year was extra special. It was unspoken, but we all wanted to make it the best Christmas we could for Daisy, and we did. The house was decorated with streamers and homemade ornaments. We strung popcorn and cranberries on the bushy tree the boys brought in from the back forty. I put a candle in every window. Mamka and I baked so many goodies that we had to take trays to Havelka's, Henry and his mother, and Mrs. Schmidlekofer, who forgave us the damage to her mailbox after George made her a new one.

Daisy enjoyed helping Addie, Albert, and Rosalie make paper chains to hang on the tree. On Christmas Eve, George strummed his guitar as we sang carols, and on Christmas Day, we celebrated with games and Mamka's famous pork and dumplings.

Henry came over as well. He stopped in often, but just as a friend. He respected that I needed to focus on Daisy and my family.

As 1935 rolled around, our time was spent outdoors as much as possible. One day in particular.

It was a heavily overcast Saturday in February, with snow drifting down in large, hungry flakes. George was home from the logging camp. We bundled up, all but Rosalie, who was sick with a cold, and trudged through the knee-deep snow to the hill off the far field. George pulled Daisy on the toboggan while Joey and I pulled Addie and Albert on the sled. Henry came behind with a pair of skis that Tata had made. Halfway there, we all broke out into *Jingle Bells* at the top of our lungs. Our rag-tag rendition echoed over the field and forest, surely scaring any wildlife into heading for the opposite direction.

The fellas built a big fire at the top of the hill with dried brush and dead limbs. Once the fire roared to life, we set Daisy on a stump near the warmth and covered her with quilts.

We went up and down that hill so many times that I lost track. Georgie and Joey raced each other a few times, but Joey was a sore loser and settled for taking Albert on his lap. Addie and I doubled up as well.

Our laughter danced over the snow, and curtains of snow drifted from the evergreen branches. Often, I looked at Daisy to see her laughing and cheering us on. I saw in her eyes a glint of longing to be included.

I stood before her with chunks of packy snow clinging to my jacket, mittens, and hat. "Come on, Daisy-do. Let's get you on a sled."

"I don't know." Yet her eyes sparked with the invitation.

"Oh, hell. You have to go once." I knelt before her. "We'll take it easy. You and me. I'll make sure we don't go too fast or head into the toolies."

Daisy straightened. "Let's do it!"

The boys got Daisy on the toboggan behind me, her woolen legs circling me, her arms around my middle, and scooted as close as she could.

"I want to go fast!" Daisy shouted, coughed, then, "Push us off, boys!"

I blinked away the snowflakes, and we were off down the uneven slope. The others cheered us on. The wind bit our noses and cheeks.

"Whoo, hoo!" I hollered. My hat flew off, freeing my hair to cover my eyes. As I tried to push it out of the way, my weight shifted, and we spilled sideways, rolling down the rest of the way.

"Daisy!" I screamed, not able to stop rolling. When I did, I heard a belly laugh from her that I hadn't realized I'd missed. Trying to catch my breath, I rolled to my side to see Daisy splayed on her back in the snow, nearly covered in white.

She rolled to face me, leaning on her elbows, her hat buried somewhere on the hill, her mask nowhere to be seen. Gloppy snow caked her black hair and everything she wore. Her nose was as rosy-pink as her cheeks, and her eyes shone icy blue. Giant snowflakes rested on her lashes and brows while her laughter danced in the frosty air.

That picture of her is burned in my memory. I'd never seen anything so lovely.

TWENTY-TWO

Daisy

Spring blew in warm, and I was grateful. I wanted to spend as much time outside as possible. I watched Tata in the fields and the barn. He welcomed my being there, although he'd never say it out loud, and we had conversations like we'd never had before. We talked about his life in 'the old country' before he came to America, landing on Ellis Island and going to Cleveland, where others from his village had settled. Soon, the rest of his siblings came as well and still lived in Ohio. He was the adventurer of the family.

He told me of the first time he saw Mamka. She wore a white dress with a high neck and long sleeves, bustled up in the back with a big bow, her light brown hair piled high. He learned she worked in the basket-weaving factory just down from where he worked as a carpenter apprentice with, of all people, Mamka's father.

He and our grandfather became good friends, and that's how he was introduced to our Mamka. It wasn't long, and he had her father's approval to marry. They were married at the courthouse and celebrated with all their family, friends, and neighbors at the Sokol.

"Josie wasn't so keen on moving north," he said, "but I heard about the fertile farmland the government was nearly giving away. It called to me. It's been hard, but we've made a good life." Then he looked at me, and I saw a slight tremor in his chin before he quickly turned away, clearing his throat.

I stared at the barn floor, unsure of what to do and hating that I was causing him pain.

Tata kept his back to me. "Must be time for supper. You'd best get yourself inside. Do you need help?"

"No, I'm fine." I stood.

He nodded and quickly climbed the ladder into the hay mow. I watched him go, then left through the granary and barnyard, where I had to sit on a bench put there for just that purpose. That way, I didn't have to bother anyone if I wanted to go to the barn.

I was getting weaker. My body was betraying me in little ways every day. I tried to keep it to myself, but Mamka and Willa Grace could tell. They hovered constantly. Sometimes, I wanted to shout at them to stop, but I couldn't. I needed them.

I napped more, ate less, lost weight, and had trouble controlling my bodily functions. I was forced to use canning jars for my increasingly frequent urination, which was painful and bloody at times. I tried to hide it, forcing myself out of bed to empty the jars outside my window. There were days Rosalie was easier to take care of than I. The embarrassment was more than I could take.

"You've got another letter from your young man," Mamka was at the door of my room.

I shook my head and rolled toward the wall.

Mamka sat on the edge of my bed and, with a hand on my arm, turned me toward her.

"Daisy, have you read any of them?'

"I can't. Put it in my top drawer with the others."

"Why don't you read them? You don't know what he writes."

Tears rolled down my cheeks.

"Oh, my girl." Mamka kissed my forehead.

"It's just so cruel. I fell in love with him, and it was all taken away." I wiped my face, but it did no good. The tears kept coming. "My friend June went to church at the San when she could. What good did it do her?"

Mamka was thoughtful for a time. "I would think it gave her a sense of comfort in the moment. I don't have the answers to that. I wish I did."

"I don't understand why such things happen." Then, I was thinking of Teddy, and I'm sure she was too.

"Life has many mysteries. We do the best we can with what we're handed." She had a faraway look in her eyes.

"I get so angry sometimes." I tried to scoot up on my pillows but gave up until Mamka helped.

"Emmett and I...we could have had a life together. In our short time together, I can't bear to have him tell me he still loves me, or worse, that he's moved on to someone else."

"If he truly loves you, he is not moving on. He's probably worried sick over you being taken from him. He's suffering the same as you. Reading his letters may bring you comfort. You may comfort each other."

We sat in silence for a time.

"Think about it, my dear." She kissed my forehead again, squeezed my arm, and left.

I took Emmett's letter and held it to my chest. The letter remained unopened.

Willa Grace

"Joey, put that chicken down," I hollered from the kitchen window.

He screwed up his face at me. I glared and raised a fist. He put the chicken down, then went to slop the pigs as he'd been told.

I was at the sink washing the breakfast dishes, staring out the window at a drizzly, slushy morning in March, when a figure walked through the morning mist carrying a carpet bag. It was a young woman—our Isabelle.

I turned away from the window, unsure of how to react. I dried my hands and went out onto the stoop.

Issy stopped when she saw me waiting.

"Where the hell have you been?" I asked. "You haven't answered a letter in nearly two months. Do you know how Mamka worries?"

Issy shifted the bag to her other hand, shrugged, and bit her lower lip. Was she going to cry, or did she not care? This sister of mine…I could never read her.

"So, where's your husband?"

"I left him." She stared me down. "You going to let me in?"

"What were you thinking, running off like that? As if our parents didn't have enough to worry about! You have a sister who's dying." I hissed, trying to keep my voice down so no one else would hear. I wanted to throttle her.

"You don't think I know that!"

"So, you just don't care? Is that it?"

"I care."

"You'd better hope you're not pregnant. Mamka doesn't need to raise a baby for you on top of everything else. Why'd you leave him?"

"What do you care?" Her green eyes flashed with anger.

"Answer me!"

"He wanted nothing more than to sweat all over me at night, clean his house, cook his meals, and wash his dirty underwear. Piss on that!" Then her eyes glistened and her chin trembled. No matter how angry Issy made me at times, she was my sister and…I loved her.

"Lesson learned there." I bit down on my lower lip and took a breath. "We can't be fighting now. It's not the time."

"I know. Where's Daisy?" Issy's face crumpled, and tears ran down her face.

"She's napping. Come here," I said, and opened my arms. Issy dropped the bag at her feet and ran forward. We embraced and rocked each other as she cried.

Soon, Addie came out, and we sisters formed a circle of arms and tears. Mamka was in the window watching. She brought a hand to her mouth.

Just like that, Issy was taken back in as though nothing had happened. Family is like that.

While Mamka was grateful Issy was home, our mother was having a harder time doing simple things around the house. She was forgetful, unable to focus on the tasks at hand, and always exhausted. The girls and I took care of everything we could so she could spend time with Daisy, but the change in her was alarming.

One afternoon in April, as I sat at the kitchen table mending one of Joey's socks, Mamka sat across from me staring at the wall, her gaze sorrowful and distant.

"Can I get you a cup of coffee, Mamka? Maybe some tea?"

She shook her head. Her face was so red. I noticed sweat beading on her forehead.

A drip formed at the end of her nose, and she angrily swiped it away.

"Are you all right?"

"Fine."

She wasn't. I set aside the mending and stood. "Let me get you a cool glass of water."

"I said no! I don't need a glass of water or anything else you have to offer. I want to be left alone, that's all. I don't want anybody watching over me. I'm not a child!"

Abruptly, she stood, sending the chair falling back to the floor with a bang.

"Mamka!" I'd never seen her act that way.

"Stay away from me!" She turned and bolted for the door.

"Where are you going?"

The back door slammed as she rushed across the yard toward the woods.

"Issy," I called, and she came running, "watch Albert and Rosa." I ran for the door.

"What's happening?"

"I don't know." I grabbed a sweater on a hook by the door and ran after our mother, who continued across the yard, past the garden, and through the orchard, heading toward the forest with a determined gait that had the bun at the back of her head rocking from side to side, what snow and ice remained causing her to slip here and there.

Mamka disappeared into a thick cover of evergreen, slapping branches aside as she went. Then, she started running as fast as her plump form would allow. She'd wanted to be left alone, but something told me to follow. I was terrified.

Mamka ran further into the forest, stumbling over exposed roots and grasping branches for support. The farm was no longer in sight. She headed toward the sugar shack where Tata made maple syrup every spring. It was difficult to stay a respectful distance behind her.

Mamka ran past the shack, stopping at an enormous maple tree ringed in snow from which she tugged a piece of rusty chain, maybe two feet long, and swung it at the trunk over and over, a frightening, desperate cry the likes of which I'd never heard.

From my hiding place behind Tata's firewood pile, I watched Mamka beat on the maple's trunk, bark flying off in angry directions, her white hair creating a fuzzy halo around her reddened face, and, despite the cold day, sweat stained the bodice of her dress and under her arms. Suddenly, with a final sob, she dropped the chain, fell to her knees amid the frost-covered spoils of last season's wildflowers, and wept, covering her face with her work-worn hands.

I turned from the horror, and with my back against a tree, I wept for the unbearable pain of my mother. With my hands clasped in front of me, I asked for guidance.

Suddenly, all was quiet. I stole a glance from around the tree to see Mamka, her face tear-streaked, her eyes swollen, her body shaking, staring off toward the creek.

I gave her a few moments, then cautiously went forward, trying not to frighten her. I knelt beside her and wrapped her in my arms. One of her hands gripped the folds of my skirt as if I might keep her afloat, while the other covered her face.

"Mamka, I'm sorry." I cradled her from side to side. "Please let me help you." I buried my face in the softness of her hair and breathed in the scent of the bread she'd baked that morning. I'd hugged my mother before, but never truly felt her heart against mine, as I did then. It was an honor to have her lean on me.

After a time, her breathing returned to normal, and she stopped shaking.

I whispered, "Let's get you home." It was getting cold, and the sky was heavy with a coming spring snow.

Mamka pushed away from me and sat on the wet forest grasses, wiping her face with her palms. "You shouldn't have had to see me like that."

I looked up at the tree and saw that the side of the trunk was bare. This wasn't the first time she'd done this.

"Too much," Mamka said finally. "There's been too much." She sighed heavily, her eyes on the sky, shoulders slumped, hands in her lap, palms up in surrender.

"I know." I touched her arm with an inadequate pat.

"Not again," she sighed as her neck flamed, sweat ran in rivers down her face, and her breathing deepened. Within moments, her hair was wet.

"Are you feeling all right?" I worried selfishly. How could we withstand her being ill on top of everything else?

Mamka pulled the wet bodice of her dress away from her chest and pushed the hair from her face.

"It's the change," she said.

"The change?" Then, understanding dawned. I'd heard women her age talk about the awful symptoms of what they called 'the change.' Now, it was the monster before me.

“One minute, I’m burning up. Next, I’m cold as an icicle. I can’t think straight. I forget. I don’t think I put salt in the bread this morning.” She shook her head with a grim smile. “That’s the least of our worries, isn’t it?”

“Let’s have Joey take the first bite.” I nudged her and grinned.

One corner of Mamka’s mouth turned up, and the corners of her eyes crinkled a tad.

“I can’t lose another child, Willa Grace. I can’t.”

“We’ll do this together. All of us.”

She nodded. There was no more pretending that Daisy would beat her disease. We, all of us, had a dark time ahead.

“I love you.” I don’t know that I’d ever said that to her, but it was all I could say.

TWENTY-THREE

Daisy

I sat across the kitchen table from Rosalie, she in her high chair, as we drew pictures of animals and flowers. I wanted this little girl to remember me, but I knew she wouldn't. She was so sweet and innocent, and nothing she drew resembled anything recognizable, but I pretended. I especially loved making her laugh, which was easy enough. I tried to sing Rosalie a few songs, but the effort was exhausting and only caused me to cough, which frightened her. I sometimes pulled my mask down when Rosalie was far across the room. I wanted her to know what I looked like. The same was true for Albert.

Often, I would catch my parents and siblings staring at me. It was as though they were trying to etch a picture of me in their mind, the sound of my voice, the way I moved.

Addie was such a dear. She hovered over my every need. Issy and Joey were good at making me laugh, which I sorely needed.

I found some peace in the yard, gazing at the garden or the creek. Wildflowers were starting to bloom, painting a lovely spring picture outside my window.

"You need to slow down, Willsy," I told my sister as she sat outside with me to do some mending. Willa Grace had helped me outside to where Tata'd put two wooden chairs facing Mamaka's garden as it was starting to sprout. "You're going to wear yourself out."

Willa Grace was running herself ragged, trying to take care of everyone. She cooked and cleaned, mended clothing, did the laundry, helped in the barn if needed, wiped drippy chins, canned, and sensed my every need. Everyone in the family tried to help, but my stubborn sister didn't stop from sunup to sundown. She became the big sister.

"I'm fine, Daisy-do." She put a smile on her face that failed to reach her eyes.

I put a hand on the sleeve of her blouse. "Let's talk about you and Henry."

She gave me a sideways glance that told me to mind my business. I'd vowed not to intrude on her life, but I couldn't help myself at times. Every time I saw them together, it was as though they fit like colors of an exquisite painting. Besides, it had been weeks since I'd brought it up.

"There's nothing to tell." Willa Grace stuck herself with the needle, yelped, and sucked on her finger.

"I know that, but couldn't the situation change? Just a tad for starters. You know how he feels about you. Everyone does."

Willa Grace in her chin, narrowed her eyes, and pursed her lips.

"Oh, come on, Willsy." I laughed. "You know you like him. Nothing would make me happier than knowing you two will marry someday and fill a house with children. You've proved you'd be a great wife and mother."

"How long have you known me? You know that's never been what I want."

I hesitated a moment before continuing.

"Are you waiting for me to die before you return to the city?"

"Daisy!"

"Well, are you?" My tone was just over a whisper.

Willa Grace's chin trembled, and she looked away. "Please don't talk like that."

We were silent for a short time. Willa Grace was swallowing hard to keep from crying.

"What are your plans?" I asked.

"I don't know. I don't think beyond tomorrow." She resumed her mending, but stuck herself again. "Damn. I haven't given this much blood to the mosquitoes."

"I'm sorry to be pushy about you and Henry. He loves you." I tried to shift in the chair but couldn't manage on my own. Willa Grace reached over to help.

"I'm sorry, Willsy. Of all people, I shouldn't be telling you to settle in life. You need to follow your own path. Do what you want. Go back to Chicago. Work in those skyscrapers if that makes you happy, but I think you love him, too. I see it in your eyes when you look at him. Can you tell me you don't?"

"You know, before you got sick, I could wallop you good. Now, it wouldn't take any effort at all." Her face was the cutest shade of red.

I laughed, and she did, too, until she started to cry, holding the shirt up to her face in a ball.

I reached for her hand. She put the shirt down and sandwiched my hand with both of hers.

"What will I do without you, Daisy?" She sobbed like I'd never seen before. "Please don't leave me." Tears dripped off her chin.

A few weeks ago, I'd be crying with her, but now, my tears had been spent, and reality. I don't know if I'd say I was at peace with dying, but it's what I'd been dealt, and I was tired of fighting. I wanted to die with grace.

"Tell you what, Teddy, and I will haunt you every chance we get." I squeezed her hand.

"That isn't funny." Willa Grace pulled her hands away and picked up the shirt that was now on the grass at our feet.

"Sorry. I don't want to die, but it's going to happen. I can feel it deep inside. My body isn't working the way it once did. There's no stopping what's ahead."

"How can you be so accepting?" She turned to me.

"Oh, Willa Grace. I can't win this. I did my raging against it when Doc Thompson explained it all. I screamed and cried. I even went to church and prayed. Sitting in the pew…it was there that I could see the truth of the situation. I'm too tired to fight anymore."

"Twenty years is not enough. You're too young."

"Live for me. Please." I leaned over and put my head on her shoulder.

Albert came around my chair and stood before us, holding something behind his back, his little body quivering excitedly.

"Present," he said, extending his arm. He'd brought me a bouquet of wildflowers.

"Oh, Alby."

Willa Grace

Henry stopped on a dreary, misty day to bring a batch of kolaches his mother had made. He looked so handsome in a blue plaid shirt and brown trousers.

He sat with Mamka and me for coffee and a sample of the treats. Daisy was napping. After we finished, he asked me to walk with him. It had been easy to see something was on his mind. I feared this would be the moment I would break his heart forever. The truth was screaming to be told, and shame on me for holding it back so long.

We strolled along the creek heading south. White trilliums bowed in the breeze as we passed. I wore a pink dress I'd sewn myself. It was plain in style, but the material had wild roses, and I thought it would be pretty with my brown hair. The willows along the creek swayed gently. We sat on a fallen log under a maple that shielded us from the midday sun.

"How are you holding up?" Sunlight glinted from his wire-rimmed glasses.

"Oh, I'm fine." I had a tough time making eye contact with him.

Henry angled his head and studied me, making me feel self-conscious as I picked at a fingernail.

"I am fine. Really." I wanted to get this over with, but the words hadn't come yet.

"I doubt that. You know, working as hard as you can won't change the outcome."

"Can we forget about death for a moment? I'm so sick and tired of thinking about it."

"Willa Grace, I'm here for you. I always have been. I think you know that."

And just like that, I felt like a fool. A lying fool. The time had come.

"I'm sorry, Henry. Yes, you've been a good friend. A great friend."

He stood, his brown eyes heavy with disappointment as though he knew what was coming.

"What is it, Henry? What do you want to say?"

"I want to say…um…that I am completely in love with you, Willa Grace. I have waited for you for so long." He shifted his gaze to the creek. "You have a light about you. I don't know how to describe it, but you're so alive and so strong." Then he looked back at me. "Do you remember the 4th of July picnic at Viola Villa when you read an essay you wrote for everyone about our freedoms here in America? It was so moving. You have a real talent for that, Willa Grace. I'll never forget it. It was then that I respected your intelligence along with all your other wonderful traits."

But then he did something I didn't see coming.

He got down on one knee.

"No, Henry. Don't do that."

"It's too late, Willa Grace. Have I told you how I love saying your name? I want to say it for the rest of my life." He looked down for a moment, then back at me. "I don't have a ring to give you just yet, but I'd sure like it if you would marry me, Willa Grace."

Oh, sweet hell. "You don't want me, Henry. I'm not the girl I was when I left here." I wanted to get up, but he was in front of me. He took my hand.

"You were the same girl when I visited you in the city only a few months ago. We had such a great time together."

I put my hands on his shoulders and eased him back so I could rise. He sat on the log.

"We did, but…there are a few things I need to tell you. You're a good person, Henry, and it wasn't kind of me to have led you on if that's what you feel I did. I didn't mean to."

"But I love you." He wasn't making this easy, but what in life is? He reached for one of my hands again, but I held it up and away from him.

"What you don't know is that…is that…oh, I'm so sorry." Then I began to cry stupid, ugly tears. He handed me a handkerchief.

"You're scaring me, Willa Grace."

"I'm damaged goods." I held the handkerchief and let the tears run.

He stared at me, eyes narrowed, mouth downturned.

"I've been with a boy. I'm not…pure… anymore."

"Not pure? What are you saying?" He pulled in his chin. I think he knew very well what I meant.

"I'm not a girl anymore."

He wasn't saying a word and staring at a trillium at his feet.

"I met a boy at Thorpe's who I let…you know. This is so difficult to tell you." My heart was beating so hard I could barely hear myself. I watched him as the words set in. The lines of his face smoothed as understanding sank in.

"There's more. I was…with child."

"Willa Grace, if you don't want to marry me, say so. You don't have to come up with this…this stupid story."

"I'm telling you the truth. As awful as it is. I was pregnant."

"You…you had…a baby? I don't believe you. Why are you being so cruel?" I'd never seen a more hurt expression on his sweet face.

"I could have lied to you, but you deserve the truth. I lost the baby the night I was attacked by the vagrant on my way home from work. No one knows but you. I was so ashamed I couldn't even tell Daisy."

Henry looked like he was going to be sick.

I wrung my hands before me. "It's the only secret I've ever kept from her. It's too humiliating. I couldn't have her worrying about me."

"What happened to your boyfriend?" I'd never heard such a harsh tone from him, and it stung.

"He ran away when I told him I was pregnant."

"Were you in love with him?"

"I thought I was. I would never do something like that if I weren't. I was foolish. He took advantage of my feelings for him." My voice hitched as I tried to gain control. "I hate him now."

Henry shifted his gaze to the ground. I would have given all I had to know his thoughts and feelings. If this ended with Henry hating me, I would be devastated. And I would deserve every bit of it.

"I'm sorry, Henry. I truly am." I crossed my arms over my chest and hung on to stop shaking. "I do have feelings for you, but this awful truth kept getting in the way because I knew you needed to be told. You deserve that."

Henry stood, turned away from me, and ran a hand over his hair. I closed my eyes and waited. When he said nothing, I said, "Please say something."

Henry shook his head sadly. Then, without one word, he turned and walked away with my heart.

TWENTY-FOUR

Daisy

I was weaker with each passing day. Some days, it was a challenge to raise my arms, my skinny legs failed to hold me up for more than a minute, and I slept a lot.

On a beautiful sunny day in May, in the late afternoon, I had a sudden need to be outdoors. Mamka warned of the still cool air, but I insisted. Willa Grace was washing dishes, grabbed a towel to dry her hands, and said she'd take me, offering to pad the toboggan to carry me. Just then, George came in. He carried me to the chair on the hill, looking out on the creek where I'd been spending so much time lately.

"Want me to stay?" My handsome brother asked as he tucked me into the quilt Mamka had insisted upon bringing.

I shook my head. "I need some alone time with no one fussing over me."

He hesitated a moment, hands in his pockets. A cow bawled from the back field.

"I'll be fine, Georgie."

"You sure? Cuz I don't have anything to do."

I raised my near skeletal hand and waved him off.

"Well, okay then." From far off, our rooster crowed.

He started to leave when I said, "Georgie?" He stopped.

"You're a good egg."

"I'll be back to get you." He lumbered off through the trees, stopping once to look back.

I tipped my head back against the chair, chin to the soft spring breeze, feeling the pinkish sun warm my skin. I closed my eyes, my thoughts drifting.

I would miss my twenty-first birthday in August. This I knew. Life would move on without me. Willa Grace would find her path, whatever that might be. My brothers and sisters as well. If only I could spare my parents the pain of my leaving.

The passage of my time there could have been long or short. I might have fallen asleep, or not. The song of a robin brought me back to the view stretched out before me of the crooked creek, the roll of distant hills, fields green with new growth, and a forest sturdy and sheltering. I was able to pull in a full breath of pure country air filled with the scent of daisies, grasses, and wild roses.

Then, a soft rustle of leaves, and I wasn't alone.

That graceful deer, half white, half brown, with wide and wondering eyes, grazed along the creek just as gracefully as Willa Grace and I had seen her at Viola Villa Hall that night, not so long ago.

Beyond her, sunset gathered with whisps of pink, orange, and lavender. Long fingers of gold reached out across the land.

I raised my right hand over the quilt, gracefully moving it back and forth as though I were painting upon a canvas provided by Mother Nature herself. As I moved my hand, the colors of my imaginary brush came alive. The field filled with wildflowers of every hue rolled out before me like an exquisite carpet.

A breeze hushed through the grasses, as the slowing thump, thump, thump of my heart marked time. My hand dropped to my lap, and all I could see was the bright sun moving nearer as though sunset and dawn were one in the same.

All the pain and heartbreak of the last few years flew from my broken body, replaced by a peace and love that compared to nothing I'd ever known.

And from the center of that warm, loving light, Teddy ran toward me with his arms open wide and a dimpled grin upon his freckled face. June waited off in the distance.

I was so happy.

Willa Grace

From the kitchen window, I watched George return from taking Daisy to the creek. Rather than come to the house, he crossed the barnyard, wiping his nose on a hanky, then slipped behind the granary where I was certain he was having a good cry. There was lots of that these days.

We all knew it wouldn't be long now.

"I don't like her being out there alone," Mamka said from the table where she picked through mushrooms she harvested, while Issy and Addie chopped rhubarb for a cobbler.

Turning from the window, I said, "I'll take a cup of tea to her." No one said a word.

I filled a cup with hot water and set a tea bag inside. I then put a saucer, a spoon, and a jar of honey on a tray. Before leaving, I grabbed cinnamon cookies, her favorite.

Gently, so as not to spill, I went across the lawn, through the orchard, and up the hill to the field overlooking the creek. Almost there, I glanced up. Daisy was seated with her back to me, and beyond, the most beautiful sunset I'd ever seen. I stopped to take it in.

"Oh, Daisy, look at that sunset. I bet you'd love to paint that." There was no movement as if she'd heard me. Carefully, I took a few more steps.

And then, I saw it.

The deer. Reaper. It moved into view at the far end of the field, ignoring me.

My hand started to shake, and the jar of honey tumbled to the ground.

"Daisy?" I asked gently. No answer. "Daisy, I'm bringing tea." Nothing. "DAISY?"

No, oh no.

The tray tumbled to the ground, water sloshed out of the cup, the saucer cartwheeled away, and the cookies landed in the grass.

I clutched my stomach with shaking hands, and my lungs refused to expand. I fought the urge to faint, to make it all go away, but I couldn't. I don't remember the steps it took to reach her.

My dear Daisy, her chin resting on a shoulder, her black hair, now longer since we've been back, pillowed her pale face, her cheeks still rosy, looked as though she were napping. I bent over her, kissing her forehead, stroking her hair, touching her face. I took her cold hand lying on the quilt, wrapped it in the warmth of my hand, and sank to the grass.

She and I remained there until George came looking for us as the last glow of the sun held on the horizon.

EPILOGUE

I stood at the open door of Viola Villa Hall on a gorgeous Saturday afternoon, looking in on all those who came to say goodbye to Daisy. Row after row of chairs had been arranged, and most were taken, with more mourners standing. The people of Emery Township were so kind in the face of our loss. Women brought food, and the men offered help with the chores.

I stepped back from the doorway and took stock of the people still coming, and wondered where we would put them all.

Looking up, I thought, *'How dare the sun shine so brightly today?'* I suppose sending Daisy off on such a fine day was fitting. After all, she'd been a ray of sunshine all her life, but I wanted the whole world to be as miserable as I felt.

"Oh my dear," Mrs. Havelka wrapped me in her generous arms. I hugged her back and nodded. She released me and went inside. I followed her to the door.

Mamka and Tata sat in the front row. Mamka held a hanky to her face, her shoulders heaving. Tata kept his head down, spine straight as the flagpole out front. I worried the weight of this sadness would never lift.

Addie sat in the second row, looking so grown up next to Issy, who, not surprisingly, was pregnant and getting bigger every day. Her husband was nowhere to be found. George sat in the third row with his new girlfriend, Jenny. Next to them was Joey, with his leg in a cast after he tried to jump off the woodshed onto our old mare and missed. Served him right.

I felt a light touch on my arm. Henry, my rock, was behind me. What a treasure he'd been these last few days. I looked up at him as he slipped a steadying arm around me.

He'd forgiven my terrible mistake. Said it didn't matter to him. He wanted me in his life and said we could work through anything if our love were strong enough. I knew it was.

I leaned into him, knowing I would always be safe in his arms. All my dreams of city life didn't mean a thing. I wanted my family, and I wanted Henry.

He and I went inside and took a seat next to my parents.

In front of the hall, Daisy lay in the coffin George and others from the township had made for her. Issy and I dressed her in her best pink dress, and Mamka tied a matching ribbon in her hair. Addie sewed the rose-patterned pillow under Daisy's head. Albert and Rosalie drew pictures for her that Mamka put in an envelope, along with a letter from her, which is tucked under her crossed hands. Vases of wildflowers, particularly daisies, decorated the room, and I brought the framed picture of her from the Milwaukee Journal to sit alongside the coffin. The locket from Emmett lay softly on the stillness of her bodice. A large bouquet of roses was delivered from town and placed before the coffin. The card read, 'Love, Emmett.'

I had kept my promise to keep him informed of Daisy's condition. He'd been released from Statesan, taken up college again, this time studying pharmaceutical research. I truly hoped he'd find happiness and live a full and healthy life. Daisy would have wanted that.

Viola Villa Hall was standing room only when the Pastor called the service to order.

1993

I talk to my dear sister every day as I go about my chores. I consult her, commiserate with her, and share good news and bad. I live for us both.

Daisy taught me to pay attention to those simple joys: the smell of a baby's downy head, the beauty in a bouquet of wildflowers, the bawl of a newborn calf, the peek of seed above the soil, and the loveliness of life unfolding as Henry and I lived our lives. A stroke stole him from me ten years ago.

Henry and I adopted Josephine Jane when Issy gave birth, using Mamka's first name and Daisy's middle. Janie, as we called her, has been a gift from the very first. After burying Daisy, the arrival of a new life in the family was a blessing.

Issy divorced Stephan and ran off to Chicago, where she worked in a bank and married three more times. Issy lived the life I thought I'd wanted, minus the husbands, but she was never truly happy, whereas I was.

Henry and I took over the farm from his mother. I became an avid gardener, a damn good cook, and built a life of peace and quiet joy. We never had a child of our own, not knowing if he was the cause or I, so we focused on Janie, the light of our lives. She now owns a greenhouse and orchard with her husband, Michael. Together, they gave us three wonderful grandchildren, all of whom are now following dreams of their own.

More than anything, I am grateful for a long life that allowed me to witness the lives of my siblings, joyous and heartbreaking. We lost George over Germany in World War II. Issy died at fifty-six from cancer, not having had more children. Addie became a beloved grade-school teacher and passed from cancer at sixty-five, leaving a large family, and Albert is a building contractor with a wonderful wife and three daughters. Both Addie and Albert remained in the Phillips area.

Rosalie sang in the theater, first in Chicago and then on to New York City. We were all so proud of her. Henry and I took Janie on a memorable trip to Chicago for one of Rosalie's productions years ago. Being in that monstrous city again, I wondered why I'd ever thought it was for me. One never knows the twists and turns in life's path.

And then there's Joey. He remained the same little shit all his life that he'd been as a child. He never married, spent his life on a rundown farm in Emery Township, saved every penny he'd ever earned, pestered his neighbors every evening to see what's on the television, and has been happier than a pig in slop.

After burying Daisy in Emery Cemetery, Tata moved into the bedroom he'd built for her. I suppose that was his way of staying close to her. Mamka endured as she always had, focusing on the family she had left, a family that would continue to be blessed with new life amid the heartbreak, as we scattered off on our own like seeds on the breeze, blooming where planted.

Such is life.

Daisy

Willa Grace thinks I am with her every time she sees a cardinal. Isn't that cute? She doesn't know that I linger far more often than that. I am in the wildflowers dancing at her feet, the creek water where she cools on a hot summer day, the apple blossoms that float on the breeze, and I sit on her shoulder as she writes her wonderful stories. When she stops by what was once Viola Villa Hall to take in those happy memories, the band still plays in the whisper of the wind, and I twirl among the ruins until Willa Grace takes us home.

THE END

Roto Section
Sunday, December 1, 1940
CHRISTMAS

ACKNOWLEDGMENTS

The writing of *Wildflowers* has been a journey filled with nostalgia for those who came before me, the challenges they faced, and the resilience they had to unearth.

So many people to thank…

I want to thank my sons, Thomas, who graciously shares his editorial insight and never says no when Mom needs advice, and Bill, who gives me a giggle when I need it and much-appreciated support. Many thanks to the White Bear Center for the Arts in White Bear Lake, MN, for providing me with a creative home and precious friendship. You took me in when I needed it most. To Amber Guetebier of the Writers Well at the WBCA for her mentorship and her example of strength in dealing with whatever life has in store. Women of Words (WOW) East for being my people. Their sage advice has been priceless, and they forever remind me that we all have our own chaos to navigate. The Wisconsin Writers Association has been a valuable resource for honing my craft, and to Annie Mydla for "telling me like it is." To Laurie Scheer, you are a legend, and I will be forever grateful for the opportunity to have worked with you. Your support for this story means a great deal. Thank you to Barbara Lobermeier for her assistance with research and plot.

Thank you to Dr. Charles Bransford for your kindness in sharing your knowledge and your copy of Frederick Manfred's *Boy Almighty*, based on the author's time in Glen Lake Sanitarium in MN. Also helpful in my research was *The Girl in Building C*, edited by Mary Krugerud, the story and letters of Marilyn Barnes Robertz, who spent three years of her teenage life in the Ah-gwah-ching Sanatorium in Walker, MN. I highly recommend these books. I also found a helpful article in the Journal of the Royal Society of Medicine, titled "Tuberculosis Sanatorium Regimen in the 1940s: a patient's personal diary."

Danna Mathias Steele did a fantastic job on the interior of this book, and the team at BuzBooks designed a beautiful cover. Also, thank you to Krista Soukup at Blue Cottage Agency, and a well-deserved shout-out to Minnesota's Springboard for the Arts and the Loft Literary Center in downtown Minneapolis. I also want to mention Midwest Fiction Writers in MN, who, in the early days of my writing, were beyond helpful.

Historical Societies are a wealth of information. A huge well of thanks to the Waukesha Historical Society and Museum in Waukesha, WI, and Michele Pollard at the Hennepin County History Museum in Minneapolis, MN. And while I'm at it, I want to acknowledge the Price County Historical Society in Fifield, WI, for their efforts to keep WI history alive and accessible.

The sharing of memories is so important. Few people are still around who remember the family that inspired this story. Special thanks to my mother, Arlene Loula Morrison, and Aunt Sally Huml for sharing. Talk to your elders, people. They are a treasure trove of information.

There have been some key people who have been my book-selling champions: Judy Holden, Julie Washatka, Gail Angone, Sarah Muender, Colleen Baldrica, Kayla Bablick, and Kristen Harper. And of course, thank you to the brick-and-mortar stores for your support.

Finally, my great-aunt Ann Huml, my grandmother, Frances Huml Loula Prezak, and my great-grandmother, Anna Janovsky Huml. Their courage to face what fate had in store is nothing short of heroic. This book is loosely based on the story of my grandmother, Frances, and her older sister, Ann, who left their farm in Emery Township, east of Phillips, WI, to work in Chicago in the early 1930s. While there, Ann, like Daisy, contracted TB and was sent to live at Statesan in Waukesha County, WI. Unlike Daisy, Ann spent 8 years there battling that awful disease, starting at age 21. She lost the fight in 1941 at age 29.

In my story, Daisy creates a copy of the Christmas Seals holiday poster, fully crafted with canceled stamps she collected at the San. She and her creation are featured in a full-page ad in the Milwaukee Journal to generate support for the WI Anti-Tuberculosis Association. This is true. Aunt Ann's picture was published in the December 1940 edition of the Roto Section. Although Ann looks healthy in the picture, she passed away the following year. I am blessed to have an original on my wall. Also, while Ann was living in the San, her 14-year-old sister Helen was sent there for a 5-year stay as well, being released at 19 after having one lung removed.

My grandmother, Frances, was the inspiration for Willa Grace. In writing Willa Grace's story, it was heart-wrenching to dredge up the fear and sadness she must have felt watching her sister's decline. In my story, Willa Grace becomes pregnant while in Chicago. My grandmother does not and would chastise me greatly for not clarifying that fact. In *Wildflowers*, the two sisters are bonded by the tragic loss of a little brother, Teddy. This is true. Ann and Frances witnessed the loss of four-year-old John in a different way, but traumatizing nonetheless.

My great-grandmother, Anna, suffered many harsh, tragic events in her life, but never did they chip away at her kindness and love for her family. In the span of four years, she lost little John, her own mother, and her two younger sisters. Ten years later, she lost a baby daughter to a horrific accident, saw another daughter sent to the San (Helen), after worrying so long over Ann, and then lost her. WWII claimed a son-in-law, while two of her sons were fighting as well. As Mamka in my story remarks, "When the train pulled into Phillips, all I saw was mud. I wanted to run right back to Cleveland," so did my great-grandmother when she arrived in 1915. When I visited my grandmother, Frances, years ago, she had fond memories of her mother humming and singing as she bustled about the kitchen and the farm. Anna Huml was never given the grace of time to grieve; there was too much to do, and too many mouths to feed.

The town of Phillips and Emery Township have always held a special place in my heart. It's where my mother was raised and where my ancestors chose to make their lives. I have many warm memories of my grandparents' farm and later splashing in Long Lake and Whispering Pines Resort. If a cemetery can be charming, then such is the one in Emery, which has nearly thirty of my relatives buried there. I will join them someday, although I'm in no rush.

As Willa Grace learns, a wildflower must bloom where the wind plants the seed.

www.ingramcontent.com/pod-product-compliance
Lightning Source LLC
Chambersburg PA
CBHW020821260626
47169CB00003B/769

9798993600406